HIBERNIA

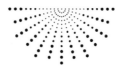

AMANDA APTHORPE

For Ez

Sometimes a sanctuary has to be hard won if it's to live up to its promise.

INTRODUCTION

Audrey put her foot to the accelerator. 'What on earth was I thinking?' she said aloud, the tone of her voice sounding insipid to her ears as it dissipated into the fabric of the empty passenger seats. She stole a glance at the old house retreating in the rearview mirror, just as a breeze rustled through the onion weeds protruding through the wire fence, their flowers bidding her a cheery farewell.

She'd been driving past it on her way back to the ferry and something about it had made her stop. It wasn't enchantment —the right light, a sunny day full of potential and optimism. Instead, it was cold, and grey, the sort of Sunday afternoon that sometimes resulted in a hefty dose of melancholy. But she'd gotten out of the car, had stepped onto the house's sinking verandah, inspected boards and had gone as far as the back garden with its overgrown beds, and even entertained the idea that she and the house had a destiny. That was, until the veil of optimism cleared, and she saw it for what it was, for surely what everyone else would see—that it was crumbling; a house that had passed its time. If it were to survive, it would need to find someone else, someone wealthier. Just as Campbell had done. Since her separation, Audrey was learning that what her idea of life should be, and what it really was, were poles apart.

Rain slapped at the windscreen in pulsing sheets, with such force that she was tempted to construe it as a punishment. It's just rain, she told herself, pulling over to the curb and turning off the engine and the wipers before they broke under the strain; the noise of it on the roof so loud it muffled her thoughts. When she felt the car tilt slightly in the back-left-hand corner, it didn't require too much imagination to know what had happened.

Restarting the engine, she applied a light pressure to the accelerator. The front wheels strained to move forward but the back wheels resisted and were making a sinister, grinding sound. She released her foot and slapped the steering wheel as though it had been part of a conspiracy.

'Damn it!'

Riffling through her handbag on the passenger seat, she took out her mobile phone, checked its reception and tossed it back with frustration.

As suddenly as it had started, the rain stopped, and Audrey saw through her side window that she was parallel with the double-storied villa she'd observed earlier from the yard of the old house. To its left, set back from the road, was a small vineyard, the gnarled and leafless arms of the vines looking tortured as they spread across the supporting wires.

The force of the rain on the unsealed road had carved out muddy rivulets that flowed beneath her feet as she stepped out of the car. Zipping up her jacket and slinging her bag over her shoulder, she crossed the road to the villa's driveway. It was long and covered in scoria that had freshened in the rain to highlight its red tint, providing a striking contrast to the soft green of the olive trees that she saw were the predominant planting.

The driveway widened at its end, then forked, with one prong directing right towards the broad marble portico of the house, and the other left to a three-car garage with a black and muddied Land Cruiser parked in front.

She double-checked her phone in hope—still no signal. As if to hurl a further insult, a thick cloud unleashed a new torrent that had her running up the steps into the shelter of the portico.

A dribble of water meandered down her forehead. Feeling her hair plastering around her ears and neck, Audrey clasped the large knocker clenched in the jaws of a brass lion head. She knocked once and was poised to knock again when the door was opened, and she was faced with four people standing inside the wide entrance as though they'd been anticipating her arrival.

'Buongiorno.' A small and robust middle-aged woman stepped forward. Audrey could hear the small tut of her tongue. 'Bella ragazza... come... come in.'

Audrey obeyed, sensing that this was how it would be for anyone in her presence. Still mute with surprise, she stepped over the threshold and quickly took in the others—an equally stocky middle-aged man and a young man with bright, dark eyes who had the colouring of the other two who were immediately in front of her. The man to her left, still holding the door open, was taller than the others and bordering on being underweight. She hadn't yet turned to face him fully but sensed an aura of darkness, a brooding about him, though in comparison to the others who were beaming at her, she wondered if she appeared the same.

The woman who had now gripped her arm was attempting to move her further into the house that was radiating terracotta warmth, even on this dull day.

The ferry! The thought brought Audrey to a standstill, resisting the woman's effort to propel her forward.

'The ferry,' she said, turning back to the others. 'I'm bogged and I'm going to miss it.'

'You've already missed it,' the man by the door said as he closed it. 'The next one's not for two hours and there's a good chance Bill will decide not to cross in this sort of weather.'

Audrey turned to face him. This "prophet of doom" had an expression of concern that Audrey guessed he might wear regularly, suggested by the shadowed creases at the sides of his mouth and the deep line between his eyebrows. The implication of what he was saying began to sink in and she could feel a familiar rise of anxiety. Had she lost time? How could she have missed the ferry? 'But I need to get back,' she said, looking at each of them in turn, hoping that one of them would manifest a solution.

'I...' Audrey hesitated. What good would it do to explain to them that she had an important meeting at work in the morning... that she should have been working on a presentation for it at home right now?

Earlier that morning, she'd been sitting at her desk in Melbourne pondering the correct choice of words for *another* PowerPoint presentation when she became distracted by her surroundings. It was as though she were suddenly seeing them for the first time; a bland room in a bland apartment she'd had to rent while waiting for the settlement on the property—*her* warehouse apartment that Campbell had never paid a cent towards but had successfully claimed half the proceeds of its sale. She could have stayed there until it was sold, but there were too many memories that haunted her, especially at night as she lay awake in their bed.

It had been impulse and anger that had propelled her out of

the apartment. Impulse had taken her driving for hours east to the coast and had her boarding an old ferry to cross a narrow section of the Pacific to an island she'd never heard of—Hibernia. And impulse had her stopping at an old, abandoned house.

The *For Sale* sign, hanging diagonally between two rudimentary pine posts, flapped in the wind. With her head aligned with it in parallel, Audrey had read its lean description. Two bathrooms were a surprise—the house was old, in the Federation style of the early 1900s, and while three bedrooms might be common, certainly a second bathroom was not. It must have been added later, she reasoned, though from the front perspective it didn't look as though anything else had been touched since the house was built. The once white paint was peeling off the lower weatherboards. From where she was standing, she could see that although the exposed boards beneath had deep fissures from weathering, they looked solid and were still in place. The verandah was another matter, sagging almost to the ground at the right-hand corner like a crooked smile that had reminded her of her grandmother, Florence, after the stroke, and she wondered if the house in front of her held as many memories as her grandmother had held behind the drooping facade.

Placing her hand on the gate and confident that no-one could see her, she pushed it open. She smiled to herself—the fences either side had long gone, just a few remnants of rusted wire disappearing amongst the onion weed. But the gate had a dignity that called her to respect its purpose. Again, she thought of Florence.

The house sat off-centre, to the right of the block. On the left, there was a broad expanse of ground covered in couch grass that had been recently mown. Here and there, tall stalks ran in a line, suggesting that whoever had mown it was either short-sighted, or rushed. In the middle stood a large and healthy date palm, so commonly seen in the yard of farmhouses of this era that, despite its size, it hadn't been the first thing to attract Audrey's eye. She'd been pleased that it was there and imagined it casting shade on the patio she would have built... imagined herself sitting there in a wicker chair sipping a gin and tonic, watching the entry and exit of parrots into the fronds and listening to them squabble over its fruit. The thought had formed a small knot in her viscera, a reminder that as a divorcee, she would be sitting there alone.

And now, here she was in damp clothes and sodden hair in the home of these strangers, on an island cut off from civilisation because its old ferry couldn't handle a storm. It wasn't even that far across to the mainland, and Audrey thought with resentment of the house down the road that had waylaid her, knowing full well that it was all her fault. Because it usually was.

The woman had returned her arm around her waist. 'What is your name?'

Audrey felt herself flush with embarrassment that she'd all but storm-trooped this home and was mentally railing against this archaic island and the whimsy of "Bill", the ferry operator.

'Audrey, Audrey Spencer,' she said, humbled.

'Audrey,' the woman said, 'I am Rosa, and this is my husband Beppe, and our grandson Dion. And this is Quentin, our friend.'

'Just Quin,' the man said with a nod in Audrey's direction, as he reopened the door. 'Beppe,' he continued, 'I'll have a look at Audrey's car. I've got a tow in the back of mine.'

'I'll help!' Dion's movement towards the door prompted a rush of instruction from his grandmother in rapid-fire Italian.

'Si, Nonna,' he said, a broad smile stretching his face as he lifted a raincoat from a brass coat rack. Although Audrey would have thought him to be in his mid to late twenties, his response and his movements were those of a much younger boy.

Rosa issued a further instruction, this time directed to her husband, who halted in his tracks as he moved to accompany the other two.

Audrey didn't need to understand the language to know that the older man, who moved with stiff hips and bowed legs, would be of little help. She saw his shoulders slump and felt a rush of sympathy, but when his wife turned from him, he slipped out the door. *Good for you*, she thought. There was something about him that was vulnerable, as though he'd lost his way and was trying to reclaim it. She could relate to that. It seemed to Audrey that she'd spent the last twelve months clawing her way back to something that resembled herself.

'You stay here tonight,' Rosa said, patting Audrey's arm and steering her again towards the living room.

Audrey stopped again; this time alarmed.

'Thank you, Rosa, but no. I'll just go back into town.' What she could remember of the "town" was a scattering of shops; a general store that doubled as a post office, a small visitors' centre, a sign that advertised yoga—that had surprised her— and, of course, a hotel offering cheap counter lunches, dinner, pool table and *Live Music*. Perhaps they had accommodation, too, she wondered.

'There's nowhere to stay, *mio caro*,' Rosa said, voicing Audrey's worst fear.

Anxiety sent her thoughts spinning. If "Bill" decided not to take the ferry across, she would be stranded in this house with people she didn't know, though, she had to acknowledge, they didn't feel like strangers. There was such warmth and generosity in their open-heartedness—something she hadn't experienced in a long time. There had been no inquisition at the door, no reserve or assessment of her, just a genuine response of kindness to someone in need. Whatever their plan for the afternoon had been, it was adjusting for her.

Rosa guided her through the living area with its view through concertinaed glass doors to the expansive vegetable garden. To its right was a small orchard. Though the trees were bare of leaves, the thick swelling of buds and first bursts of blossom were evidence of their vitality. Audrey thought of the twenty trees she'd counted in the overgrown and abandoned garden down the road and was surprised by a feeling of protectiveness towards them.

There had been a lull in the wind as Audrey had made her way down the side of the old house and, in the relative calm, she'd heard a soft, regular thud coming from its rear. The noise had drawn her on and when she reached the end of the house and turned its corner, she'd come to an abrupt stop. The backyard, dense with bare-limbed fruit trees and garden beds blanketed in weeds and herbs going to seed, sprawled the width of the building. Audrey moved into a central position behind the house to get a better view. A brick path mottled with mould like age spots extended ahead of her and, at its furthermost limit, a thick band of dark grey ocean met the sky in its paler version. She realised that the sound she could hear was that of the waves beating against the coastline.

Audrey followed the path, mentally counting the fruit trees in varying degrees of vitality. Some, she saw, needed heavy pruning, but the tips of many of the branches were already swelling with the new buds of early spring. Twenty, she'd counted, and soon they would blossom. Wondering what this garden would look like when they did, she'd turned around to take in the rear of the house and the vantage point of its one-time occupants. A window that ran its length revealed, through skewed and broken bamboo blinds, a deep room—a typical sunroom extension. The sight of it had pleased her and as the sun cracked through a small break in the clouds and cast its light and warmth on the weatherboards of the original rear of the house, her smile had broadened.

She snapped back to the present. 'Rosa, who owns the old white house down the road?'

They'd stopped at the base of staircase. Rosa's face seemed to cloud over.

'This belong to Harold, our neighbour.'

'Is he still alive?'

'Si,' Rosa breathed the word out with a long sigh. 'In a home for old people. Harold's daughter put him there!' Rosa threw her hands up. She looked bewildered. 'Now she sell. What if he want to come home?'

They made their way up the stairs.

Audrey knew the scenario well enough and knew, too, that many such as Rosa saw this as an abandonment of family. In some cases, Audrey would agree, but she also knew from first-hand experience that there were times when there was little choice. Her parents had been adamant that Florence, her father's mother, would live with them when she was no longer able to take care of herself, but after the stroke she went downhill so quickly and needed constant medical care beyond her parents' capacity and community home help.

'The house is old,' Audrey said. 'And needs a lot of work.'

'Si.' Rosa nodded and paused, holding onto the banister. Audrey waited. 'Beppe help fix, but... he getting old too!' She laughed spontaneously as she said it and Audrey could tell that she would do this often.

'You like it, Audrey?' she said more seriously, but with a glint in her eye.

'The old house?'

'Si.'

Audrey had been intrigued by it. She'd never renovated a house, having lived in one new apartment after another, and more recently in a converted warehouse with Cam, but there was something about this one that had sparked a desire to create. As co-director of a chain of popular art galleries, there was plenty of mental stimulation and the opportunity to meet and mix with the highly creative. Once, it would have been enough but, these last twelve months, she'd begun to feel dissatisfied, as though enhancing others' creative visions was leaving her as dry as a bone. This had been made more acute since Cam, whom she had not only nurtured in exhibiting his art but had also provided with a steady income stream when he couldn't work because he felt 'burnt out' by public expectation, had left her for another woman—not younger, but certainly wealthier.

Audrey considered Rosa's question. Yes, she'd imagined the old house's renovation, but the sharp eye of rationality had made her see it for what it really was. That's how she would see things now, she told herself—without whimsy, without romantic notions.

She shook her head. 'No, Rosa. I'm a city girl.'

At the top of the stairs, several rooms opened off a wide landing.

'This way, Audrey,' Rosa said, leading her to a bedroom on the far right and ushering her into its modern ensuite. She brought out a lilac robe and a bath towel from a cupboard behind the door. 'You give me clothes to dry and have warm shower.'

Audrey took them from her and undressed behind the closed door. The robe was soft against her skin as she handed the damp jeans and jumper to Rosa, who was waiting on the other side.

'*Bene*. When you ready, come down to kitchen for a cuppa.' Rosa closed the door behind her.

'Cuppa'. Audrey smiled and knew that Rosa had said it to make her feel at home. She hadn't considered having a shower, but as she eyed the wide recess, the thought was very appealing.

Warmed by the flow of blood from the shower's heat and comforted by the softness of the robe against her skin, Audrey stood at the bedroom window and marvelled at the same view of the Pacific Ocean she had seen from the end of the garden down the road. The wind had calmed and shafts of sunlight breaking through the clouds spot-lit sections of the water. Had a dolphin leapt and arched through the rays, she wouldn't have been surprised.

She looked towards the old house. Though the back garden was obscured by tall gums and tea-trees that ran its length, she recalled the charm of its overgrown beds and the pleasure of finding the leaves of the crocus plant that offered themselves like a secret.

As she'd picked her way between the garden beds that revealed herbal treasures of the hardiest varieties—lavender, rosemary, a thyme bush with a dense mat of tiny new leaves at the base of its old stalks that looked like a grounded sea urchin —Audrey had pulled aside delicate and fleshy stalks of spurge to reveal crocus leaves already flaccid and browning. Amongst them were the remnants of wilting purple flowers. Though she was no expert on crocuses, she recognised this variety from her mother's prized kitchen garden.

'Be careful, *Mi niña querida*,' her mother, Isabel, would whisper as she handed her daughter the tweezers. 'Take it gently.' There was reverence in her voice as, together, they harvested the plants' stigmas.

Audrey closed her eyes as the memory prompted another—

the odour of slow-cooked lamb simmering in onions, turmeric, cardamom and cumin seeds as her mother would take the lid from the tagine to add just a few of the precious stigmas. There had been a time when she had been embarrassed by these very odours coming from their kitchen and had wished that Isabel would adapt to the simple, if not bland, Australian diet that her friends' mothers cooked. Audrey's forty years had seen considerable changes in the culture of her country of birth.

The house itself seemed to be more expansive in this view from the villa, and she counted five chimneys in the tiled roof that, she noted, looked to be in good condition.

Turning away, she took in the room behind her. She'd expected to see photographs and evidence of family life, but it was surprisingly bare—a queen-sized bed with a thick and richly textured spread in gold and black, a mahogany dressing table with curved barley-sugar legs, but without adornments, and a long mirror with pedestal legs in the far corner. She wondered if there were other grandchildren besides Dion.

At the sound of a heavy thud of the front door closing, Audrey gathered her handbag and stole another glance at the ocean beyond the window before she left the room.

From the landing, she could hear voices in a languid murmur of familiarity, punctuated now and then by a bass tone. Quin, she thought, the man at the door. Audrey hoped that he'd been able to extract the car from the ditch, though what she would do then was another matter.

As she reached the bottom of the stairs, the volume of the voices became louder and there they were—all four of them, standing beside the dining room table. Dion and Quin were facing her as she came into the room and her hand automatically tugged together the gown's lapels at her chest.

Dion's eyes widened when he saw her, but Quin, she saw, had cast his down.

'You're beautiful!' Dion said, breaking free of the others and approaching her. His wide smile revealed irregular teeth that enhanced rather than detracted from his looks. His eyes were almost too wide, too bright, and Audrey realised then that he was not like other twenty-year-olds.

Rosa placed a steaming cup of tea on a coaster on the table and let out a low growl. Dion paused in his tracks but gave Audrey a wink before he returned to the others.

'Good news, Audrey,' Rosa said, smiling at her, then scowling at her grandson as he moved back to stand beside Quin.

Audrey saw the older man's hand move to pat Dion's shoulder.

'The ferry,' Rosa continued, 'she's going. Milk? Sugar?'

Audrey shook her head and thanked Rosa as she picked up the cup and sipped the welcome brew. It never failed to comfort her, but she suddenly longed to be sharing tea and hummingbird cake with her parents at their kitchen table in Ballina.

Beppe cleared his throat as though unused to speaking. 'The weather is good now.' It was a gentle voice, and Audrey already felt endeared to this man. Though he bore no physical resemblance to her own father, his unassuming way reminded her of him. She resolved to call her parents as soon as she returned home.

'That's not good news!' Dion's voice contrasted sharply with his grandfather's. 'I was hoping you'd stay.' He'd said it without guile and Audrey felt certain that this would always be the way with him. 'Don't we?' he continued, looking at Quin for support who smiled at him.

'Audrey has to get back to work, remember?' Quin said, passing her a fleeting glance.

Work. How dull that sounded to her. Audrey could feel a

heaviness around her heart as she pictured herself presenting at tomorrow's meeting—if she ever got there.

'I'm afraid so, Dion. But thank you. I'm disappointed, too,' she added.

'Then stay.'

'Enough, enough, Dion.' Rosa clapped her hands as though conducting primary school children. 'I get your clothes, Audrey. How long until ferry, Quin?'

'Fifty minutes. It will only take you five to get there,' Quin said, addressing Audrey.

Rosa hurried off to the rear of the house. Quin stepped forward. 'The car's fine.'

He was standing only a few feet away and Audrey was able to take him in. Closer, in the light of the living room, he looked younger than he had in the shadowed entrance. Mid-late forties perhaps. She'd thought that he might be a farmer from the island, but his complexion was not weathered like other farmers she'd known. There were lines, some deep, between his eyebrows and around the sides of his mouth. His eyes, though, were soft, coloured the green end of hazel. His hair was fair but beginning to grey around his temples and in the fine stubble around his chin and cheeks. He was dressed in jeans and a pale blue denim shirt and Audrey noticed that one side of the collar had not folded down completely, as though he'd dressed quickly. She wondered about his relationship with this family. He and Dion were obviously close, but the style of the man in front of her seemed somehow at odds with the others. He had an educated tone and she pictured him living on a large property that had an expansive home with a wide verandah. But, she decided, he could equally be at home in the corporate world of the city, a maverick who, in a quiet way, called the shots.

Audrey shook her head to clear her thoughts, reminding

herself of her resolve not to give in to whimsy. He probably owns the local pub, she thought.

'Q, I told you that you need accommodation at The Island."

Dion's voice cut through her thoughts, and she realised that this was the name of the hotel she'd seen in the "town".

'Q owns our only pub,' Dion continued, as though plucking Audrey's thoughts from her as fast as they came.

'I've only recently bought it,' Quin said, in what sounded like an apology.

'And I'm going to be working there, aren't I?' Dion said, with apparent pride. 'When it's ready.'

Audrey felt as though her mental dialogue was starting to dictate her reality.

'Yes, I saw the hotel. Hard to miss it,' she said. She remembered that it was an imposing single-storied building of red brick, with a laced, wrought-iron verandah, typical of those built in the early 1900s.

'It's in need of a lot of work,' Quin said, and Audrey had to agree.

'And he's going to open a restaurant,' Dion's voice was becoming louder with excitement, 'and I will be... What'll I do again?'

'You'll have an important role,' Quin said, turning to the boy with a smile.

Dion coloured with pleasure.

'Have you owned a hotel before, Quin?' Audrey hoped her curiosity wasn't too apparent. In her mind, he just didn't fit the bill as the owner of a country pub, though she knew that some hotels were becoming gentrified. In her travels with Campbell, a self-asserted wine buff, they'd visited a few that successfully catered to both the tourist and local trades and Audrey had sometimes envied the tree-change lifestyle of the once-urban owners.

'No, this is the first.' There was a steely look on his face, not directed at her, but as though he was lost in a thought.

What's his story? she wondered and was forming another question when Rosa reappeared with jeans and jumper in hand.

'All good for you now, Audrey.' Still holding the clothes, Rosa beckoned her back in the direction she'd come from.

Audrey turned back to Quin and Dion and saw that Beppe had disappeared once again.

She thanked the others for their kindness, though the words didn't seem to convey the depth of her appreciation.

'I'll follow you to the ferry,' Quin said, 'in case there's a problem.'

'There's no need.' Her reply sounded too quick in her ears, and she reconsidered. 'But if it's not too much trouble, I'd be grateful,' she added.

'I'll come, too,' Dion said, with his trademark enthusiasm.

'I've got to go home from there, mate.' Quin's tone was patient.

Rosa's voice cut across them all, first in Italian to her grandson and then apologetically to Audrey. 'Come, Audrey, or you miss the ferry.'

In a smaller and older bathroom than the one upstairs, Audrey took off the robe, reminding herself to look for one exactly like it when she got home. Her clothes were still warm from the dryer when she put them on, and their familiarity was comforting.

Still in socked feet, she returned to the living area. The others had moved from where she'd left them and Beppe came towards her, holding her shoes that she had left, wet, at the door. When she took them from him, they too felt warm, and she realised that he'd dried them. He coloured as she thanked him.

It was like a different day outside the villa than when she'd arrived only an hour or so beforehand. The thick band of clouds had deconstructed and the sunlight that now bathed the portico held the promise of the warmer months to come.

Her car was waiting for her in the driveway. It looked cleaner than she remembered and there was no caked mud on the back wheels. Just inside the doorway of the opened garage door, she saw a pressure cleaner. She knew it was Beppe who had cleaned the car and turned back to see him, Rosa and Dion standing in the entrance to see her off.

'Thank you, Beppe.'

Beppe smiled and nodded his head.

'Come back soon, Audra,' Dion said, moving towards her with arms outstretched.

Another instruction in Italian was issued from his grandmother that included the correction of her name, but Rosa smiled when Audrey accepted his embrace. Despite his occasional bravado, the hug was tentative. When he released, he stepped back and tucked his chin to his chest. Audrey could see that his face was flushed with colour.

This time, Rosa's voice was soft and crooning as Dion stepped back to stand between his grandparents and Audrey was surprised by a thick ball of emotion forming in her throat. She swallowed.

As she said her goodbyes, thanking them again, she resolved to return before long with a gift for their generous hospitality. The thought of coming back sat well with her.

Audrey checked her rear-view more often than she needed to on the muddy road to the ferry. Quin had offered to lead, but she'd insisted that she was fine and knew her way, as much to regain a sense of her own composure as anything else. He would follow then, he'd said, just in case there was a problem at the other end. Now she felt somehow exposed and wished she hadn't been so hasty. When she checked the mirror again, he flashed his lights and she saw that she'd almost missed the turn-off to the jetty.

As they turned into the car park she saw, to her relief, that the ferry was docked. She drove towards it and waited at the start of the metal ramp until she received the green light to board. Checking her mirror again, she saw that Quin had parked his car and was walking towards her. There was a quiet confidence in his gait, and he held himself very formally, almost rigidly. Audrey wondered if he'd ever served time in the military. He came to her window as she opened it and leaned in.

'All's well. I spoke to Bill earlier and he'd have waited for you, anyway. He'd remembered that you were only planning on coming for the day.'

Audrey now recalled the brief conversation with the ferry driver that she now knew as Bill and felt guilty that she'd remembered so little about him. Had she been so inattentive? Had she even been dismissive?

'Thanks again, Quin, for all you've done. I don't know what I...'

'Think nothing of it,' he said as her voice trailed off. 'Perhaps we'll see you another time, if you would ever want to come back to the island.'

Audrey wasn't sure if she could hear the trace of an invitation. 'I could stay at the hotel... if you had any room.' She'd meant it as a joke and laughed to cover her embarrassment.

'You'd always be welcome. But we're a way off that yet.' He was smiling, but there it was again, that far-off look.

Whimsy! she warned herself. He was probably just a daydreamer, or vague.

'The light's green,' she said, and he drew his head back and stood upright.

'Safe journey, Audrey.' Quin patted the leather padding of the window and stepped away.

She moved the car forward, her heart racing at the thump and clang onto the metal ramp that was the only thing between her and this shallow strip of the Pacific Ocean. Once fully aboard, she looked once more into her rear-vision to see Quin standing beside his car with one hand on his hip and the other waving her goodbye.

CHAPTER ONE

A udrey stirred the hot chocolate with absorbed attention as though searching for life's meaning in its mocha froth. The presentation had gone over very well, Bruce had said with what seemed to be genuine appreciation, indicating that the investors were happy with the galleries' profit margins. Once, she would have been buoyed by the praise, but not now. Once the production of exhibitions would have satisfied her creativity—she was good at it, there was no doubt—but increasingly, she came to realise that, in the end, she was merely an administrator of other people's creativity. She was great at enabling their dreams, but not her own. The bigger problem was, she didn't even know what her dreams were.

There had been a moment, a pause when the investors were discussing aspects of the new proposal to expand the city venue, when her attention had been caught by something outside the window—two horizontal bands of grey, one on top of the other, that mimicked that of the sea and the sky she'd seen on the island from the garden of the old white house.

. . .

Seagulls flew overhead and her ears tuned again to the pounding of the sea. *How does this garden survive its salty blasts?* she'd wondered, as she continued the path's subtle ascent. At the top of the land's rise, she stood in wonder at the sight before her. The ocean was vast, and she could hear it hurling itself violently against the cliffs fifty metres below.

In front of her was a low fence and a gate. Behind it was an expanse of grass only marginally protected by the salt bushes and low tea trees at the cliff's edge. She opened the gate and walked to its centre. The wind buffeted so strongly that her cheeks stung as though from a slap. The sight before her was wild—whitecapped waves angled in irregular patterns, evidence of the wind's fickle mood. It could have been foreboding—the ingredients to fuel melancholia that seemed to visit her more often now, thickening and deepening since the separation—but she felt calm as though she'd stumbled upon a moment when unseen forces coalesced; a moment to savour...

Flashes of memory like this had visited her often over the three weeks since she'd been to the island, taking her by surprise. She'd remembered the verandah sagging at its right-hand corner, the stem of wisteria thick as a man's forearm wrapped around one of its posts. When she'd looked through one of the front windows veiled in thin terylene, cupping her hands around her temples to keep out light, she'd just been able to make out the bare floorboards, solid but hungry for oil, and at the rear of the room, the black marble mantle. Through the other—a bay window whose curtain didn't quite reach the sill— she could make out a faded brown Westminster carpet. Lying on it was a cardboard coaster with an upside-down photo of a building and *The Island* written across the top, the words almost obscured by the round stain where a glass had been regularly placed. She'd forgotten about that coaster until she'd come home. Quin's hotel. She remembered how excited Dion was to work there when it was renovated, the gentle tone of Quin's voice when he spoke to the boy, and the sight of him in the rearview waving goodbye.

'Thanks, Nina.'

Audrey's fingers hesitated on the keypad of her phone until the cup had been removed, then typed in her search and waited for the real estate listings to load. There were several in the region and she scrolled quickly through the new subdivisions on the mainland to the only one on the island—the old white house. Audrey stared at the banner across the top of the photo —*Under Offer*—unsure if she felt disappointment or relief. The price at the bottom of the photo was affordable, and too high given the amount of work it needed, but her argument lacked conviction.

'That's that then,' she muttered, putting the phone on the table. Her shoulders relaxed and she began to feel lighter, as though the house and the memory of that day had become a slight weight. But she knew it wasn't over yet; there was a promise she'd made to herself, to return to the island with a gift for Rosa, Beppe, Dion, and Quin.

Audrey was putting the phone into her handbag when it rang in her hand. The sight of the name on the phone startled her and she considered ignoring it, though she was slightly intrigued.

'Cam.'

'Audrey.'

His tone was soft, and she was momentarily caught in a time warp, a residue of memory when her heart would accelerate at the sound of his voice, as it did now, but, she reminded herself, for different reasons.

It was the first time they'd spoken in months. The divorce

would go ahead in a few weeks' time, but there'd been no need to speak. She didn't want to speak.

She waited for him to continue, and when he did, his voice was hesitant, nervous.

'I want to thank you...'

For what? she wondered. She'd had no choice in agreeing to splitting the assets, even though the warehouse, and the apartments—one after the other when he'd gotten bored and wanted to move on—had only been possible because she'd owned the first one outright and had made enough profit to fund subsequent moves. As much as she was upset with him about it, she was annoyed with herself for her weakness.

'Cam, what's this about?'

There was a pause at the other end. He would be pacing as he made this call, she thought, and he's stopped to consider his next move. It was always this way with him. Her suspicions rose.

'I want to see you... take you out... for lunch, as a gesture of my appreciation.'

I want. If there was a phrase that summed him up, it was that one.

She was on the verge of ending the call when his voice cut into her thoughts.

'There's something I need to talk about.'

How quickly her resolve began its disintegration. She felt it and tried to restore its integrity, but she and he had a history and, despite all that had happened, it still meant something to her.

'Talk about it with Caroline.' Audrey was aware of feeling something akin to sympathy for *her*—Caroline—the new woman who would, sooner or later, reach her use-by-date. Perhaps it was sooner than she thought.

'Aud—'

'What, Cam? I'm not your confidante anymore.' God knows she'd filled that role often enough.

'Please, Aud.'

So many times, she'd heard that appeal. *Please Aud—I need more time, I need more love, I need more...*

'You can tell me on the phone, Cam.'

She heard his sigh and something else—a catch in his voice. She gave in.

'Okay, I can meet you later today.'

'Thanks.' His tone was laboured, tired. 'Café Romano?'

No, she thought, not there. It had been their favourite place for an afternoon drink. He'd meet her there on her return from the gallery, after he'd been painting all day. They'd both be tired but pleased to see each other, to talk about their day, to relax over a drink. The little things.

But you're over him, she told herself in a challenge to her own courage. 'Sure. See you there at four.'

When they'd ended the call and she was putting her phone away, Audrey wondered if she was making a very big mistake.

It would have been quicker to catch the train, she thought as the tram ground to a halt once again. Meeting Cam at this hour when the traffic was at its worst was unwise, but Audrey doubted there was much wisdom involved in agreeing to meet him anyway. The tram was crowded and there was an uncomfortable lack of personal space between standing passengers. She was fortunate to have found a spot in a recess away from the door, but a man in a smart blue suit had moved into the space in front of her with his back to her and was reading a news article on his phone.

His collar's up. I wonder if I should tell him. Audrey could feel her fingers itching to turn it down. What if she did? How would he react? It would be misconstrued; it was an intimate thing, to turn down someone's collar. Perhaps the upturn was deliberate, she thought, but he wasn't of the generation and the style of the suit jacket suggested he was conservative. As though reading her mind, or sensing her staring at his neck, the man turned slightly towards her. Audrey averted her eyes, but the collar still bothered her. He'd want to know, but what she really meant was that Cam would have wanted to know. She imagined Cam leaving his new house—Caroline's house—the Victorian terrace in one of Melbourne's leafy, opulent suburbs, so unlike Cam to want to live there, and she, Caroline, would catch him at the door and might say, 'There, that's better,' as she turned down his collar. Would she lean into his neck to savour his aftershave? Strange, she thought, that in the absence of a scent you can still smell it, still feel the same surge of emotion. She wondered if the man in front of her was wearing the same one and felt for a moment that her mind and muscles would betray her logic to make her lean in. When she looked back at him, he'd turned away and the collar had somehow turned itself down.

Life folds and unfolds without you, Audrey, she thought, further confirmation that any control she might exert on her life was an illusion. It was a lesson she really needed to learn.

She was five minutes late and searched the crowded tables for him. *Of course he's not here,* and couldn't remember a time when he would be there before her on those afternoons, even though he'd been home all day at the apartment, just a five minute walk away.

From her vantage point at the door, she saw a couple leave their table at the rear and manoeuvred her way to claim their chairs, nodding at a few familiar faces, though the level of noise restricted all but up-close conversation.

When she was settled on the high stool at the equally high table and facing the entrance so that she could assess Cam from a distance—something she had done habitually to determine his mood—Audrey checked her mobile phone. There was a missed call from Bruce, and she dug out her earphones while she waited for the message to come through.

Bruce's voice was animated and high as though he'd been drinking. After she'd listened a fourth time, she took out her earphones, folded and then refolded the wires and returned them to her handbag in an automated sequence. Slowly, as she sat staring at the entrance of the café for reasons she couldn't quite remember, her thoughts coalesced.

'The investors want to expand the gallery franchise,' Bruce had said. 'In London, and they want you to head it up. If you agree, it will be effective immediately.'

'Aud.'

The voice so close to her ear startled her and Audrey was surprised to see Cam standing beside her.

'You were far away,' he said, as he settled onto the stool in front of her, placing wallet—new, she noted—and car keys—Audi, she couldn't fail to notice—on the table. Café Romano was a long way from where he lived now, and she doubted now that he did miss the stroll down the road.

He'd convinced her that it was perfect for them—an old, inner-city warehouse that had been renovated to perfection—open plan living, skylights that bathed the mezzanine bedrooms, studio space for him and the living area downstairs in a warm light, winter and summer, a rooftop garden with views to the city. No office space for her, though; she would set up at the end of the oak dining room table when needed. He'd offered her the studio space, but she knew as well as he did that it was impractical. 'Really, it's no problem for me,' she'd said, and Audrey knew that this had been an all-too-common expression.

It hadn't taken too much convincing; she'd loved it too, though it had meant a small mortgage, a fact that seemed to give Cam more leverage when it came to claiming half the proceeds from the sale. His elation had been contagious, and Audrey had hoped that it would finally make him happy, that he'd settle and perhaps even think about having children.

For the first year, it seemed to work. When they would meet at Romano's, he would be buoyed by the day's work, eager to tell her about the breakthroughs and progress on the latest work, sometimes several paintings on the go at the one time. On occasion, she would see paint residue in his hair and under his nails even though he'd shower before meeting her, and for some reason this gave her great joy, as though a positive portent for their future together. When he was creating, Cam was happy, calm, loving and optimistic, but the dry spells inevitably came and she came to realise that there were no external factors—the apartment, and herself included—that could prevent them. In these times, Cam alternated between a great restlessness and the need to be entertained by some new experience—travel, parties—or, more frequently, he slept for much of the day, meeting her here in a sullen and pessimistic mood.

Audrey assessed the man in front of her. Which man was he today?

It had been months since she'd last seen him, when they'd sat opposite each other at the solicitor's office, a cold shaft of light on the documents spread before them spotlighting their failure. Afterwards, he'd offered to buy her a drink at a local bar and seemed relieved when she declined. Audrey didn't want to celebrate his future freedom. For her, it would be the ending of a dream, a fanciful, hopeful and irrational dream. She'd stepped away as he tried to kiss her forehead goodbye, and headed home to her rented apartment, picking up a bottle of gin on the way.

He looked tired, she thought now, and felt a small internal sag of something in her intestines, a vestigial reaction. She took in his face as discreetly as she could, its familiarity momentarily taking her breath away as though every fair hair of his eyebrows and lashes was known to her, the scar beneath his nose an old friend. His hair was shorter than she ever remembered and made him look older. Thinking of the man on the tram with the upturned collar, her eyes wandered to his neckline, and she realised that, like today, Cam preferred a black t-shirt, very rarely wearing a shirt. How could she have forgotten?

'Hi,' she said, wondering what it was that they'd talked about in those afternoons, and it struck her that he'd seldom been genuinely interested in her day.

Audrey felt an urgency to get this meeting over with. Bruce's message was still playing in the back of her mind, and she needed time to think it through.

'You look well, Aud.'

'So do you.'

Cam looked down as though sensing her lie and studied his fingers that were reading his wallet and keys like braille.

'Drink?'

Oh, for God's sake get it over with, she thought, but nodded in agreement instead.

While he was at the bar, she listened one more time to Bruce's message, not trusting that she'd heard it correctly. It was a great opportunity and a recognition of the passion and energy she'd invested over the years. But Audrey couldn't deny that her most immediate reaction was anxiety. 'Here you go,' Cam said, as he placed the glass in front of her. It was an uncharacteristic expression and she wondered if this was how he spoke with Caroline. Was he becoming someone else? Had the Cam she'd known been a reflection of herself? The thought unsettled her.

The seconds crawled as they each took a sip from their drink. Her foot slipped from the rung of the stool, betraying her discomfort.

'Cam. What do you want to talk about?'

He placed his glass down, took a deep breath and spoke to the table.

'I miss you, Aud.'

On the way home Audrey replayed the scene she'd just left.

At first, she'd forced the feeling of indifference, reminding herself that the man in front of her had betrayed her. But she couldn't deny the history they shared; they'd seen rough moments, but also good times of love, laughter and intimacy. Cam was a paradox, but Audrey also knew that their marriage had not been a total sham—she hadn't been a fool, she hadn't been conned, and she hadn't been blameless.

His relationship with Caroline was floundering, he'd said, and had seemed sincere and humble. He'd realised that he'd made a terrible mistake, that he found himself thinking of Audrey more and more each day.

'It's funny, you know, but it's the little things I miss, the things you did for me—the cup of tea that you'd bring into the studio before you went to bed, the crustier portion of lasagne you'd serve for me, the missing button on my favourite jacket that you replaced after you'd searched the haberdasheries. I noticed, Aud.'

He'd looked up and searched her face that she'd tried to keep as impassive as possible.

'But I didn't tell you, back then. And now it's too late.'

Had she heard it as a question? There'd been a flicker of something in his eyes. Had it been hope? Audrey had felt her pulse quicken and knew that the adrenalin was working its way into her muscles. She'd placed the glass down carefully and looked away from him. At a table by the wall, a couple were sitting very closely, talking directly, lovingly, into each other's faces. As though on cue, the background music changed from a rhythm that was keeping pace with her heart, to a mellow and lazy jazz, the sound that had filled their Sunday afternoons.

She'd look back at him.

'Yes, Cam. It's too late,' she'd said.

As she stepped into the apartment, its silence felt like a scream of failure and loneliness. All the effort she'd made—leaving the warehouse and renting it out so she wouldn't be surrounded by memories, sorting through boxes and eliminating evidence of him, reducing herself to reading "self-help" books on grief and loss—had been pointless. She hadn't purged him from her mind or her heart, only buried him deeper. And now that she'd seen him, had heard him, it was as though he'd been released to wander her psyche.

She slumped onto the arm of the sofa as though she'd been drained of life force and knew that she needed to change her life. Her index finger hovered briefly over the recall button on her phone.

'Hi, Bruce.' She mustered enough energy to convey a sound of enthusiasm, even if it was a lie. 'That's such wonderful news. I'm shocked... and honoured.'

Bruce gave her the details—a one-year contract initially, flights home to visit family, settling costs, and told her she had a week to think it over. He'd be able to manage the galleries here while she was away, he said, thanks to all the work she'd put in.

'It's a wonderful opportunity, Bruce, I'd be foolish to give it up. Thanks for your endorsement of me. I'll let you know before the end of the week.'

She paused before adding, 'But I think I know what my answer will be.'

She sat a while longer on the arm of the sofa. It was a once in a lifetime chance and she would say yes. The stars were surely aligning in her favour. But she felt deflated.

CHAPTER TWO

The mainland road to the ferry had been resurfaced in bitumen since she'd travelled it only three weeks before, and Audrey noted that some of the newly subdivided housing lots had been sold, especially those closest to the tidal flats that looked towards Hibernia. The wheels on the new surface were relatively silent, and she remembered how much she'd loved the crunching sound of them on the old scoria, as though a reminder that she'd gotten off the beaten track.

Ahead, she could just see the glassed cabin of the ferry, the rest of the boat being obscured by a dense band of mangroves, and she felt a sudden acceleration of her heartbeat. She lowered the window and breathed in salty air tinged with the sulfurous odour of anaerobic sand. In the city, she was beleaguered by allergies that narrowed the internal layers of her nostrils, but now, with each breath sucked as though through a straw, she could feel them relaxing and widening. With her head angled out of the window, Audrey took a deep inhalation as a soft breeze licked her face and she exhaled a long and audible sigh.

Turning into the parking bay in front of the ferry, she was surprised how much closer the island appeared than on her last trip. That day, the wind had whipped up a salty spray that had created a veil of mist between it and the mainland, but today there was only a breeze, and, in the sun, she could see clearly to the make-shift marina on the other side, and the carpark behind where Quin had waved her goodbye.

Two other cars were boarding ahead of her, and Bill was collecting money through the driver windows. When he saw her pull up behind the ramp, he waved and smiled in recognition and, spontaneously, she returned it as though greeting an old friend. She remembered how she had thought unkindly of him when she'd been close to being stranded on the island.

He waved her forward and she edged the car onto the ramp with more confidence than she'd felt last time.

'Hello, love. Audrey, isn't it?'

'That's right. How are you, Bill?'

'Good, good, love. Can't keep away from our island, eh?'

There was no reason for her to blush, but she could feel her face warming and was about to launch into an uncalled-for explanation as she handed over the fare, but he gave her window a friendly tap and went behind her car to draw in the ramp.

There was a remnant of winter chill in the breeze as they crossed the stretch, but Audrey kept the window open. With her hands off the steering wheel and cupped instead around the eco-cup she'd had filled with espresso at the last café on the mainland, she relaxed into the seat and felt the muscles in her shoulders slowly releasing. The ferry moved slowly, giving a sense of the island being further away than it was—three kilometers, she'd read, but it would take more than thirty minutes to get there. 'I'm in no hurry,' she said aloud and repeated it to embed it into her psyche.

As the ferry moved through the water, Audrey's thoughts turned to the pressing subject of London and the job offer. She'd called her parents to tell them about the offer but didn't mention the meeting with Cam as she knew they'd be concerned. Though they'd never said anything, she was aware that they didn't think he was good enough for her and had initially put it down to their parental protectiveness.

For her sake, they'd tried to embrace him as their son-in-law, but Cam had retained an almost formal distance. When she'd questioned him on it, he'd adopted a look of bewilderment —'I don't know what you mean, Aud. Isabel and Max are... good... simple people. Of course I like them,'—and she suspected that he thought they weren't good enough for him. Her parents' life together was simple, humble, but it was through choice rather than economic circumstances. Max's long tenure as a professor of environmental science had enabled them to travel extensively, which they still did, and to fund building projects in Timor-Leste. Their house by the sea in Ballina was modest, eco-friendly and their substantial garden a permaculture haven. Over the years of her marriage to Cam, she had more often visited them alone.

There'd been a small silence when she told her mother about the job in London before Isabel finally spoke. 'It's a wonderful opportunity, my darling,' she said, and Audrey was about to agree when she continued, 'but is it what you want?'

Audrey allowed herself the admission. 'I don't know, Mum; that's the trouble.'

She had discussed it on the phone with her friend Poppy, who lived in Paris. 'The only good thing about that job is that you'll be closer to me!' Poppy's voice had the tone of a mother berating a child. 'But it's not *you* anymore, Aud. What about you? Find yourself, my darling.'

They'd been the best of friends since their first meeting

when Poppy was a struggling artist. Not in the clichéd sense that Audrey had experienced with some others—full of self-grandeur and disdain that disguised their insecurities and bitterness. No, Poppy's was a true talent, with an enthusiasm and love for her work that was contagious. She painted and sculpted purely for the love of it and took any job on to support it. When Bruce had "discovered" her work at a local market, he took a risk and signed her up for an exhibition at the gallery. A star was born. Poppy moved to Paris to study and exhibit her work, returning for a few months to support Audrey in the early days of the break-up.

'He's an arsehole anyway,' had been her first words, as she'd embraced Audrey in the arrivals lounge of the airport, making Audrey laugh for the first time in weeks. Poppy could always be relied on to make her laugh.

Finally, she decided that she would take the position. In a way, Cam had been the deciding factor, but she still had a few days left until she needed to commit and once done, there would be a whirlwind of things to do. The Board members were keen for her to come as soon as possible. The reconstruction of the old warehouse in Waterloo was near to completion and Audrey would be required to advise on the finer details of its refurbishment. Bruce was already working on contracts for some big names in the UK to exhibit at the opening in July and the next months would move at a frenetic pace.

'It seems very late in the process to be appointing a director,' she'd said to Bruce, as they studied the photos that had been sent by the Site Manager.

Something flickered across his face, and he looked guarded. 'Yes, well, the original Director they had in mind took up another offer, in New York, I believe.'

So, she'd been the second choice. Audrey wondered why she was not surprised. Bruce seemed to sense it and was quick to add that the Board members were very excited to have her if she accepted.

Audrey leaned back into the seat of the car and closed her eyes. Today, she would not think of the gallery, of London, or of Cam. He'd called her three times since their meeting, and she'd deleted the messages without listening to them. She glanced at the screen of the phone lying at the top of her open bag. There'd be no reliable signal on the island anyway, she remembered, and this time she'd be glad of it.

The ferry began to softly shudder as it slowed down on entry to Hibernia's dock. There'd be four hours to kill until the return trip and once she'd visited Rosa and Beppe and given them the gifts, she'd take another tour of the island.

The two vehicles ahead of her—an old Ute that looked as though it was held together by its rust, and a sedan with two straw sun hats sitting on the back shelf, began to disembark. Audrey couldn't see either of the drivers, but assumed they were locals by the way that Bill had stopped at each window for a chat. She smiled when she saw him tap the open driver windowsill—it seemed to be his trademark move. He approached her car.

'Y'over for the night, or heading back today?'

'Back today, Bill,' she said, liking the easy familiarity that was developing between them now.

'Okay, love. We'll be heading back at four. No weather issues today, like last time.' Bill turned around to take in the island and the sea, his smile reflecting something akin to pride and contentment.

'You're becoming a regular,' he added and there was something mischievous in his voice. He didn't wait for a response but turned away, not before patting the window as he left.

'I'll see you then,' he called over his shoulder. 'Have a good one, love.'

. . .

With the back wheels of the car safely onto land, Audrey let out a sigh of relief as she headed up the drive to the road. Fear of deep water had embedded itself in her psyche. Apart from being held underwater in a backyard pool by the teenage son of family friend when she was seven, she couldn't think of any other reason for it. Phobias just creep up on you without a cause, she reasoned.

There was no sign of the other two cars, or anyone else, and she eased off the accelerator to savour the island's air that tasted of salt and smelled of warm straw.

The roadside was thick with saltbush, Salicornia and low tea-tree, and small birds—a stunningly blue male wren and his harem of brown females, white-faced finches, and wattlebirds darting through the shrubs. Audrey stopped the car to watch them. On the sandy roadside, large bull ants crisscrossed each other's paths, while the small sugar ants maintained an ordered line. A cabbage moth, early for this time of the year, took a break on the bonnet of the car, then alighted and resumed its lonely journey. In the background, Audrey could hear the thudding of the sea and was reminded of the same sound that had drawn her to the backyard of the old white house, and how the Pacific Ocean had stretched out before her.

How different the island seemed to her on this calm and beautiful spring day, though its tempestuous mood had equally excited her. Before her visit three weeks ago, she had rarely left the sterile confines of the city except to visit her parents, and her grandmother when she was alive, and even then, she had flown.

The left-hand turn was coming up that would take her to the villa. Audrey mentally rehearsed what she would say to Rosa, Beppe, Dion and Quin, and hoped that they liked the gifts she'd brought for them. As she'd forgotten to ask for their landline number, and there was little to no signal in spots on the island, she hadn't been able to call beforehand, so if they weren't there, she'd simply leave the gifts at the door, with the cards she'd pre-written in case. It was a long way to come on the off-chance they'd be home, but she had to admit she was drawn to returning to the island, anyway.

Twenty metres ahead was a sign to the island's Post Office. On impulse, she turned right in its direction, crossing the bridge over a mangrove-lined river, and away from her route to Rosa and Beppe's.

The Island Hotel looked as though it was once again shrouded in a mist and, as she approached, a puff of white dust billowed from the open double doors and windows. A male figure emerged in what reminded her of a scene from an old sci-fi movie. He wore overalls and a dust mask hung on its straps below his chin. His hair was coated grey and when the cloud began to settle, she saw that it was Quin. The muscles in Audrey's foot above the accelerator began to flex, but Dion, like a powdery carbon copy, had followed Quin out and turned towards the car as she approached.

'Audra! Audra!' He was moving quickly towards her, and she slowed down to a stop.

'Dion,' she called back through the open passenger window, 'how are you?'

'It's good to see you!' As he leaned in towards the window, dust particles projected forward, some catching in the back of Audrey's throat and making her cough. In her peripheral view she saw Quin coming towards her.

'Hello, Audrey.' He stood beside Dion and removed the mask to below his chin. The fine layer of dust on his face accentuated the lines around his mouth and forehead and the ends of his eyelashes were tipped in white. 'It *is* good to see you.'

When he smiles, his eyes crinkle, she thought.

She cleared her throat. 'I was on my way to see Rosa and Beppe, to thank them... and both of you... for all your help the other week.'

'You've come the wrong way then, Audra,' Dion said. 'You turned right when...'

'It's "Audrey", Dion, but lucky for us she did,' Quin cut in.

'Are you staying this time, Audra?' Dion said, his eyes wide with hope. 'You're welcome, you know.'

'No, Dion, but thank you. I'll just visit Rosa and Beppe and I'll have to get back.'

'You've got four hours. Don't let Nonna talk to you for that long. Come back and I'll cook you lunch. I'll wash first, I promise.'

'Actually, that's a good idea,' Quin said, smiling approvingly at Dion then turning to Audrey. 'Will you?'

It didn't take too much consideration before Audrey agreed, thinking that it would provide her with a chance to give them their gifts. She wondered, on looking back at the hotel, where he would be doing the cooking. Dion beamed as she accepted.

'How's the renovation going?' she said to Quin.

He turned to look at the hotel, then back to her. 'It's a bigger project than I thought. But we'll get there.'

'Yes, we'll get there,' Dion added. 'One hour with Nonna and Nonno, Audra. That's all, okay? He consulted his watch again. 'See you at twelve-thirty.'

Audrey couldn't help but smile at his serious expression.

'Will do,' she said.

'Perfect. I'm setting my timer now.'

Quin, who was standing back, smiled at her over Dion's shoulder.

'You better not be late,' he said, 'or we'll hear about it all afternoon.'

'Right. I'll be here.'

Both men stood back as she took off.

There were smiles on all their faces.

Audrey placed the large bag she was carrying on the portico before accepting Rosa's embrace.

'What pleasure, Audrey,' Rosa said, stepping back to take her in. She turned and called through the open doorway behind her. 'Beppe, Beppe!'

Audrey could hear the shuffle of feet on the terrazzo floor. Beppe came into view and her heart was stirred once again by the sight of his gentle face and humble demeanour.

'Hello, Beppe,' she said, moving forward and resisting the urge to hug him in case she embarrassed him.

He nodded shyly in acknowledgement. 'Hello, Audrey. Is good to see you.'

'Come in. Come in, *mio caro*,' Rosa said and slipped her arm around Audrey's waist as she guided her forward in a replay of three weeks earlier.

The living space ahead, Audrey remembered, had been filled with light even on that dull day weeks ago, but today it looked as though it was aflame as the sun hit the terracotta tiles and off-white walls. Beyond the glass doors, the bright green of new citrus leaves provided an almost shocking contrast, and tall leaves of fennel softened the herb gardens in a feathery blur. A cabbage moth dipped and rose, and Audrey was pleased that the solitary one she'd seen on the road near the ferry might find a mate after all—that is, if Rosa or Beppe didn't see it first.

This time, Rosa steered her to the right of the living area

and to the kitchen, which, unlike the open plan of many newer homes, was a separate room. Every bit of wall space seemed to be utilised—Blackwood cupboards, racks with jars, hooks for cooking utensils and pots of various sizes. A very large stove was centrally placed directly ahead of the doorway and was surrounded by marble-topped benches. In contrast to the walls, they were bare except for a knife rack, a large, green-glassed bottle that she assumed contained olive oil, and a salt cellar. In the middle of the room was a wooden table that, although clean, had a washed look as though permanently coated in flour. An industrial-sized pasta machine sat at the end closest to her. The room had retained the odour of garlic and onions and rich sauces that conjured thoughts of delicious, hearty Italian fare.

Rosa issued an instruction to Beppe who had followed them in, and he quickly brought forward a chair that had been nestled in a corner of the room.

'Sit, darling,' Rosa said, and Audrey obeyed, placing the bag at her feet.

'I make you tea? Nettle? And you stay for lunch,' she said, having already taken an apron from the back of the door and was tying it around her waist.

'Oh... thank you, Rosa, but... you see, Dion is cooking me lunch at the hotel.'

Rosa paused. 'You see Dion?

'Yes, I drove past the hotel. They were working—'

'You see Quin too?'

'Yes,' Audrey said, noticing the look that Rosa gave to Beppe.

'*Bella*. This is good, Audrey. Dion will cook you a good meal. This,' she said with her hands out to encompass the kitchen, 'is where he lives to be. This is right, Beppe?'

'Yes,' Beppe said, coming from behind Audrey into view. 'He's very... talen... tal ...'

'Talented?' Audrey offered.

He nodded, kissed the tips of his pinched fingers and spread them in an almost clichéd gesture that made Audrey smile.

Remembering her purpose in being there, she lifted the bag beside her to her lap and took out a potted white orchid in a protective cardboard surround.

'I want to thank you, for all you did for me a few weeks ago,' she said as they moved in beside her. She stood up and gave it to Rosa. 'You were so kind to do that.'

'Oh, Audrey, it is beautiful... isn't it, Beppe?... but it was our pleasure.'

While Rosa carried the orchid to a bench near the sink, Audrey took out a smaller gift that she had wrapped in layers of red tissue paper and tied with bright blue string.

'And this is for you, Beppe,' she said, 'for cleaning my car, and drying my boots.'

Beppe moved in closer to accept it. He fumbled with the string, but as it released and the tissue paper unravelled, Audrey held her breath. His face was a mixture of curiosity and pleasure as he lifted out the square wooden box and studied the sepia painting on its lid—a single olive tree with a thick, gnarled trunk and wide branches that seemed to bend under the weight of its fruit.

He looked up and his broad smile almost brought a tear to her eye.

Rosa returned with the Moth orchid now out of its box and sitting on a white saucer of fine bone china. She placed it in the middle of the table, and they marvelled at its single long stem and five delicate white flowers that seemed even more fragile in this hard-surfaced and utility-style kitchen.

'Oh Beppe, this is lovely,' Rosa said, as she moved next to him and took in the box that was still in his hand. 'What is it used for, Audrey?'

Audrey shook her head and laughed. 'To be honest, Rosa, I have no idea. For some reason, when I saw it I thought of Beppe.'

Beppe suddenly turned and left the room, taking the box with him. When he returned, moments later, he placed it on the table and nodded to Audrey to open it. Inside were five small plant bulbs.

'What are they?' she said, not understanding what he was showing her.

'The future,' he said, looking at her directly.

On closer inspection, Audrey recognised them as the bulbs of the crocus plant that her mother had grown to harvest saffron. She knew, too, that they grew here, remembering the remnants of the purple flower she had found in the garden of the old house next door.

'Good luck for London,' Rosa said through the window and Beppe confirmed it with a nod and a smile as they stood beside the car. 'Send us a postcard of Big Bill. You have our address now.'

'I will. It's been lovely seeing you again,' Audrey said and, on impulse added, 'I'll call you before I leave, now that I have your number.'

'Yes. Do that,' Beppe said, leaning forward. 'Come back to see us when you can.'

'Most definitely.' Audrey checked the time. 'Well, I'd better get back to the hotel.'

'Sì. You don't want to keep Dion waiting,' Rosa said, rolling her eyes in mock frustration. 'Or Quin,' she added, giving Beppe "that look" again.

When Audrey checked the mirror and saw them standing in the middle of the road waving her goodbye, she resolved to come back on a return trip from London. Once they were out of sight, she paused by the old white house. The *Under Offer* sticker that she'd seen on her web search was still in place, though curling at the corners, and she hoped that whoever was buying it would not pull the house down but see its existing potential. With its face in the morning sun, the house seemed to cast a benevolent eye over the buttercups and onion weed that had taken hold and were flaunting their blooms at the foot of the tilting verandah. The thick and twisted trunk of the wisteria wrapped around the post had sprouted tendrils that swayed in the soft breeze in search of somewhere to anchor. A swallow darted from beneath the bullnose, flew in a wide arc and returned. Through the open window of the car, she could hear the manic chirping of her babies in their nest.

There was a glint of metal in the sunlight on the wall near the front door. When Audrey looked closely, she saw the name *Hibernia* written in fading gold letters on a white metal plate and wondered that she hadn't seen it before. She was tempted to get out of the car to study it closer, to follow the line of the house past the palm tree whose fronds trembled under the onslaught of parrots, to see again that wild garden at the rear and check if the fruit trees were blossoming, and to hear the roar of the ocean behind. But the house was not hers and would belong to someone else, and soon she would be far away, this house on the island forgotten in the pace of London life. Audrey drove on to the hotel with a heavy heart and the sense of another dream abandoned.

. . .

The dust had settled around The Island Hotel and there was no sign of Dion or Quin outside. As Audrey drove into the carpark, she was surprised to see that a section of the wetland she had crossed earlier in the day curved inwards towards the hotel like a glistening lagoon. Each time she'd been here, it had been obscured by either low lying cloud, or dust.

Fastening her hair in a loose bun with a tortoiseshell comb, she checked her reflection before applying a stroke of clear lip gloss and got out. There was a light, cool breeze so she grabbed her jacket from the back seat.

After taking the gifts from the back of the car and locking it, she paused to take in the view. This section of the island sat halfway on ascending land that fanned from the marina and mangrove flats opposite the mainland, to the high cliffs that butted against the Pacific Ocean. Most of the land had been cleared many years before for farming, though here and there were clusters of densely planted trees—eucalypts, she assumed —that suggested there were attempts to regenerate the natural flora and to act as wind breaks.

As Audrey approached the back of the hotel, her sense of smell was blasted by the odours of toasting seeds—cardamom, cumin and fennel—familiar and welcome, that conjured memories of coming in the back door of her childhood home after school, where warmed and fragrant za'atar bread would be waiting for her alongside a small bowl of her mother's version of baba ghanoush. Audrey remembered that, beneath the knife beside the china bread and butter plate, would be a starched and carefully folded white napkin. It was a simple gesture bursting with the complexity and richness of a mother's love.

Ahead of her, she saw that, on a rough-bricked patio, a table had been set for three, complete with colourful Moroccan-styled plates, cutlery and glass tumblers on an Italian-styled red and white check tablecloth. A glass pitcher containing banksia flowers took centre place, and three old wrought-iron chairs with mismatching cushions on vinyl seats were positioned to take in the view.

'Hello, Audrey.'

Quin had come out from a door at the rear of the hotel. She could see that he had washed and changed into a cream shirt and jeans, though his well-worn Blundstones retained evidence of the morning's labour.

His hair was damp and swept back from his forehead and his skin had a sheen from washing and the astringent effect of a subtle aftershave.

'It smells beautiful... the cooking.'

He smiled in response. 'Oh, Dion's cooking you up a storm. I hope you like spices.'

Audrey was surprised as she'd been expecting something Italian. She told him about her mother's heritage, and how she had learned from her how to cook Spanish and Middle Eastern dishes.

'I have a passion for spices,' she added, taking herself by surprise. She'd *had* a passion, she really meant, until it was subdued over the years spent cooking bland meals. Despite the persona that Cam projected—well-travelled, cosmopolitan and spontaneous—in Audrey's mind his taste in food was mediocre.

'Yes, I can see the Spanish in you,' Quin said. 'Your dark hair and eyes. Quite beautiful,' he added, looking down at his boots as though studying the patterns formed by the dried concrete dust.

Silence hung briefly in the space between them until Dion erupted from the door, resplendent in a black chef's apron and cap.

'Right on time, Audra,' he said coming over to greet her.

'Audrey,' Quin reminded him gently.

Audrey quite liked the new name and gave Quin a look of

reassurance. 'I didn't want to miss it,' she said and meant it. 'The smell is amazing.'

Dion moved with something like a proud swagger to the table and pulled out a chair, gesturing with a flourish for her to sit down.

Quin offered her a drink as she placed the bag containing the gifts beside her and took a seat. She'd give them later, she decided, not wanting to steal any of Dion's thunder.

'Water would be great, thanks,' Audrey said and then, turning to Dion, she asked, 'What's on the menu?'

He paused and turned to Quin. 'Audra's our first customer!' Straightening his back and turning to her, he continued in a suddenly formal voice, 'Stewed lamb and preserved lemon tagine with fragrant couscous. I'm afraid,' he added, with a serious expression, 'that we don't have, and never will have, quinoa.'

There was a sudden burst of laughter from Quin that took her by surprise, and she noticed how much younger he looked. Something inside her smiled.

'Audrey might like quinoa, mate,' he said, smiling broadly.

'Do you?' Dion said, alarmed. 'Are you vegetarian? Vegan?'

Audrey couldn't hold back her own laugh at the look of horror on his face. 'No, no, Dion, I'm a proud omnivore and lamb tagine with couscous is perfect. I can't wait.'

'Whew,' he said, with an exaggerated bend at the waist in relief. Straightening up, he checked his watch. 'Right. I'd better get back to it. It won't be long.'

At the wire door to the rear of the hotel, he paused and turned back to them. 'In the meantime, you two can get acquainted.'

When he'd gone inside, Quin gave Audrey a look of mock exasperation.

'I'll be back in a moment,' he said, 'with your water.'

Audrey settled into the chair. The wetland extended from the base of the rise on which the hotel stood—approximately fifty metres ahead of her—to another elevated area she estimated to be two kilometres away. Light filtered through the tall canopy formed by Redgums, their feet submerged in the mud beneath the water. A wood duck appeared from its hiding place in the thick reeds at the water's edge and was quickly followed by four babies who slid into the water behind her.

She closed her eyes and watched as her lids became a crimson-tinted screen lit by the gentle sun. Woven into the odour of spices from the kitchen behind her was the scent of saltbush, mud and detritus, not unpleasant, but rich and organic. Close by, she could hear the warble of crested doves and, further away in a harsh contrast, the screech of a sulphur-crested cockatoo.

Audrey heard the wire door softly close and opened her eyes. Quin was holding a jug of water. A sprig of mint and ice cubes swirled as he poured into the glass in front of her, the ice clinking against the side of her glass in a happy sound that reminded her that hot summer days were approaching.

He poured one for himself and sat down next to her rather than opposite and she was pleased. It seemed somehow less confronting. Together, they sat in silence looking at the wetland until he spoke.

'Are you warm enough?' he asked. She nodded, glad she'd put on the jacket.

'It's a different view in summer.'

'I was just wondering about that,' Audrey said. 'Does any of the water remain?'

'Some. It recedes to about half that size.' He was still looking ahead. 'Then it reveals another version of itself, another beauty—wildflowers and grasses. It's never dried out, at least in my memory.'

'How long is that? Your memory of this place,' she said, turning in her seat towards him.

He did the same and when he faced her squarely, she felt a rise of blood in her cheeks.

'I was born on the island, though I've spent most of my years away from here, boarding at school and university in Melbourne, and then overseas—the US and South-East Asia mostly.'

'For work or leisure?' she asked, curious about this man in front of her.

'Work mostly. Sustainable construction.'

'It's a growing industry, I believe.' She was intrigued but confessed to him then that she knew very little about it other than what her father, Max, had told her. In recent years, he'd been an advisor for a project in south-east Asia.

'Yes, it is growing.'

There it was again, that look that she'd seen on his face the first time she'd met him. He looked down to his lap and she hesitated to ask anything further, sensing that his return to the island was part of whatever it was that troubled him.

'And you live here now?' she said into the gap that had opened between them, hoping that the question sounded as benign as she'd meant.

'Yes. I needed to return. For Dion, Rosa and Beppe... and for Hibernia.'

He smiled, but it didn't disguise an emotion that was clouding his eyes. Audrey waited for him to go on but, at the sound of the door behind them, he turned towards Dion who was carrying the tagine between mitted hands.

'Are you okay with that, mate?' he said, as Dion placed it carefully on the table. 'You should have called me, and I could have brought it out.' He stood up. 'What else needs to come?'

'All good, Q,' Dion said, standing back and looking with

pride at the lid of the tagine, as though it concealed a great and wonderful mystery. 'I'll get the couscous. What if you get a bottle of the wine?'

'Would you have some?' Quin said to Audrey, and she saw that, although he was smiling, it seemed forced, as though for her sake and for Dion's. 'It's a special drop.'

'Yes,' she said. Despite the wine-tasting trips with Cam, she couldn't count herself as any expert. Fleetingly, she wondered if wine held as much interest for Quin, too. For some reason she hoped not.

They both went inside, and Audrey could hear a clink of glasses and the two of them murmuring in a tone that suggested great familiarity.

She wondered what Quin might have told her if Dion had not come out.

He seemed more relaxed when they returned with three small glasses stacked inside each other in one hand, and a bottle of honey-gold wine in a clear glass bottle with stopper in the other. He was smiling as though he and Dion had just shared a joke. Dion, too, seemed content as he placed serving implements and a bowl with golden couscous and dates next to the tagine. She proffered her plate to him at his request.

'One spoon or two, Audra?'

She eyed the large portion he was placing on the plate. 'Just one, thanks, Dion.'

When done, he removed the lid of the tagine with all the theatrics of a magician, to release a heady aroma of rich meat and spices, then scooped up thick, glistening lamb that he placed tenderly, almost reverently, on top of the couscous. He whipped a cloth from the belt of his apron to wipe the rim of her plate, and she marvelled at the visual impact of the turmeric-stained juice against the mosaic of the deep blue and jade green earthenware.

31

When Dion had served Quin, and then sat opposite her and served himself, Audrey felt the desire to offer a blessing—still a ritual in her parents' home. They weren't religious, though Isabel had been educated in a Catholic convent in Spain. Their simple prayer was one of gratitude and it was a tradition that Audrey had carried on into her marriage, only silently. As she took in her companions and glanced beyond Dion to the wetland dappled with light and shadows as the sunlight filtered through swaying branches of the red gums, she felt in that moment to be blessed.

'*Salute*,' Dion said as the three of them clinked their glasses together.

As Audrey took a sip, she noticed that the other two seemed to be watching her keenly, but quickly forgot about it as the wine coated her mouth like cool silk. She waited for the flavours to reveal themselves—cashew, something that reminded her of verdant fields, and a hint of honey, but it was that silken texture that lingered.

They were still watching her as she replaced her glass.

'Nice, isn't it, Audra?'

'"Nice" isn't the first word that comes to mind,' she said. '"Exquisite" suits it better,' she added and meant it. She looked at Quin in surprise, who nodded his head.

'It is, isn't it?' he said. 'Very special.'

'Where's it from?' Audrey was still savouring the aftertaste.

'It's local,' Quin said.

'It's Nonno's,' Dion added.

'Beppe's?' she said, amazed and wondered what other talents he had. She thought of his enthusiasm for the bulbs in the box she had given him and wondered what he planned.

'He's struck gold this time,' Quin said. 'Hopefully, he can reproduce it.'

'Red wine would have been more... appropriate... Is that

right, Quin? With lamb? Nonno's working on one,' Dion said, then added, 'Audra, are you going to eat?'

When her fork touched the lamb, it fell apart, revealing just-pink meat that still oozed its own juices. Breaking some off and mixing it with a small amount of the couscous, she brought it to her mouth, pausing to savour the mix of aromas. When she took a bite, the meat felt as though it was truly melting in her mouth.

Dion was intent on her reaction until a sudden thought came to him.

'I forgot the bread!' he said, jumping up and heading for the kitchen.

'My goodness,' she said to Quin when he had gone, 'this is amazing. But it usually takes hours to cook.'

He nodded as he swallowed a mouthful and they both paused to take another sip of Beppe's wine.

'Where did he learn to cook like this?' Audrey asked, thinking that this was one of the most delicious meals she had ever eaten. The combination of spices was perfect, and Audrey felt her spirits rise at the hint of the return of a passion and knowledge that she thought she had lost.

Quin was quiet for a moment beside her. 'From his mother,' he said finally.

'She must be remarkable herself,' Audrey said turning to him. 'Dion's parents are here on the island, I assume?'

He didn't answer immediately, and she was shocked at the look on his face. It was one of deep grief.

'She died,' he said after some time. 'Both his mother and father were killed in a boating accident eighteen months ago.'

Pieces of the jigsaw began to come together. 'Was she Beppe and Rosa's daughter?'

'No,' Quin said looking ahead. 'His father, Michael, was

their son. Their only child.' He took a deep breath and let it out as he said, 'Dion's mother, Fionnuala, was my sister.'

Audrey was at a loss to know what to say. 'I'm sorry,' she said at last, jarred by the inadequacy of the words.

Quin looked at her. 'Thank you. It was a great shock, for all of us, but especially for Dion, of course.'

'This is why you've come back?' Audrey ventured hesitantly.

'Yes.' He ran a hand through his hair as though a reflex action of stress. 'Rosa and Beppe are getting on. Dion lives with them, but it's not easy for them. He has,' Quin looked towards the door then back to her, 'special needs. I'm sure you've noticed.'

'Yes,' she said, 'it would be hard on them.'

'Oh, they don't complain. And really, they manage him very well. But I didn't think it was fair on them, so I came back. I help where I can and,' Quin's eyes softened and there was the hint of a smile on his lips, 'I love him. In time, when he's ready, he'll live with me.'

The region around Audrey's heart felt like it had expanded and momentarily took her breath away.

'I can see that, and that he loves you, too,' she said gently. 'It must be very hard for him.'

Quin was about to answer when Dion returned. He opened his eyes widely as a silent affirmation.

They each took another sip of their wine.

'You two are getting along,' Dion said with a grin, as he placed a wire basket filled with quarters of warm flat bread on the table. When he sat, he lifted his glass. 'To friends,' he said, and Audrey noticed that, for the second time, he didn't take a sip but placed the wine back on the table and drank a glass of water instead.

'To friends,' Quin echoed and tilted his glass towards each of them.

'*Salud!*' Audrey replied in her mother's tongue. 'To friends.'

After wiping up the last of the juices with a section of bread, Audrey sat back in the seat with her senses more sated than they had been for a long time.

Since separating from Campbell, she'd had little interest in the things that had given her pleasure. She ate, but only practical, easy to prepare meals eaten in the gaps between working. She no longer listened to music as it seemed that even the most innocuous lyrics made her feel low. She donated to the local primary school fair the herbs and basic leafy vegetables that she had tended with such care on the rooftop garden of the warehouse apartment, after Poppy had eyed her and the plants with the same sympathy.

'Don't,' Audrey had said to her, when she could sense a well-meant reprimand coming her way.

To friends, she thought now, wishing that Poppy were there, and took another sip of the wine.

Quin stood up to clear the plates, but Dion insisted, with a mischievous smile that he made no attempt to disguise, that he was to stay where he was.

Once he went inside, Audrey broached the question she'd been wondering about.

'You mentioned that you also returned for Hibernia.'

'Yes,' Quin said immediately. There was something in the way he shifted to sit up straighter and seemed to bristle slightly, that suggested a problem of a different kind.

'The island is losing its people,' he said. 'Industries are closing and there's little to keep the next generation here, and the environment is under threat.'

There was a small rush of adrenalin when Audrey heard the words 'under threat', as though she had something at stake in the island's survival. She glanced at the wetland in front of her, then back to Quin.

'The wetland?' she said.

'Not all of it will be drained, but substantially enough to affect the bird migrations. This section won't be touched, I have the leasehold on it.'

Audrey was surprised.

'It came with the hotel... an old arrangement with the council and...'

'That's why you bought it!' she said. 'To protect the wetland!'

Quin's eyes crinkled with a mixture of amusement and kindness.

'Yes, and to save the hotel. Is the incongruence of my owning a pub that obvious?' he said, with a grin.

Audrey smiled. 'Oh... I didn't mean... well, maybe just a bit.'

'What plans do you have for the hotel?' she added.

Quin paused, deep in thought before answering. 'To save it from collapse. That's the number one priority,' he said. 'The building's a hundred and twenty years old now, and it's starting to show. Redesign the bar, refurbish the restaurant.'

In the entire time they'd been sitting there Audrey had not heard a car. Other than the two on the ferry with her, she could count having seen only three on the trip from Rosa and Beppe's to the hotel.

'The patrons?' she ventured. 'Would they come in from farms?'

Quin seemed unconcerned. 'I'm hoping to tempt them,' he said, with another grin.

They were laughing together when Dion came out. To

Audrey's surprise, he came to stand behind Quin, placing his arms around the older man's shoulders and nestling his head against the back of Quin's neck.

Audrey saw the young boy that he still was, despite his age, and her heart went out to him for what he had lost. From Quin's reaction—an affectionate pat on Dion's ear, then a turn of his head to kiss the boy on the forehead—she could tell that this sort of contact was common between them, though she could see, too, the sorrow in Quin's eyes. She looked away.

'So, Audra, what do you think of the first meal from our hotel?'

'Extraordinary. You're quite a chef, Dion,' she said and meant it. 'That was one of the best meals I've ever had.'

Dion looked suddenly concerned. '*One* of the best, Audra?'

She held back a smile. 'My mother's is the other best.'

He seemed to approve of her answer and looked at Quin with a broad grin.

'Do you cook other cuisines?' she said, wondering about the extent of the boy's talent.

'Oh yes. Thai, African, and Italian of course.'

'Good heavens!' Audrey said, raising her eyebrows to Quin who confirmed the truth of it with a nod. She wondered if the restaurant idea was for Dion's sake and hoped it would work.

'And Spanish,' Quin added. 'He might give your mother a run.'

'Your mother is Spanish, Audra? That explains it.'

Audrey was puzzled.

'Why you're so beautiful,' he said. 'I like Spanish ladies.'

'Dion!' Although he intended the scolding, there was a gentle tone in Quin's voice.

'Sorry, Audra.'

'It's okay, Dion,' she said, knowing that there was no harm

in the boy. 'Now that we've eaten, I've got some things here for you.' She gestured to the bag beside her.

Dion took his seat, eagerly awaiting his gift.

She took out the green-tissue-wrapped parcel first and placed it in front of him, then handed the red-wrapped one to Quin.

'This is to thank you both for your help the other week. I would have been stuck without you.'

'I wished you'd been stuck to us,' Dion added, as he began to undo the wrapping. 'So did you, didn't you, Quin?'

There was silence from the older man and Audrey avoided looking at him.

'Oh, this is *great!*' Dion yelled, holding out the black apron with *The Island* in bold white lettering for Quin to see. 'It's perfect, Audra.'

Audrey could feel herself grinning at his enthusiasm. 'That's good,' she said, 'I'm glad you like it.'

'What did you get?' he asked his uncle.

Audrey turned to Quin, who was holding the hand-painted tie with the same design across it in both hands, with a look of surprise.

'Thank you. But how did you...'

She told him about the coaster on the floor of the old white house and how she'd tried to remember the detail of the building and the font used for *The Island* that was written across the top. 'It's a novelty, not really intended for wear.'

Dion jumped up and went inside, quickly returning with something white in his hand.

'Here. Look, Audra,' he said, almost bursting with excitement. 'See, it's perfect.'

He placed the coaster on the table. This one was old, too, but unused and she was pleased to see that her memory had not betrayed her.

'It's so... thoughtful of you,' Quin said and there was something in his expression that made her look away, though she wished that she could have held that gaze.

'Do you mind if I keep this' she said, still holding the coaster, 'as a memento?'

'You don't need a memento, Audra,' Dion said. 'Just come back.'

She told them then about the job offer in London.

'And I'll be accepting it,' she said, noticing Dion's face fall.

There was a brief silence when she'd finished.

'That's... good news for you,' Quin said quietly.

Dion still hadn't said anything and when Audrey looked at him again, his eyes were glazed with tears.

'No, it isn't, Q,' he said suddenly. 'Audra is going away, and we'll never see her again. Why do people do that?' He got up from the chair and strode down the embankment towards the wetland.

She didn't know what to do and looked to Quin.

'He's okay. It's just... well, he's not adjusted to the idea of loss yet. None of us are, to be honest.'

'Of course. I shouldn't have—'

'No, no, it's fine. It's not your fault. After all, you hardly know us. It's a significant offer so of course you're going to talk about it. Congratulations, by the way.'

He sounded sincere and Audrey appreciated his reassurance, but as she watched Dion throwing chips of bark into the lagoon, she couldn't feel an ounce of enthusiasm for the "opportunity of a lifetime", as Bruce had called it more than once. But she had all but accepted and there was no going back now.

She checked the time on her phone. 'I'd better be getting back to the ferry,' she said.

'Do you need a guide?' Quin said with a smile, then, more seriously, 'I'm sure Dion would want to see you off, too.'

She considered his offer. 'Thanks, Quin, but I think it might be better if I just go alone.' What she meant was that she didn't think she wanted to remember the two of them in her rear vision mirror waving her goodbye because, despite her best intentions, she might never return.

Dion returned and seemed to have recovered. They both walked her to the car, thanking her for the trouble she'd taken in returning, and from the tightness of Dion's hug goodbye, Audrey knew she'd been forgiven. Quin's embrace, on the other hand, was tentative, and when he stood back away from her, he was smiling but his eyes told a different story.

'Good luck,' he said, and she found it difficult to reply.

Her heart was heavy as she drove away from the hotel, the taste of that exquisite wine lingering on her lips as a reminder. Three hundred metres down the optimistically named, but deserted, Main Street, past the General Store that doubled as the Post Office, past the half-dozen or so shops that included a butcher and a baker that had Audrey mentally chanting an old nursery rhyme as a distraction from the invasion of other thoughts, she saw again the sign that indicated yoga, in the side road simply named Church Street.

As she turned the corner, she saw clearly why. A hundred yards ahead on the right was a beautiful church rendered in white-grey cement with tall, but narrow stained-glass windows. On the far side of the church were two other buildings—one a single storied red brick house with a wide verandah, and the other, which was furthest away, was double-storied, rendered, and with deep verandahs on the top and bottom floors that looked as though it was, or had been, a convent. On the opposite side of the road was a primary school in the same red bricks as the house. Although the gardens around the church, house and convent had been tended, and the grass mown, the school and yard looked abandoned. Audrey felt a chill as she drove down the street, as though she'd entered a ghost town.

As she got closer to the convent, she slowed down and came to a stop when she saw a rainbow-coloured banner made of sari material advertising *The Sanctuary*, strung between the gateposts. Hanging across the top of the arches of the ground floor verandah, Tibetan prayer flags rippled in the breeze, offering a welcome riot of colour. Her phone rang in her bag with an unknown number.

'Hello, Audrey Spencer here.'

'Oh, great, love. It's Bill here... from the ferry. I got your number from the Cazonis... hope that's okay. There's a delay, I'm afraid... old Mick Prescott needs to cross but he's run into a spot of bother. A tree down or somethin' across the road, so it's holdin' him up. Reckon we'll be another hour and a half. Sorry, love.'

Bill was talking so quickly that it took Audrey a moment to digest it, but there was little she could say. Fortunately, she wasn't in a hurry, but having that much time to kill would be challenging. She briefly entertained the thought of going back to the hotel but thought better of it. She'd already said her good-byes and didn't want to put herself, or Dion, through that again. She wondered if his quick attachment to her was common for him, perhaps part of his condition, or whether it was indicative of a need since the death of his parents.

'Okay, thanks, Bill.'

'Good on you, love,' Bill added, with an audible sound of relief, 'I don't always get that sort of reaction. You're a good sport.'

She was about to reply but he'd already clicked off, leaving her wondering how she'd received the call at all. She checked her screen—three bars—and put it back in the bag.

'Interested?'

Audrey's heart leapt with surprise at the sound of the voice through the open passenger window and she turned quickly to see a woman bending at the waist towards the window, with her head cocked to the side.

White-grey hair was piled haphazardly in a loose bun and held in place with two black chopsticks, and she was wearing a garish, rainbow-coloured top in the same material, it seemed, as the banner. Audrey assessed that she was middle-aged—perhaps in her sixties. The tone of her skin, the bright blue of her eyes and the definition of her forearms as she leaned in and rested them on the sill, suggested vitality. Audrey liked her immediately.

'Oh... I was just driving by...'

'It's okay, my love, that's what everyone says. Lucky for me I like a solo practice.'

Audrey was confused.

'Of yoga,' the woman said, with a laugh. 'It's just me; it's only ever me.'

Audrey smiled and thought about The Island Hotel and her concern regarding the lack of potential patrons.

'Well,' she said, 'if I lived here, I would be interested.'

The woman looked at her directly. 'Want to come in for a bit?'

'Yes,' she said, taking herself by surprise. 'I would.'

'You'll have to fight for a parking spot though,' the woman said with a deep and throaty laugh, as she stood back from the car and waited for Audrey to merge into the curb.

When Audrey followed the woman through the heavy oak front door, she had to adjust to the sudden change of light. The entrance, with its mosaic patterned tiles, was bathed in soft rose, an effect of the sunlight through the long, ruby, stained-glass window that depicted a woman in a nun's habit, gazing

upward towards a dove, set above the landing of the wide staircase directly ahead. The air was cooler in here and, while it
would be a welcome relief in the summer months to come, she
doubted a building of this age and size could ever be warmed.

A grandfather clock struck the hour and it felt to her as
though the building trembled with the reminder of its own
mortality.

'It's beautiful,' she said and heard her voice resonating.

'It's a special place, that's for sure,' the woman said, slowly
closing the heavy oak front door and draining more of the light
from the entrance. 'This way,' she added, veering right, past the
staircase.

'I'm Lola, by the way. And it's a long shot, but I reckon you
might be Audra,' she said over her shoulder.

Audrey was taken by surprise. 'You know Dion?'

'My love, everyone knows everyone on Hibernia, and he's
painted a very vivid picture of you. Welcome to the island,
Audra.'

Away from the austerity of the entrance, the rooms they passed
through were used for more homely purposes. In the first,
several worn but sturdy armchairs were positioned close to a
gas heater; in the next, a large mahogany table was framed by a
dozen or so chairs. In here, there was carpet in various stages of
wear becoming almost threadbare in the trail that extended
through the rooms. Audrey felt as though she was at the edge of
a movie set from a period film—everything meticulously
sourced and positioned, the light through the windows casting a
sepia wash. Only the actors were missing. In front of her, the
now dulled brilliance of Lola's garment was still a stark, almost
shocking contrast, like a gaudy tourist at the edge of a set in
Downton Abbey.

Audrey walked on the balls of her feet and felt that anything said in these rooms should be whispered so as not to offend its ghosts. She wondered if Lola thought the same and saw that despite her broad and well-defined torso and the strong muscles of her calves that flexed as she walked, she moved lithely, noiselessly.

Despite the apparent age of the building, and rooms that had been preserved perhaps for decades in their current state, there was no smell of must or decay, but instead the scents were light and fresh, as though the woman in front of her resuscitated them as she swept through. There was something fortifying in the clarity of her eyes and the energy that rippled through her, tempered by the gracious flow of her loose-fitting dress.

Lola veered to the left and they entered a large kitchen that was lit so brightly by the sunlight through the clear arched window that Audrey had to blink. When her vision had settled, she saw that a jacaranda tree with blooms that were about to burst was leaning towards the window, as though looking in.

'Take a seat,' Lola invited, turning to her with a broad smile. Her strong and healthy-looking front teeth were slightly crooked and swept in an angle to her right. She'd gestured to a small table and two wicker chairs with cushions in the same violet that the jacaranda was promising. Audrey wished that she could be here when that tree erupted. 'Cup of tea? I'm afraid I've only got black, though. It's a bit hard to get anything else here and, anyway, it's still my favourite.'

Audrey agreed and sat down next to the slow combustion stove and nestled into the seat, imagining Lola in this kitchen in winter and decided that it would be a very pleasant place to be. Unlike the rest of the building, this room was painted an off-white and was bright. Though not modern, it looked as though it might have seen some renovation in its more recent history.

In addition to the combustion oven, there was an oversized stove on the opposite side of the room and large, wooden benches extended from both sides. This kitchen, Audrey could see, had been designed to cater for a number of people and she thought of the dining table in one of the other rooms.

'How long have you lived here, Lola?'

The woman was at the sink and looked over her shoulder as she spooned tea leaves into a black and gold pot. 'Coming up for two years. The best thing I ever did.'

She brought two mugs with hand-painted slogans on them and placed the blue one in front of Audrey. It bore the slogan, *You are entirely up to you*, written in gold. The other, red with black writing, was placed at Lola's spot at the table. Audrey tilted her head and smiled as she read it out loud: *'Die, my dear? Why, that's the last thing I'll do'*.

'Groucho Marx. A great philosopher,' Lola said, returning to the bench and pouring the water from the kettle into the pot. 'Sugar?' She took a small plate from the cupboard to her left and placed on it two slices from a jar on the bench and brought pot and plate to the table.

'No sugar, thanks. Is Hibernia a good place to live then?' Audrey said, as Lola took her seat.

The woman paused. 'Oh, it is. But it has its idiosyncrasies, that's for sure. And perhaps now I'm one of them!' She laughed, then, just as Audrey was thinking that this would be the way with her—to laugh and to be light—Lola's expression suddenly became more serious. 'It's a very precious place,' she said and leaning forward, added in a quiet, conspiratorial tone, 'and it needs protection.'

Quin's words replayed in Audrey's mind.

'Developers, you mean?'

'Hmm.' Lola leaned back into her chair and looked at Audrey directly. 'Yes, development... and abandonment.'

. . .

With the soft, swollen tips of the jacaranda tree brushing the window in a gentle breeze, Audrey learned more about the island and the threats to its survival. The younger generation, educated on the mainland and seduced by its opportunities, were not returning to the farms—mainly dairy—or to the once-thriving fishing industry.

'The network's so bloody unpredictable here,' Lola said, 'thank God. But that's old school talking and even I miss feeling connected to a bigger world at times. It's frustrating for the younger generation. Hibernia, it seems, is not a candidate for the NBN—too hard or something—but there's been promises to remedy it all somehow. I don't think that's going to happen anytime soon.'

The old dairy that had employed most of the island's other inhabitants—two hundred of the island's twelve hundred—had become obsolete and a new, high-tech one had been built on the mainland.

'They offered positions to Hibernia's dairy workers first, to their credit, but the problem is that the only access across is by private boat, which many islanders have, or by ferry, and I'm sure you know how slow and unpredictable that is. The dairy is a few kilometres out from the mainland marina so it's hard for them to get there. Many took up the job offer and moved across.'

When Audrey told Lola about the day's delay, she just nodded her head. 'Bill does a great job, and he's a really good bloke, but the ferry is getting old now, and there's been some talk of replacing it with... I don't know... a hydrofoil or something.'

Audrey could tell by the expression on Lola's face that she didn't think this was a good thing.

'Why? Who would come across from the mainland?' she said. In the two trips she'd made, Audrey had not seen a crowd waiting on either side to board the ferry.

'Well,' Lola said, offering Audrey a home-made muesli slice, 'that's the other and perhaps bigger problem. It's an ageing population here and many of the farmers are thinking of selling, but the land prices are at rock bottom. There's an anonymous developer, used to be a Hibernian apparently,' Lola's eyes widened, 'who's offering them more than they'd get on the free market. Wants to build an eco-resort or something.'

Audrey thought that it didn't sound such a bad idea, but chose not to voice it, sensing that there might be much more to this story. 'What about the wetland areas? Are they at risk?'

Lola looked surprised. 'Yes. Have you heard?'

Audrey shook her head. 'Not any details, it was just that Quin...'

'Quin O'Rourke?' Lola sat back in her chair and seemed to be considering what she would say. 'That's interesting,' she said, pouring more tea into each cup.

'Why's that?' Audrey's curiosity was spiking.

'Rumour has it that he's the anonymous developer.'

Audrey was about to refute it—after all, it had been Quin who had raised the issue in the first place, and he'd seen genuinely concerned—but Lola continued:

'He's been buying up land all over the place, apparently and The Island Hotel, so I hear, is the first part of his plan.'

Audrey had no comeback. Once, she would have trusted her instincts—that Quin was a good man and was genuine in his concern for Hibernia—but all up, she'd known him for only a few hours, and she had also come to realise over the last few years how wrong her instincts could be.

'I don't know him at all,' Lola was saying, 'and this is second-hand information. I've seen him with Dion, though, and

47

the boy loves him. That's got to say something about him. It was a terrible thing that happened—the accident. Some say he came back for the boy, after his sister died, but others say it's something else. How do you find him?'

Audrey took a deep breath while she considered her answer. She thought of Dion placing his arms around his uncle's neck and the gentle way that Quin had responded, of them coming out from the hotel kitchen laughing at a shared joke, and of Quin's face when he talked of the accident, and of the threats to Hibernia.

'Kind, genuine,' she said.

Lola's eyes smiled over the edge of her cup as she took a sip of tea.

'Then that's how I'll see him, love. I know what small-town gossip can be like—God knows I've been the subject of enough of it. And probably still am!' Her laugh and lightness had returned.

'Lola, what's the history of this place?' Audrey was grateful that the conversation about Quin seemed to have ended and was warming even more to the woman in front of her.

Lola stood up. 'Come on,' she said, 'let me show you around and I'll tell you all about it. It's fascinating. Got enough time?'

Audrey checked her phone that, she noted, had lost the network bars. She still had forty-five minutes until she needed to be back to the ferry.

They paused at the top of the staircase that had dominated the entrance. Narrow corridors extended left and right and were flanked by numerous closed wooden doors, only metres apart.

Lola saw Audrey eyeing them.

'There's twenty all-up,' she said. 'There were that many nuns here in the convent's heyday.'

'When was that?' Audrey was intrigued by the apparent narrowness of the rooms.

'Nineteen-hundred to nineteen-fifties saw the biggest congregation—fifty years, but it started to wane in the nineteen sixties after Vatican 2.'

Audrey remembered her mother talking about the pre- and post-Vatican 2 eras and how the changes to bring the Catholic Church into the modern world were embraced by many, while others, particularly those who'd chosen the religious life in its older form, found it difficult to adapt.

Isabel had told the story of how some of her religious teachers went quietly, and one very publicly, mad. 'Their world changed,' she'd said. 'They were not ready.'

Audrey had been surprised at her mother's compassion because she knew that she'd experienced unnecessary and now illegal punishment at the hands of some of the nuns and wondered if Isabel had been reflecting more on changes in her own life.

'I'll show you one of the rooms,' Lola said, breaking through her reminiscences and going to the nearest door.

When she opened it, Audrey could smell orange-blossom. At Lola's invitation, she stepped into the room that comprised a single bed covered in a blue candlewick spread, a small vinyl-topped table and single chair, a small cupboard and a wash-basin. The walls were bare other than a small crucifix that hung opposite the bed above the doorway.

There was no window, just a vent high in the wall and Audrey suspected that if she stood in the centre of the room and extended both arms to the side, she'd be able to touch the walls.

'How long ago did the last nuns leave?' She was fascinated that someone could choose to live a life such as this.

'Well...' Lola paused to think, then continued, 'the school

closed about five years ago, I'm told—for some of the reasons I mentioned before. In its day, the school had up to a hundred children attending, but as it waned and some of the nuns were called back to Ireland, or died, or went into nursing homes, there were only two remaining here. They were too old to teach by then and in the last years of the school, lay teachers were employed.'

'You've kept it preserved.'

Lola laughed. 'Well, yes, most of it. I don't have the money yet to renovate completely, so I keep it as clean as I can and... a bit out of respect, if you know what I mean, for what's gone before me here. I was raised a Catholic but abandoned it as soon as I could. It's funny, though, this place sort of brings me back to my roots,' Lola's face momentarily darkened, 'to gentler times.'

Audrey knew well that many would not view those years of the Catholic Church in such a light, and for good reason, but there was something in the way Lola said it that made her wonder what had happened in this woman's life. She was vibrant, healthy, and seemed to be happy, but her decision to live on Hibernia, and in this old convent, in an almost self-imposed exile had Audrey guessing.

'I'll show you what I *have* done, and the latest project.' Lola closed the door to the cell and led Audrey further on towards the front of the building. At the corridor's end were double doors with frosted panes. In front, against the wall, was a statue of Mary in iconic blue and white lit by a small blue glass lamp. As they passed, Audrey noticed that the table beneath them had a just-polished satin sheen that scattered the blue light into its creases.

Lola pushed open one of the doors that creaked its complaint.

Audrey wasn't prepared for the scene in front of her and let out an audible gasp. Gone were the heavy furniture pieces of downstairs, the dulled furnishings and sepia tones. The room ahead of her shouted with vibrant colours. Two large yolk-coloured couches, with sapphire blue and emerald-green cushions that reminded her of the plates at The Island Hotel, were placed centrally around a muted, well-loved and well-worn Persian rug. Indoor palms in lurid ceramic pots created ghostly silhouettes on the polished wooden floor. Large, mismatching cushions were bunched in groups in an invitation for languid afternoons with close friends. But the highlight, directly ahead, was the glass concertina doors that extended the width of the room that Audrey estimated to be ten metres. Beyond the doors was the deep, mosaic-tiled balcony, framed by the rendered arches she'd seen from the street. Large fans that matched the ones inside were poised to take on the summer.

'Wow! It's stunning.'

'Isn't it?' Lola said, with such a contented smile that Audrey envied her in that moment.

Lola moved to the glass doors, unlocked them and folded two back. A breeze licked through the room and the parlour palms nodded in approval.

On the balcony, two sets of white wicker chairs and cushions were positioned around small brass-topped tables with carved wooden legs. Though Audrey had seen tables similar to these in the more mass-production stores in Melbourne, she could tell that these were heavier, hand-carved and authentic.

'I lived in Morocco for years,' Lola said as they moved to the edge of the balcony, 'as if you couldn't tell. It's hardly the same view that I had there, but in summer this room is divine.'

From their vantage point, they had an almost bird's-eye view of the primary school yards from the convent. In one section was a playground equipped with iron monkey bars, slides and swings and at their feet grass tussocks had broken through the asphalt. She remembered a playground like this near her childhood home. In summer, the iron heated to scorching point, but it didn't deter her and her friends.

Beyond the school, she could see the roofs of the buildings in Main Street, dulled by years of salt and sun, except for one sitting higher than the others at the furthest end that reflected light off its new metal. Audrey could see the side of the building and recognised it as The Island Hotel. She thought of what Lola had said about Quin and decided to remember, instead, the man and the boy, and the peace she felt in their company.

'The other side's a whole different view,' Lola said from behind her. 'Come on, I'll show you the latest project.'

Before they returned along the passage, Audrey stole a final view of the room and, beyond it, the glint of sun on the new metal roof of the hotel.

Past the top of the staircase, the corridor extended ahead of them towards the rear of the building. There were more doors —bedrooms, and one with a small plaque indicating a bathroom. Audrey had seen only one other of these in the area behind them. The light was brighter here, and she could see that the doors at the end of the corridor were open, revealing a room as wide as the vibrant space she had just left. As they entered, she saw that at the far side and sitting centrally on a raised wooden platform, was a large marble altar. In the concave wall, a metre or so behind it, were three long, stained-glass windows, the centre one depicting Jesus Christ with crown and sceptre, on its left, a more humble version of Jesus of Nazareth with hand resting on his chest and finger indicating his bleeding heart, and on the right, Mary, his mother, with up-cast eyes and surrounded by doves. Though Audrey could see that they had been made by a skilled craftsman, they looked sombre without the light behind them, as the sun was already tracking overhead to ignite the colours of the room at the other end of the corridor. Most of the light was entering from the left-hand side of the chapel, through a plastic sheet that was fixed around a gaping and jagged hole about three metres high in the concrete wall.

'Have a look at this,' Lola said, moving towards the plastic. She bent to loosen the industrial-strength tape that adhered it to the wall and peeled back a section.

Audrey stood beside her. Beyond the scaffold fixed to the outside of the building she could see the wetland to the left, and across the green pastures directly ahead, the blue Pacific rolled benignly towards a low-lying section of the island's coast.

'Most of this wall will be replaced with reinforced glass,' Lola said, turning towards her. 'Whenever that will be,' she added, rolling her eyes in mock exasperation. 'It's been one interruption after the other—weather, mostly. I'm hoping it'll be finished before New Year... sign of a new start.'

Although she was still smiling, there was something in the tone of Lola's voice that had Audrey wondering again about her story, but she was concerned that even carefully placed questions might stir emotions that Lola would be left to sort through alone.

'It will look amazing,' she said. 'What will you use this room for?'

'This,' Lola let go off the plastic and turned towards Audrey and the chapel behind her with her arms outstretched, 'will be the yoga, qigong and meditation space.' She turned full circle then stopped, her face lit with a thought that made her appear more youthful. 'Come back and see it when it's done. By the New Year, I should have it all up and running—The Sanctuary. Actually, Audra, come back and stay.'

Come back and stay... It seemed to Audrey that the sound

waves echoed off the walls and the hard surfaces of the chapel to resonate somewhere inside her.

'Well, it was great to meet you, my love,' Lola said, as they walked to the car. 'If you're back on a visit from London, you're welcome, you know.'

'It was great meeting you, too, and good luck with The Sanctuary. I'll spread the word.'

'Thanks. I'd appreciate it.'

As Audrey was doing up her seat belt, Lola leaned once again on the sill of open window.

'I hope you don't mind me saying this, love,' she said, with an expression of concern, 'but... I don't think it's your path. I'm sorry if that sounds presumptuous,' and added with that uninhibited laugh, 'or loony, more like it.'

Audrey was momentarily taken aback but thought of her mother's concern about whether this was what she wanted, and Poppy's advice to find herself.

'But I don't know what my path is,' she found herself admitting to this woman she barely knew.

'You need to be quiet for a while, Audra. Allow yourself to be heard.'

Audrey could feel tears pricking around the edges of her eyes. 'I will. Well, I'll try at least.'

She drove back to the ferry feeling strange. The slogan on the cup in Lola's kitchen brought a smile to her lips: *You are entirely up to you.* She wondered if she was beginning to change.

CHAPTER THREE

A breeze caressed Audrey's closed lids and her body vibrated as the ocean waves thwacked the shore. She opened her eyes and scanned the wetland, surprised to see that it had spread from the left across the flat land in front of her. When she looked down, her body jerked in shock and her hand grasped for the substance of the bricks behind her, searching for something to stop her plummeting thirty metres to the ground. Closing her eyes in terror, she inched back into the gaping hole, relying on the flapping of the plastic strip to guide her.

Gasping for air, Audrey propelled herself to sit upright, startling a bird that had been preening its wings on the verandah rail. Its shadow was stretched in grotesque proportions on the bed cover as it eclipsed the low morning sun.

She was home—not in the cold and empty Melbourne apartment that never would deserve that title, but in the comfort and familiarity of her parents' house in Ballina.

Still groggy from the dream, she nestled under the covers

and savoured the smell of clean linen—a particular scent she associated with her mother and childhood.

In the background, she could hear the clunk of a heavy pan on the stove and the metallic ring of cutlery being collected from the drawer. Her mother would be up, and normally her father before her, but Audrey couldn't hear his voice.

She thought back to the evening before when they'd picked her up from the airport. They'd been very quiet with each other and a strain between them was evident at first, but as they listened to her news, they'd seemed much better.

Isabel looked up as her daughter came into the kitchen. 'Good morning,' she said with a smile. The deep set of lines around her mouth suggested a different internal monologue.

Audrey bypassed the place set for her at the table and went over to her mother, who was standing at the stove poking the edges of the chorizo omelette with the wooden-handled egg-lifter. When she carefully embraced her from behind, she heard the sudden intake of air and a sob that rebelled to be released.

'Mama,' she said softly into Isabel's ear as she stroked her hair. Once lush and sleek, it now felt brittle under her fingers, as though it had sacrificed its life force to sustain its host.

'Sit down,' her mother said, releasing herself from the embrace with a half-turn towards her. In one deft move, she flipped the omelette to its other side then, easing it out, placed it gently on the plate beside her. Putting the utensils down, she wiped her hands on the half apron, unscrewed a waiting jar of smoked paprika and sprinkled a fine dust over the glistening omelette, its scent filling the space between them. Despite her frenetic movements, Isabel's expression confirmed there was something wrong.

'What is it, Mum?' Audrey said, as they pondered the plate in front of them.

'*Él es deprimido.*' Her mother's reply was immediate, as though it had been waiting on her tongue.

'English, Mama.' Audrey knew that her mother reverted to her native tongue in times of stress and wondered if it was a form of protection and comfort to her.

'He is depressed,' she said.

The very word startled Audrey. She knew that, like herself, her mother was prone to melancholic episodes, but her father had always been the epitome of positivity. With little encouragement, Isabel opened up about it and Audrey learned that he had been slipping so quietly into depression that it had caught them both off-guard.

'Little things should have warned me,' she said, wiping at the sprinkle of paprika on the bench. 'His eyes wandering past me as I speak, no answer to ordinary remarks. I had thought that he was going deaf, or that I bored him.'

Isabel spoke quickly, as though her emotions had breached the wall that had contained them.

The little things... Audrey watched her mother's expression as she spoke and wondered how it was that she had not seen the deepening of the line between Isabel's eyebrows, the look of both despair and pleading in her dark eyes as her voice became more animated in the voicing of it. But it was her hands that Audrey watched more keenly. She had come to read her mother's gesticulations as a type of sign language that revealed more than she would allow her face to do, and it was this that she had missed on the telephone.

Her mother, Audrey realised, was lonely. She knew with some shame that she had been so engrossed in her own concerns that she hadn't even noticed.

'Here, Mama... I'll take this one to Dad,' Audrey said, settling the plate on the round tray with the glass bottom that she had bought for her parents years ago at a school fair.

'Give me a moment with him and I'll come back and eat with you.'

Isabel didn't object and positioned a knife and fork she'd tucked inside a cloth serviette next to the plate on the tray.

'Dad.' When there was no response, Audrey balanced the tray as she manoeuvred through the half open doorway.

The room was dimly lit, and she'd assumed her father was still asleep, but as she approached the bed, she was surprised to see that he was half sitting up against the bedhead, the pillows haphazardly tucked behind him.

'Hello, sweetheart,' he said, his voice deep and croaky.

Audrey placed the tray on his lap when he had shuffled to sit more upright and sat on the edge of the bed.

'Dad... what's going on? Are you alright?'

She could tell that he was forcing a surprised expression.

'Yes, love. Of course. Just a bit tired this morning, that's all.'

He looks tired, she thought, but Audrey knew now that there was more to it and she wasn't letting him get away with that. There'd been too many things left unsaid between her and Cam, leading to the breakup, and she'd sometimes wondered if only they had spoken of their feelings earlier, could they have been able to salvage it?

'Mum's told me—'

'Ah,' he said, looking down at the omelette as though hoping it would help him out.

'Do you want to talk about it?' she said, shuffling a bit closer.

He looked up and she noticed how the little light coming through the blinds accentuated the glassy look of his eyes.

'Not much to tell you, love.'

Audrey selected her words carefully. 'Is it boredom?'

He gave a soft chuckle. 'Put like that, it sounds... like I'm a spoiled brat. But yes... I suppose that's it.'

Audrey laughed, relieved to see a small return of her father's good humour. 'Spoilt brat? *Nooo!* That was Cam!'

Max's eyes rolled upward in agreement.

'The redundancy... that's hit you hard?' she said, more seriously now. When he'd told her about it on the telephone, she'd wondered how he'd cope, but he'd been his usual cheery self. 'I can relax at last,' he'd said with a laugh.

His face clouded and he shifted his lap beneath the tray. 'Yes, I can't deny it, vain old fool that I am. I just... don't feel old, Aud. Well, I didn't feel old, but I'm not sure now.'

Despite the ageing of the man in front of her, Audrey couldn't relate to her father as being old. The usual Max was vibrant, but gentle, physically and emotionally strong and was only sixty-six. It hadn't been unusual for his fellow academics to be working well into their seventies, but new departmental policies had seen several others like himself being packaged off. It was, she agreed, far too early for her father to retire.

'Well, you're definitely not old, Dad. Perhaps another university...'

'No, love. I think I've lost it for institutions.'

Audrey nodded in agreement and felt it resonate at a deeper level.

A thought came to her.

'I might need some advice, Dad. Some sleuthing perhaps. It's about this island called Hibernia...'

As Audrey told her father about the island, the wetlands and the mysterious developer, there was no mistaking that a glint was beginning to replace the glassy look of his eyes.

Max listened closely and posed questions in between mouthfuls of omelette.

'What's your interest in this, love?'

She paused to consider her response. It was a question she'd asked herself, but the answer was elusive.

When she hadn't answered, he continued, 'This fellow... Quin...'

Blood rushed to her cheeks.

'... do you think he's the developer?' Her father was watching her carefully.

'I'm only repeating what Lola, the woman at the convent said, but no, I don't think so.' Audrey paused, trying to conjure Quin's face though it was already fading. 'But then again, I don't really know him at all.'

Her father was silent for a moment as though sensing something.

'Leave it with me. I'll see what I can find out.'

'Babe!'

'Poppy? What's wrong? It must be three am in Paris!' Audrey could feel her heart pounding.

There was a laugh at the other end of the phone. 'No, actually it's eleven am. I'm here. In Ballina.'

Poppy's voice held its trademark exuberance, but Audrey's mind was too scrambled to make sense of it.

'What? You're here? But...'

'I was going to tell you, but when you said you'd be visiting Max and Issy, I thought I'd surprise you instead.'

Audrey felt herself calm as her best friend sped through her explanation—an unexpected trip to Sydney for her sister's wedding that had taken everyone by surprise... a few days spare before she had to fly back to Paris to get ready for an exhibition...

'I did, didn't I? Surprise you, I mean.' There was an uncharacteristic silence at the other end of the line.

'Oh, Pop... it's the best surprise,' Audrey said, to counter her best friend's sudden lack of confidence, and she meant it.

They shared a few anecdotes about their week, holding details until in each other's company.

'So...' Poppy's voice was conspiratorial, 'this Quin guy ...'

Audrey hesitated. There was an implication in her father's and now her friend's question and she thought of the "look" that had passed between Rosa and Beppe.

'Nothing more to tell you, really,' she said, feeling again the rise of warmth in her face and a note of defensiveness in her reply.

'Okay, okay. I need to talk with you about Cam the Bastard, though,' Poppy said, 'when we meet. I'm free this afternoon. You?'

Audrey smiled. She'd always found a strange comfort in her friend's direct, even blunt approach. An image of Poppy at her and Cam's wedding came to mind. Audrey could tell she was forcing composure because her body language was rigid under the strain of it. She remembered, too, seeing her talking with Isabel and Max, whose faces, she recalled, were not so transparent in hiding their concern.

'Bye, darling. Say hello to Poppy.'

When Audrey had come into the kitchen moments before, she'd been surprised to see both her parents seated at the table.

Isabel had looked up to say her farewell and Audrey thought that her face was more relaxed, her eyes a little brighter.

Her father had his laptop on the table and was typing. 'Have a good day, love. Give Pop a kiss from us,' he'd said. As he looked up, there was a furrow between his eyebrows. 'It's too slow,' he said, turning to his wife. 'I think I need a new one.' Then back to Audrey: 'Thought I'd do a bit of a search... see what I can find...'

Audrey left them to the to-ing and fro-ing of domestic interchange. Her father's depression was not going to be so easily fixed, she knew, and her mother's predisposition for anxiety would not be cured, but it was a start and as she set out to meet her best friend, Audrey could feel pieces of herself aligning once more in fundamental ways.

There was no missing the jet-black hair and red streak from the forehead to crown above the open pages of the newspaper. Audrey paused to take in the startling effect, musing on the thought of her friend as one of Australia's deadliest spiders. Oh, she'd come out fighting, alright, to protect those she loved. Though Audrey had never been subjected to it herself, she knew that below Poppy's laissez-faire demeanour was a venemous bite—she'd seen her in action with Cam.

'Don't be such a fucking tosser,' she'd said to him across the table at dinner in an upmarket restaurant. Audrey couldn't remember what had prompted this reaction and had had to console Cam afterwards. She'd called Poppy out on it the next day over the phone.

'Sorry, my love, but my opinion remains,' was all she'd said.

Had Audrey paid attention to the small twist in her gut then, she might have saved herself years of quiet discontent. She'd argued with Poppy at the time but realised later that it was more to convince herself that she hadn't made a mistake.

Her phone buzzed in the pocket of her coat. She didn't recognise the phosphorescent number on her screen and stepped into the alcove of a building to accept the call.

'Hello, Audrey speaking.'

'I know, Audra. Who else would you be!'

Her pleasure had her smiling into the concrete wall of the nearest building as she leaned in to hear more clearly over the noise of the traffic.

'Dion? How are you? But how...?'

'... did I get your number? Nonna and Nonno of course.'

'Well, it's a lovely surprise.' When he didn't respond, she continued, 'Is everything okay?'

'*Todo... está... bien,*' he said, faltering over some of the vowels.

Audrey's Spanish had become rusty over the years away from home and her mother's spontaneous outpourings, usually when Isabel was excited, but she knew this one well. "Everything is okay." She thought of how frequently she'd heard it from her mother over recent months—too many times to be convincing, she thought now, still admonishing herself for not picking up on what now seemed so obvious; a trait she was acutely aware was becoming a signature.

'That's wonderful, Dion. You're a natural!' She felt as though his blush came through the phone, the boy with the wide grin and flushed cheeks. 'How are Beppe and Rosa?'

'And Quin,' he added with a soft scold. '*Todo está bien,*' he said, this time with more confidence. 'Quin won't be away too long.'

'Away?' Audrey hesitated, but the question was burning on her lips. 'Where's he gone?'

His reply came as a series of staccato sounds, and she held a hand over her other ear to listen more closely.

'Dion? I can't hear you.'

'Bloody phone!' It sounded as though he was shaking it at the other end. 'Is that better?'

'Yes, that's better. I can hear you clearly now. You were saying that Quin had gone somewhere...'

'Back to his wife. That's where Quin's gone.'

She felt it first like a soft slap, then as a turmoil in her gut—as though her insides were collapsing.

'Audra? Are you still there?' Dion's voice trailed away then returned with more volume. '*Audra?*'

'I'm here... must have been my phone this time. Sorry.'

'Great. Now for my other reason for ringing, other than to say hello.'

Audrey's eyes were locked on the irregular pores in the rendered concrete wall and the dried paint that bled from the larger ones.

'Do you know your mother's recipe?' The boy's voice brought her back to the moment.

'Recipe? For the dish I mentioned at the hotel?'

'Yes, the one that was better than mine.'

Audrey felt herself smiling and an idea came to her. Her mother had been fascinated with the story about the lunch at The Island Hotel. 'Aah... no, but... how about I give you her number and you can ask her yourself?'

'Really? Oh, yes please, Audra. I'd love to talk to your mum.'

As she gave him the number, Audrey remembered that the boy had lost his own mother only recently. 'I've already told her about you and that amazing meal,' she said. 'She'll know who you are, and I think the two of you will get along just fine.'

'She'll know me? That's... stupendous. Oh... and before I forget, Lola said to say hello. So "hello".'

Audrey felt a sudden desire to be in that fabulous and vibrant room at the convent, in the company of the equally vibrant Lola. The easy familiarity of the greeting sent via Dion stirred her, though Audrey wondered if Hibernia might have now lost some of its charm.

'Quin will be back soon,' he said, and not for the first time Audrey wondered if her thoughts were exposed. She turned away from the building and saw that Poppy had put down the paper and, although she was wearing sunglasses, Audrey knew she was watching her keenly. She knew who Poppy would be thinking she was talking to.

'Well, say hello to Lola from me, Dion,' she said, resuming her walk to the café. 'You know, now might be a good time to ring Mum... Isabel. Between you and me, though, I think she might have been a little bit envious about that meal you cooked.'

'Do you think so? What... that I might be better than her?'

She could hear the excitement in his voice. 'Hmm, perhaps that's it. She'll love talking to you.' She gave him the phone number.

'Okay. I'll do that now.' She heard him pause. 'Audra, is it all right if I call you sometimes?'

There was a part of her that wanted to dissuade him, to put Hibernia behind her. But she had to admit, the boy had gotten to her.

'I'd love that, but... I'll be in London next week.'

There was a moment of silence at the other end, and she remembered how upset he'd been when she'd first told him that she would be leaving.

'Don't go, Audra.' His voice was almost a whisper at the other end of the phone. 'I miss Quin,' he added, 'but he'll be back soon, I guess.'

'I'll be back. I'll come and visit you,' she said, wondering why he'd attached to her so quickly. 'I promise.'

Dion seemed reassured with this, and Audrey knew that

she must not let him down. She felt strangely relieved to make the commitment.

Poppy had stood up and was edging around the table to greet her. Audrey couldn't help noticing how much weight her friend had lost since she'd last seen her on one of her flying visits to Melbourne. Perhaps, she thought, this perspective was exaggerated by the tight black dress she was wearing. When Poppy removed her sunglasses though, Audrey was shocked to see that the flesh around her eye sockets seemed to have lost its fullness and there were lines she hadn't noticed when they'd last met only a few months before. Poppy's dark eyes, accentuated by black kohl and false lashes, seemed to have lost their light.

They exchanged kisses, and Audrey was on the verge of questioning her, but Poppy broke across the words still forming on her lips. 'Was that him?'

Audrey feigned ignorance. 'Who? Cam, do you mean? No.'

Poppy nodded with approval. 'The new bloke then?'

It stung, but Audrey couldn't help but laugh at her friend's lack of guile. She pulled back a chair at the table. 'Let's sit down and I'll tell you all you ever wanted to know but were afraid to ask.' When they sat, she leaned in conspiratorially. 'But first, tell me the goss about your sister's sudden wedding and, of course, life in the City of Love.'

Over tea and lush hummingbird cake, Poppy related the most recent event in her family life that, Audrey knew well, was never short on dramas—some petty and others more serious, such as her brother's arrest for the illegal importation of exotic birds. Poppy's sister, Clementine, was often at the centre of the smaller ones. At thirteen, she'd announced that she was a boy, and that she should be known as "Charles", but when hormone therapy was offered to begin the transition, she changed her mind and, in a strange twist, embraced her femaleness with gusto. From sixteen, there had been a series of unhappy relationships, and, by her late twenties, she had sworn off men and joined a dubious religious cult that worshipped goats. Clementine's paradox was that she was a gifted sculptor, but she had never achieved Poppy's success, blaming the industry, the government, and sometimes, her sister. Bruce had offered to display her work at the gallery, but she'd proven to be so difficult to please that he gave up on her. Audrey wondered if Poppy's expat life in Paris was really an escape from her family, and she couldn't blame her if it was.

Between sips of tea, Poppy entertained Audrey with her sister's latest escapade—she'd abandoned the goat-worshipping for a sudden marriage to a moderately famous rap artist from Argentina whom she'd met at a club in Sydney.

'The vows were sung in rap!' Poppy laughed at the memory, but Audrey couldn't help noticing that something of her usual spark had gone. 'Okay, your turn,' she continued, leaning in and sliding her sunglasses along the red stripe to her crown.

Audrey shuffled in her seat, not sure of what she actually had to contribute. Yes, she'd seen Cam, as she'd confessed to her on the phone, but that at least seemed to have died down for the moment. She knew that her friend was fishing for news about Quin, but what did she have to tell her? They'd met, shared a lunch, and he was now with his wife. Case closed.

She told Poppy all of this, emphasising her time spent with Dion, Rosa and Beppe, and Lola. 'Anyway, London awaits. That's exciting.'

Poppy sat back and was still scrutinising her friend. 'Who are you trying to kid, my darling? Your enthusiasm is as convincing as an amateur magician.'

Audrey mustered some indignation. 'Oh, but you're wrong. It's such a—'

'Wonderful opportunity? I'm not convinced, Aud, but... who am I to know?'

As her voice trailed off, Audrey was startled by the look on her face.

'Pop, what's wrong?'

'Everything ... And nothing.'

Poppy had turned as though her attention had been caught by something on the other side of the road. From Audrey's vantage point, she could see light pooling in the fluid building in her eyes. Poppy turned back to her, blinking rapidly.

'I'm pregnant.'

'What?' Audrey's thoughts were raddled. Had her friend just told her...?

Poppy leaned in and repeated her bombshell news. 'Aud, I'm pregnant.'

Audrey's breath caught in the back of her throat. She breathed deeply as she gathered her thoughts. 'But... Who?'

'It doesn't matter.' Her reply was short, almost abrupt, but Audrey wasn't letting her get away with it.

'Tell me. What's going on? You've never mentioned—'

'I know.' Poppy spoke to her cup. Her face was distressed. 'I know, I know... I just thought that if I told you—'

'That I'd be hurt? Jealous? Pop, I'm so... so happy for you...' Her words faded as she looked at Poppy's face.

'It's over. He's gone.' Poppy was looking directly at her now and her face was like a stone.

Audrey reached for her hand across the table and Poppy clasped it with a gentle squeeze. 'I'm here, darling. Now tell me.'

She'd heard Poppy mention the name Didier several times in past months, but it had been in the company of other names—a group of friends who gathered regularly in the Parisian club scene.

In phone conversations more recently, Audrey had an inkling that her friend was slowing down, was becoming tired of the constant partying—fewer names had been mentioned, including that of Didier. Now she knew why. He had been a relatively new member of the group; a producer of documentaries and Poppy had fallen in love with him. They'd shared an intimate relationship and then, without warning, he'd left, with no reply to her messages. When she'd questioned a mutual friend, he'd told her very matter-of-factly, as though Poppy would have known, that Didier had returned to Nice for his wedding.

'The next day... the very day before I had to fly out here... I did the test. Before I looked at the result, I knew. I'm such a fucking idiot.'

'What will you do? Have you had time to think it through? And... are you sure? The test could be wrong. It's only been two weeks—'

'More than two weeks, in fact. More like sixteen.'

'What!'

'Yes, I know. Don't look at me like that, though I can't blame you. I'd been ignoring it. It's not so unusual for my cycle to be erratic. But now that I've faced it, I've retested every day,' Poppy said, sitting back in the chair and sliding her glasses down over her eyes.

Audrey knew that Poppy had never wanted children. At thirty-eight and with a successful career, it had never been on her radar.

'I'm keeping it.' Her arms were folded across her chest as though in defiance.

Audrey felt assaulted by her own conflicting thoughts; she couldn't envisage this as her friend's future. Words wouldn't form to express it.

'It's okay,' Poppy said, leaning forward to pat the back of Audrey's hand which was still lying motionless on the table. 'It's a lot to get your head around.'

'I'm here for you, darling. Like you've always been here for me,' Audrey responded, and knew that she meant every word.

'Except...' the skin on Poppy's forehead concertinaed above the glasses in a small expression of an idea, 'this time... this is life giving. And about time, for us both, don't you think... Auntie?' Deep creases formed around her mouth as she smiled.

The thought of having her friend just across the Channel pleased Audrey and now, a baby would make it even better. For the first time, Audrey felt a rise of something akin to pleasure and she felt a sense of purpose. Without siblings, this was as close as she'd be to having a niece or nephew. Cam's sister had three children, but they lived in the States and Audrey had only met them twice.

Now, picnics in St James Park seemed appealing, and they could take "Junior" for trips along the Seine... when 'they' were older, of course. 'You're right,' she said, 'we do need this. New life, new hope, and a sense of purpose.'

Poppy's face beneath the glasses tightened and she looked suddenly sheepish. 'Will you be godmother?'

Audrey was surprised. She hadn't heard the term for years and Poppy had been opposed to the Greek Orthodox tradition of her family.

'I know... it seems weird coming from me,' she continued, 'but... I don't know... I feel like I'm changing.'

'I'd love to,' Audrey said without hesitation. She didn't know much about the role, but she was honoured to be asked. She felt protective of this new life. Her eyes wandered to Poppy's abdomen bound tightly in the dress. When she looked up, Poppy seemed even paler, and sad.

'I'm scared, Aud.'

'We'll do this together, okay? You're not alone.'

Poppy shook her head. 'I know. Thanks, babe. I don't think my parents could cope with any more sudden news. They were devastated at Clemie's wedding, though they tried hard not to show it.'

'But you need to tell them—'

'I can't. Not yet. It will be apparent soon enough. Mum's eyes follow me and... well, I think she's guessed. She keeps offering me food.'

'Are you feeling okay?' Audrey could understand her mother's concern over Poppy's loss of weight. She noticed that she stabbed at the edges of her cake, but very little had been eaten.

'No. I feel terrible. I had morning sickness I think but put it down to stress, but I just feel... hollow. Though obviously I'm not!' she added, with a small laugh. There was a pause as she seemed to be ruminating over some other thought.

'Aud, to be honest, I'm not actually sure that I can go back —to the apartment, to that life. It's not good for me anymore, or...' she placed a protective hand over her belly, 'for little one here.'

London collapsed around Audrey, and she felt a weight in her neck and shoulders. The biggest plus of her move there was that her best friend would be close and now she saw herself isolated and unhappy. She knew she was being selfish.

'But what about the exhibition?'

'I'll go back for that, but... I'm sorry, darling.'

'It's okay. I understand. You're right, of course. It is best that you stay here, but... I wanted to be there for you, especially now.'

'Don't go to London, Aud. You don't want it, I can tell. Stay. We can find a place together in Melbourne.'

How appealing it sounded—a perfect excuse to stay. But

Audrey knew that this was not her future. Poppy might find love again, someone good and willing to raise the baby with her. Where would she be then? A third wheel, watching others' lives unfolding. And what work would she do? The thought of staying on at the gallery brought a sinking feeling. At least London was the promise of something new.

Isabel was kneeling in the herb garden weeding and staking young tomato plants in preparation for the warm months ahead. Audrey thought of the crocus leaves in the garden of the old white house on Hibernia, and the bulbs that Beppe had nestled in the tissue of the box.

'How's Poppy?' she enquired, with emphasis on the last syllable as her daughter came to stand next to her.

Audrey was about to give a positive account but reconsidered. 'She's expecting a child,' she said, carefully choosing her words to accommodate her mother's sensibilities.

'Oh!' Isabel straightened her back and stood up without effort. 'Is this... good news?'

No doubt about it, Audrey thought. Right onto it. She told her mother the facts as she knew them.

Isabel exaggerated her nod of approval when she learned that Poppy wanted to return to Australia.

'She need to be here with family,' she said and Audrey knew that the message was as much pointed to herself as it was to Poppy.

'Did Dion call you?' she said, to deflect it.

Her mother smiled broadly. 'Sí. Oh, he's a very sweet boy! I give him the recipe he wants. He knows much about Spanish food, and we agreed to speak again soon.'

Audrey sensed a strange liaison happening between the unlikely pair. 'That's great. He'd love that.'

'Yes, yes,' Isabel said, still smiling as she returned to the garden bed.

Audrey returned indoors. Max was in the study and the rear view of him stooped slightly over the computer was a heartwarmingly familiar sight.

'What are you up to, Dad?' Audrey said, coming up behind him.

He turned to look over his shoulder. 'Hello, love. How's the girl?'

Audrey recounted Poppy's news. Her father's reaction was similar to her mother's. No judgement, just concern.

'A shame you're going away if she comes back home,' he said. 'She'll need her friend.'

Audrey nodded, noting the sense of a conspiracy between her parents.

'It's another great reason to come back as often as I can,' she said.

Max turned back to the computer. 'You're mother's quite chuffed about that phone call. Dion, is it? Sounds like quite a character. It's good to see her smile like that, you know, Aud. I realised when she got off the phone that I haven't see her do that for a while.'

Even though his back was to her, Audrey knew that her father felt guilty. She went to him and placed a hand on his shoulder.

'Found anything interesting?' She leant in towards the screen.

'Mmm... I came across this.' He brought up a page. The company's logo read *Foster-O'Rourke Holdings*. In the first paragraph of its spiel beneath it he highlighted a section.

Company Directors Quentin O'Rourke and Marion Foster.

Audrey's hand clasped the seat behind her father's back. 'That could be him, Dad. I don't remember hearing his last name and he was introduced as Quin.'

'Well, I can do better than that,' Max said, half turning towards her. 'I'm familiar with the company, though I didn't have personal dealings with them, but one of my colleagues did and, as far as I know, found them to be reputable. I gave her a call. She mentioned the name "Quin" and spoke highly of the company. They contributed a substantial donation to the Sustainability Fund."

Audrey moved around the chair to lean against the desk to face him. 'Okay.' She wasn't sure what she was thinking but felt some comfort in this news. If it was the same Quin, he had a good reputation. 'Did you find anything about Hibernia? It's only a smallish island so—'

'Well, it's not just an island, love. A preliminary search says it's a significant habitat—wetlands, saltmarsh and a mangrove that doesn't normally grow that far south. If someone's developing it... well, that would be a great pity. The main industries —dairy and fishing—have declined significantly.'

Audrey nodded in agreement and was impressed with how much her father had already discovered. 'They've been considerate of the ecology, in as much as those older, established industries were.' He rolled his eyes. 'So much logging for farming, of course—the usual problem. But they left the wetlands be... didn't have the technology to drain them, perhaps. It was first settled by Irish monastics apparently. You might already know.'

Audrey hadn't heard that and shook her head, though it fitted with Lola's story about the nuns who'd lived there. She mentioned it to Max.

'Yes. The convent makes sense. There's an old abbey there somewhere, too. Did you see that?'

'No, I didn't.' It might be a small island, she thought, but Hibernia seemed to keep revealing little gems. 'Nobody lives there now, I assume?'

'I don't know but doubt it. Are you familiar with the name, "Hibernia"?'

Audrey was but played ignorant. She could see in his eyes that her father had a fire in his belly.

'It's the old Latin name for Ireland. An interesting little island, though—Irish religious settlement, the once-thriving dairy and fishing industry and, remarkably, it still has unspoiled sections of natural habitats. I wouldn't mind having a look myself.'

Audrey thought of the view from the lunch table at The Island Hotel and Quin's seemingly genuine appreciation of the wetland. If he did own this company her father was referring to, there didn't seem to be conflict. She was relieved.

She turned back to the screen and took in again the directors' names. Dion had said that Quin would be coming back soon. Would "Marion" be with him, she wondered? Audrey had promised Dion that she would return to Hibernia to see him but wondered if time and distance would make it impossible. Perhaps it was better, she thought, if she didn't go back.

The evening was spent cooking with her mother. Since her conversation with Dion, Isabel seemed to be more energised and moved around the kitchen with quick, light steps as she checked the cupboards for ingredients for the *Estofado de Carne con Verduras*, or "Spanish Beef Stew", the very recipe that had prompted Dion to call.

Little else, besides food, had been discussed between the two over the telephone, but there was no doubting the effect that Dion had had on her.

'How old is he?' Isabel asked. She had picked up on the discrepancy between the tone of the young man's voice and the conversation of the boy.

Audrey filled her in with what she knew—that he was in his twenties, that he had a condition, though she didn't know its nature, and that he'd lost both parents in a boating accident only eighteen months before.

'Ah, poor little one,' Isabel said. She'd paused at the island bench where Audrey was stripping and chopping fresh chard from the garden, and her face held genuine concern.

'His grandparents look after him, no?'

'Yes, his father was Rosa and Beppe's only child.'

Her mother's eyes widened and held a look that Audrey knew meant she was assessing the enormity of their loss. Sometimes, Audrey wished that she wasn't an only child.

'Quin, the man that I met at their house, is his uncle— Dion's mother's brother. He's moved back to the island to help Rosa and Beppe.'

'*Sí... sí.*' Audrey saw the furrow in her mother's brow as she returned to the stove. 'Poor little one,' she said again, less audibly, and to herself.

Audrey freshened up for dinner and joined Max at the dining table, where he was reading a brochure from the local council. In recent years, her parents had modernised their home, demolishing walls to open out the space to include a new kitchen, dining area and living room. From the dining table positioned in the middle of the room, she watched her mother at the bench loading colourful platters with steamed vegetables and garnishing them with chopped herbs and crisp, oven-dried chard. She loves this, Audrey thought, widening her nostrils to draw in the odour of toasted and grounded cumin and fenugreek seeds. She began to look forward to shopping at Borough Market in London and cooking in her own kitchen. When she looked across to her father, he was watching his wife lovingly. Some colour had returned to his face, though the evening lighting cast deep shadows where his cheeks had sunken in recent months.

As Isabel was approaching the table with the loaded dishes, Audrey's mobile phone that she'd left on the coffee table vibrated audibly. Her mother nodded towards the phone.

'It might be important, *corazón.*'

Audrey was going to ignore it, but she was surprised that someone would be calling her now.

'If you don't mind, Mum,' she said, 'I'll just see who it's from and I can call them later.'

She saw that it had been Bruce, and that he'd left a single word as a message. 'Urgent'.

'Of course, love, call him back,' Max said, when Audrey told them.

'*Sí*... we can wait,' Isabel confirmed.

'Hi, Bruce. What's wrong?' Audrey was sitting on the edge of her bed in anticipation of something unforeseen.

'Some bad news, I'm afraid,' he said immediately. His voice sounded breathless, as though he'd run to the telephone. 'There's been a fire... in the London gallery... Squatters or vandals, they think.'

Audrey tried to digest the news. 'How badly?'

'Not gutted, thank goodness, but... it'll take a few months to repair.'

The implications were beginning to dawn on her.

'You still have your job at the Melbourne gallery in the meantime, of course. No problem there. It's just... well, you're all ready to go and you've let go of your lease... I'm so sorry, Audrey. If there's anything that we can help you with... finding another place ...' His voice trailed off.

'It's okay, Bruce,' she said, feeling sorry for him. His usual buoyancy had been replaced with embarrassment, but she felt a rise of panic about where she would live now that she'd finalised the lease on her flat. 'It's a lot to digest. I'll see you at work Monday, I suppose.'

'You're a sport, Audrey. It's only for a few months. I'll see you Monday then.'

'What is it, love?'

Audrey turned towards her father who'd gotten up from the table. Isabel had put down the plates and was wiping her hands on her apron.

Still holding the phone, Audrey was trying to make sense of the news and its implications.

'There's been a fire at the London gallery. It looks like I won't be going anywhere for a while.'

Although she knew that her parents had reservations about the move to London, nevertheless, their expressions of concern were genuine. Her mother moved towards her with arms moving automatically into the embrace position.

Max was standing still. 'Well, that's... I'm not sure what to say, Aud. That's a bit unexpected, isn't it? How do you feel?'

Her mother had paused, waiting for her answer.

Audrey tried to accurately assess her thoughts. She was shocked, and rattled, but lurking somewhere deep inside her was a small nut of relief.

That night after dinner, the three of them talked for hours about the next move. Audrey didn't need to admit that she didn't want to go back to the gallery; her parents had already determined that.

'I think you should take a break,' Max said.

'*Sì*,' her mother said, nodding in agreement. 'This might be a good thing. Time to think.'

'Your mother's right, love. Perhaps it's time to reassess your life. You've been through a lot recently. I know you're okay for money... always been pretty savvy that way,' Max said, with a small laugh. 'But we can help if—'

Audrey was considering her parents' advice. She had been under pressure, and she was starting to recognise that the last twelve months or more had taken a toll in a number of ways. 'That's lovely, Dad, Mum. Thank you, but yes, I am okay and... I think you're right. I do need a break.'

Isabel and Max relaxed back into the couch and smiled at each other. 'How long will you take off? A few weeks? A few months until the London gallery's restored?' Max asked.

Audrey let him finish, but during their conversation she'd come to a decision.

'No, Dad. I'm going to resign.'

It had only been two weeks since she'd seen them in Ballina, but Max and Isabel seemed bright and relaxed when Audrey greeted them at Melbourne airport's arrivals lounge.

'It's bare bones, I'm afraid,' she reminded them, about the flat she was renting.

'That worked well... to be able to stay on, love,' Max, who was sitting beside her, said. 'A pity you'd already packed up, though.'

'Hmm... yes, but I'm slowly getting things back out of storage. Quite liking the minimalist look, I've decided.' When she'd rented out the warehouse, she'd had taken what she could fit into the smaller apartment, and stored the rest, including more personal items—the detritus of her marriage.

'Any takers on the warehouse?' Max asked. 'Pity the other one fell through.'

'Actually, Dad... just today there was an offer made, and over the asking price. If we accept, I'll be able to avoid going to auction, which I'm considering.'

'So, he still has a say—'

'Dad, Campbell's entitled to half,' Audrey said with little conviction, anticipating what her father would say next. She knew his opinion of her soon-to-be ex-husband. 'I'll still have plenty to put down on another property. We bought the warehouse at the right time and we're selling at the right time too, it seems.'

'Max, your daughter is clever, you know that.' Isabel's voice interjected from the back. 'She always looks after herself, remember?'

Audrey smiled to herself as her parent recounted, not for the first time, her frugality as a child and when, as a teenager, she'd gotten her first job. She knew this was true of herself, though she sometimes wondered if it was a negative trait. Cam had suggested on more than one occasion that she was "tight" with money. She'd defended herself, but it was only now with hindsight that she knew that it was far from the truth. He'd had expensive tastes that he couldn't personally afford, and although his own income from art sales was significant when it came, it was sporadic. It had never been an issue for her—she knew the roller-coaster of artists' incomes and never questioned that, as a married couple, they would share that ride. Now, it seemed to her that she'd taken far more of the load than she should have, though she wondered how much of that was her own fault; he hadn't been demanding, but Audrey would have done anything to make him happy. Sometimes it worked, but it never lasted for long. She wondered if Caroline was doing the same, though his disenchantment with her might well be because she didn't so readily concede to his wishes.

'You look so well, *corazón*,' Isabel said, and Max concurred.

Audrey knew this was true and she felt it in subtle ways—a lighter feeling when she walked and more energy than before. The persistent narrowing of her nasal passages seemed to have eased and the return of her sense of smell, along with a renewed interest in cooking, had increased her appetite.

'I'm putting on weight, though,' she said with a laugh, as they pulled into the garage of her apartment.

'This is good news,' her mother said, unclasping her seatbelt.

The irony wasn't lost on Audrey. Though Isabel had a healthy appetite, she had remained reed thin her whole life.

'Then that would be good news for me, too,' Max said, patting his abdomen and half turning towards his wife.

'No.'

Audrey and her father laughed. Isabel was not always diplomatic and spoke from the heart. She and Dion would get along very well, she thought.

'Lola says that there's more than enough linen and blankets, Mum.'

Isabel was repacking her suitcase and, holding a folded quilt from Audrey's cupboard, was determining how to fit it in. She put it down and picked up the pillow and sheet she'd brought with her. 'I'll take these,' she said, and Audrey nodded, knowing her mother's fear of contracting a bug from a foreign bed.

The events of the last two weeks had unfolded quickly. Returning from Ballina, Audrey had kept true to her plan to resign from the gallery. She knew that she was taking a risk, as she'd worked there for so long that she wasn't sure what other career options would be available. 'Another gallery will snap you up,' her father had said, but she didn't want that. Audrey wanted something new, something to inspire and challenge her; just what that would be was not clear at all.

Bruce had physically taken a backward step when she'd told him. The look on his face revealed more emotion than she'd expected. They'd both worked for Lombard and Jones, or L&J as it was known, for fifteen years, but with Bruce constantly travelling between the six national galleries, they'd never formed a close relationship. He was twenty years older than she was and his personal life had always been somewhat of a mystery, though she'd met his partner Robert on a number of occasions. However, they held a deep respect for each other, and Audrey was in awe of his knowledge of art. She'd learned a great deal from him over the years—about art, about artists, and about business acumen—and had always felt incredibly lucky to have been his protégée.

Audrey remembered Bruce finally expressing his thoughts on Campbell after the breakup. 'A genius, really, but a proverbial... You're far too good for him, my dear.' Coming from the usually reserved Bruce, this was a tick of approval.

She would miss him and many of the clients who exhibited their work at the gallery on a regular basis—Finton, sombre, shy and socially awkward, but his metalwork displayed a keen dystopian eye, and Bridget, the antithesis of Finton, gregarious and colourful. Her ceramic miniatures conveyed the precision and focus that could only be created in quiet and isolation. She'd loved helping all of them to establish and maintain their careers and had formed some lasting associations, but what she wouldn't miss was the direction the gallery was taking. When she'd started, fifteen years ago, there were only two galleries in Melbourne's CBD, but the expansion to six had seen funds spread too thinly and, worse, relationships with artists become merely expedient. She'd fought against it, often working out of hours to follow up those who showed promise but were a potential risk. Most times it paid off. The artists she worked with trusted her. Cam had told her that. He'd been one she'd taken a risk recommending.

She'd called into a local gallery near her first apartment. The owner, Sharmi, was a friend from university where they'd studied Fine Arts together and who had provided helpful advice on managing a gallery in Audrey's early days at L&J. Sharmi's husband had accepted a work transfer to Mumbai, and it was in the gallery's closing days that Audrey had called in to view the latest, and last, exhibition by a little-known artist. When she'd arrived, the artist, Campbell Myers, was talking with a small group of people who were expressing interest— feigned or genuine—in his paintings. Audrey took her time, moving from one painting to another and noted that their classic style seemed to be at odds with their modern young creator. While absorbed in a depiction of the Hawkesbury River at dawn in winter, she was startled by a male voice close to her ear.

'Don't get lost in the fog,' he said, and she'd turned to find its owner, Campbell Myers, standing too close in her personal space.

'What gift can we give to Lola?'

Isabel's voice broke through Audrey's reverie. She thought back to her time with Lola in the convent and the conversation they'd shared in the kitchen. An idea sprang to mind.

'Tea. Lola would love a range of teas and... a teapot large enough for the four of us.'

'Yes,' her mother said. She was holding a towel to her chest and had paused in the packing of the case. She looked at her daughter and smiled. 'You're looking forward to it, no?'

'Yes, Mum. I am.' Audrey had felt buoyed since she'd spoken with Lola on the phone the week before. During discussions with her parents that last evening in Ballina, they'd decided that Hibernia held interest for all of them and that a few days spent on the island might be just what they all needed. She'd some reservations at first, but her parents' enthusiasm had been the deciding factor. It could be good, she decided, to take her time for a change, to visit the island not bound by the need to return to work. An unbidden memory of standing on the windswept cliff behind the old house suddenly caused a great longing, though she wondered how it would feel to her now. While pondering the practicalities of accommodation, and in the middle of searching what was available on the mainland, she'd received a text:

Hello, Audra

The opening of The Sanctuary is set for 3 Jan. Love to see you there if you're in Australia. You're welcome here anytime. More than enough rooms.

Love, Lola (from Hibernia)

'Lola, it's... it's Audra.' For some reason, she acknowledged, her new name was sitting well with her. 'Thanks for the message. How good to hear from you!'

'Hold on, my love, I just need to move into the kitchen...'

Audrey had imagined her barefoot, walking lightly through the rooms on the ground floor, her colourful shirt lapping around her solid frame.

'There, that's better. Audra? How are you? I'm pleased you

got my message then. Goodness knows, it seems to be in the lap of the gods whether Hibernia connects with the world or not.'

Lola's energy seemed to travel down the phone, lifting her own. Audrey wondered if the jacaranda blooms had opened and how they would look in the illumination of the lanterns that she'd noticed were strung through the tree.

'You're not in London, surely?'

Audrey told her the recent developments and her decision to leave the gallery. As she spoke, it seemed to her that everything was happening at a frenetic pace, and she was surprised at her honesty with a woman she'd only met once.

'Ah... the Spirit moves in mysterious ways, my dear. I'm not surprised. It's not your path,' she said, like an echo of their parting conversation on Hibernia.

Audrey was tempted to ask what her path might be. Though she had little patience with self-proclaimed psychics, there was something about Lola—wisdom born of a rich and colourful life, she suspected—that gave her credibility. Perhaps she'd ask her on another occasion, she thought and instead, told Lola about the plan to come to the island with Max and Isabel. Before she could broach the question of accommodation, Lola had interjected, her voice determined.

'And of course, you will all stay here.'

CHAPTER FOUR

S he hadn't anticipated this, to be crossing to Hibernia again so soon; her third trip in only two months. Audrey could barely identify with the self who thought she was leaving Melbourne and this island behind to start a new life.

There were no pangs of regret. She loved London but taking up the position at the gallery had been a self-enforced move, calculated to further a career she didn't think she wanted anymore. Now, as she stood with Max on the deck of the ferry, the strong wind buffeting their hair and carrying their words away, she felt something akin to excitement—for what, she still didn't know.

Isabel, anxious that her own light frame might be lifted in a gust of wind from the deck, was going through her mother's handwritten recipes in the car. She hadn't looked at them in years, she'd told Audrey, as she'd taken down the small, but thick leather-bound book from a less frequently used kitchen cupboard in Ballina.

Audrey returned to join her mother in the car while Max negotiated his way to Bill's cabin on the ferryman's invitation.

They'd struck up an immediate rapport when they'd met through the window of Audrey's car.

Max had driven to the jetty while Audrey had sat with Isabel in the back. The time spent cooking in her mother's Ballina kitchen and talking about traditional Spanish and Middle Eastern recipes had fanned the dying embers of a passion she'd discounted as being whimsy.

They'd been poring through some of the individual slips of paper wedged into the pages of the book, both marvelling at the exquisite cursive script that Isabel's mother had used, when Bill spotted Audrey in the back as he approached the car. His response was immediate.

'Audrey! Good to see you. Thought you were leaving us for greener pastures. Literally, I mean.' Bill tapped the open window in response to his own joke.

In her peripheral vision she could see her mother sit up more alertly, almost defensively.

'Change of plans, Bill,' Audrey said. 'It's good to be coming back to Hibernia. I've told Mum and Dad a lot about it. This is Max and Isabel.'

'G'day,' Bill said to Max and acknowledged Isabel with a respectful nod.

'That's good, love. Bit of tension on our island since you were last here though. Bloody nuisance. Been here all my life and, I dunno what's gunna happen.' His normally bright eyes seemed to cloud momentarily. 'We could do with someone... you know, from outside the community... someone with another viewpoint and plain common sense.'

She was at the point of asking what was wrong but thought better of it. Max, on the other hand, didn't hesitate.

'I hear there's a bit going on... development plans, is that right?'

'Yep,' Bill responded immediately. 'Bloody eco-tourist

resort or somethin'. *Eco!* They're kidding. They're gunna wreck the place. "Wrecko-tourism" more likely,' Bill said with a laugh, though his eyes didn't get the joke.

'Who's "they", do you know?' Max said.

'Nah. There's some rumours, but... that's somethin' the people of the island have always been good at—startin' rumours. Small place an' all that. But I think me days in this job are numbered.'

'Why's that?'

Audrey and Isabel listened intently to the men's exchange.

'There's talk of changes, maybe even runnin' a hydrofoil. Seems that old "Maggie" here,' he turned his head to encompass the ferry, 'is too slow. Everyone'll be in a rush, they reckon... to slow down at the 'wrecko'-lodge. Ha!'

Audrey felt a grip in her abdomen of protectiveness towards Bill and "Maggie" and briefly wondered if she'd stepped in progress and had brought it with her. She'd heard this possibility about the hydrofoil before from Lola, and now Bill's reiteration of her words gave it more weight. She wondered if Lola knew even more than she'd done at their last meeting and felt the pull of urgency to know, and to not.

———

'Audra!' Lola swept forward across the threshold to embrace Audrey. When she stepped back, still gripping Audrey's forearms, she seemed to be appraising her.

'You look... different. Something of an inner glow.' Her blue eyes, highlighted by the royal blue caftan she was wearing, were mischievous, but their expression shifted to one of curiosity and warmth when she saw Max and Isabel approaching the door from the car.

'Welcome, Isabel and Max,' she said, without need of introduction, and clasped their proffered hands in turn.

Audrey saw that her mother was relaxing and was reassured. Isabel was a sensitive and highly strung woman at times and had been concerned that they would be imposing, especially with The Sanctuary under renovation.

'You only met her once,' she'd said to her daughter when the plan was hatching in Ballina, 'and she doesn't know your father and me at all.'

Max had merely looked on from the sidelines, awaiting the outcome. In comparison to his wife, he had no such qualms because he would offer a roof to anyone and had done so over the years.

Pleasantries were exchanged and it seemed that Lola became even more alive, if that were possible. Audrey wondered again about the self-isolation that seemed so much at odds with the energy and worldliness of this woman.

'Come in, come in,' Lola said, stepping back inside, where her blue-draped figure was almost swallowed by the rose-tinted dimness of that large and expansive entrance. Audrey felt a thrill at the thought of her mother's reaction to the stained window that cast its ruby glow, and she was rewarded.

As Isabel stepped inside, her reaction was immediate and came as a soft gasp.

'*Dios mio!* It's just as I remember.' The others waited for an explanation, and she continued. 'Where I go to school... the nuns of *Orden carmelita*... It was just this way in their *convento*.'

'You were taught by the Carmelites? So was I,' Lola said, moving beside Isabel and linking an arm in hers. 'It's so true, Isabel. In my travels, I've seen a number of convents just like this. It reminds me of my schooldays, too.'

The two women smiled at each other, and Audrey

marvelled at her mother's ready acceptance of this stranger's touch.

'And it was Saint Teresa of Avila who greeted us in the entrance. Just like here,' she said, looking up at the stained-glass window.

'*Sí, sí* ...' Isabel was nodding and seemed to be deep in thought.

'It's beautiful, I suppose,' Max said, 'but it would have scared the living daylights out of me as a school kid. Never could understand all that. Mine was a very practical upbringing.'

Audrey, lagging behind the three of them, moved into the entrance and listened with amusement to her parents.

Once settled in their adjacent rooms on the first floor, they gathered to head down to the kitchen for a cup of tea. Audrey glanced at the closed door at the end of the corridor that held that vibrant sunroom like a secret. Isabel was still chuckling at the sight of her husband's face when he'd seen his room. Max was a tall man, and Lola had been concerned when she saw him that the bed might not be long enough. He'd assured her that it would be fine, that he'd slept in beds of all shapes and sizes on his travels for work. Though the decor of each room was spartan, Lola had gone to an effort to masculinise his, replacing the candlewick spread with a deep blue and purple blanket, but it was none of this that had Isabel laughing, more the context of her husband sleeping in what was formerly a nun's room, complete with crucifix and a picture of the bleeding heart of Jesus.

'Not much space,' he'd said to his wife and daughter, standing in the centre of the room with arms extended, his fingertips touching the side walls. 'Great view, though,' he added.

Lola had positioned them on the eastern side of the corridor with a view though narrow windows to the wetland and the sea in the distance. Audrey was reminded of the dream she'd had in Ballina of her standing in the open wall of the chapel and wondered if anything more had been done in that space since she had last been here.

On their way to the kitchen, through the main rooms downstairs, Audrey noted that her parents walked lightly, as she had, as though they felt they were trespassing.

From the kitchen came the chink of crockery and the deep resonance of Lola humming a familiar ballad. When they entered, the first thing Audrey looked at was the window and she smiled with pleasure when she saw the purple hue of sunlight through the open jacaranda blossoms.

Isabel and Max saw it too and their comments made Lola smile with pride.

'I know,' she said, as she placed cups and small plates on a tray. 'I like to think of it as the colour of transformation. I hope that whoever planted that tree got to enjoy this sight and I am ever grateful that "she", I imagine, knew what she was doing. I've set up a table in the garden out the back here and you'll see what I mean—there's a sense of her there.'

A door that Audrey hadn't noticed last time was open. The strong wind on the ferry was replaced here with a light breeze that rippled through a beaded curtain and carried the scent of the sea.

Carrying the gift bag containing a large teapot, four different blends of tea and Isabel's homemade fruit cake, she placed it on the benchtop next Lola.

'From the three of us, in appreciation.'

As Lola opened the parcel, her eyes widened with pleasure.

'How wonderful!' she said, thanking them all. 'You remembered about the tea, Audra, and now I have a decent sized pot. That's so lovely of you. The cake looks divine.'

'My mother's recipe,' Isabel said, with a look of pride.

'That's special,' Lola said. 'Come, I'll get you settled then I'll cut some for us. Can't wait to try it. I'm getting very bored with my muesli slices.' Her laugh was deep and throaty.

Max offered to carry the tray and followed.

Outside, a tangerine cloth, secured by a small garden gnome at its centre, covered a wrought-iron table with legs mottled with an algal green. The cloth's edges swayed in the breeze and its colour provided a startlingly beautiful contrast to November's new growth. Behind the table, set almost in a hedge to the right, was a wooden garden shed. It was old by the weathered look of the boards, but otherwise in good condition. Either side of the door were long double windows that would open outwards.

Lola removed the gnome, introduced as "Barney", a parting gift from a friend, to provide space for the tray.

'Thanks, Max.' She caught Audrey's eye. 'Are you familiar with the Cadfael mysteries?'

Audrey shook her head, confused at what she meant, though the name registered somewhere.

'They're a series of books, fiction, written by Ellis Peters, about a medieval monk who solved crimes. In his military days, before he became a monk, he learned a lot about medicine— herbal mostly at that time, of course. In the monastery grounds he set up a herbal garden and concocted his potions in a shed... I like to think not unlike this one.'

Lola's description had prompted a memory.

'Was there a movie?'

'Yes, a very popular series.'

'I know the books,' Max offered. 'Loved them as a boy.'

Isabel shook her head, not being familiar with the stories.

'Well,' Lola said with a dramatic flourish, 'follow me.'

She led them past the shed.

'I think we had our own Cadfael here, though hopefully not solving murders.'

In an open area was the outline of a bricked herbal garden complete with geometrical design, set around a circular centre that contained a big bay tree. It was a large herb garden and Audrey wondered if, in its day, it would have rivalled the lush and manicured gardens she'd seen on some of her trips to the UK and Europe. Behind the garden was an orchard—six rows, Audrey counted, of fruit trees in various states of health, though most, she saw, had sprouted new growth. Sections in one half of the herb bed had been tilled, the deep richness of the soil suggesting that it had been turned in the last few days. The other half had been planted and, as they got closer, she could just identify emerging leaves of familiar herbs.

'Parsley?' she said, bending down to a nest of leaves ready to thrust to the light.

'That's right. Coriander's over here,' Lola said, moving to a different section.

Isabel moved in closer and bent down for a closer look at the varieties Lola had planted. 'Here?' she said, peering at what seemed to be an empty bed that looked out of place.

'That's for the crocus. They grow like wildflowers here, so I just leave them to it and look forward to autumn when they bloom.'

Audrey thought of the decaying flowers she'd seen at the old house and mentioned this to Lola.

'Oh, I'm not surprised. Nobody seems to be quite sure who planted them—monks, or perhaps our sister here. But they're what brought Dion's parents to the island, as well as a return home for his mother,' she said to Audrey, 'to grow them commercially. They had a farm up the northern end. Beppe still tends it.'

Audrey thought of the look on Beppe's face when he came back into the kitchen with the box she'd given him—pleasure mixed with sorrow. 'The future,' he'd said, as he held the crocus bulbs in their tissue nest. She suddenly felt very sad.

They headed back to the table and gained a different view of the jacaranda that stood by the kitchen window like a peeping Tom. Its trunk was thick and gnarled and elbows and knees of large roots had broken through the soil as though the tree would, one day, decide to leave.

When they were seated, Audrey spoke aloud her thought.

'I'd assumed that Rosa and Beppe had lived here for a long time. Did they follow their son and daughter-in-law to Hibernia?'

'Yes,' Lola said, nodding as she poured the tea, 'they did. They moved here from the mainland—on the coast not far away, fifteen years ago, I believe. Beppe was a master boat builder and did very well, so they retired early to help with the farm and to watch their grandson grow up. Sad business,' she said, shaking her head.

It made sense to Audrey now—the relative newness of the villa that had seemed at odds with her assumption that Rosa and Beppe had been on Hibernia for a long time. She imagined their anticipation and excitement for the new life they would have together on the island. Audrey couldn't remember their son's name but knew Dion's mother's was Fionnuala because she remembered the look on Quin's face when he'd said his sister's name.

'Lola, last time I was here there was talk of a developer, and Bill said he thought that "Maggie's" days were numbered—too slow.'

'Oh yes.' Lola's cheerful expression slid from her face.

'They've been here—the surveyors, I think they were, letting it spill that they're just assessing the quality of the soil at the site that seems to be marked for the eco-lodge.'

Max leaned towards the table, his interest piqued. 'You're not convinced?'

'Well,' Lola paused before continuing, 'the site they're talking about sits right at the edge of the wetland. In winter it floods.'

'Why that site then, do you think?' Audrey asked.

'The view of the Pacific is spectacular. It's not got the high vantage point of some of the other places they could have chosen, but there's a sheltered beach it would have access to, and I think that would be the drawcard. A bit of everything there—the Pacific thundering in the distance, a safe beach for swimming, and a tranquil wetland at the door.'

'It would be good to have a look,' Max said, turning to the others, who nodded in agreement. 'And the developer? Any further word on who it is?'

Audrey saw that Lola glanced towards her before answering.

'Word is it's one of our own—Quin O'Rourke.'

Audrey took a deep breath. Something more must have happened since she was last here.

Max looked taken back by the news and told Lola what he knew of the company and its good reputation.

'We're all surprised, too,' Lola said, 'but one of the surveyors let it slip and Harry Mitchell, a local who works for the Council on the mainland, confirmed it.'

'So... what do you think his real interest is in The Island Hotel?' Audrey could feel her heart thumping in her chest.

'Mmmm, that's a strange one. Some say it's a ruse to deflect attention away from the main issue, but,' she faced Audrey squarely, 'I like to think it's for the boy—for Dion. He loves him and that, at least, is beyond doubt.'

'And the island's inhabitants?' Isabel had been listening intently. 'Are they all opposed to this eco-lodge?'

'Oh no,' Lola said, her eyes wide. 'Many people here are all for development. You wouldn't think so, would you? What's even stranger is that it's mostly the older generation who want it. They're losing their young to the mainland because there's nothing to offer them. Ironically, it's those very young ones who are most vocal about it—dead against progress here, in fact. They want Hibernia to stay as it is, or even return to what it once was, a community that was relatively independent and thrived because of its local industries. Except, the industries—dairy and fishing, mainly—don't quite fit with their personal philosophies. That's a problem. What else does Hibernia have to offer if not those?'

'The eco-lodge will create jobs, no?' Isabel offered. Her expression was uncertain, as though speaking in favour of the development might offend their host.

'You're completely right, Isabel,' Lola said immediately. 'On paper, there's nothing wrong with the idea and, yes, the young here do need something. But sadly, there's an environmental cost that could impact very badly if it's not handled well. If they could get the national broadband happening, maybe there'd be more opportunity for working at home. But I don't know that they want that.'

They nodded in agreement.

'Lola, you're on track for the opening in six weeks?' Audrey felt a need to shift the tone of the conversation.

'Yes, my love! The chapel's nearly finished. We'll have a look when you're done. Ten of the twenty bedrooms will be refitted over the next three weeks, as well the bathrooms on that floor.'

Audrey was impressed with Lola's energy and was excited to see the latest work on the chapel. She wondered, though, how much the eco-lodge would attract potential customers away from The Sanctuary, though if it worried her, Lola didn't show it.

'Ooh, it's getting warm. I think we're going to be in for a hot one. Let's leave these here, I can tidy up later. Isabel, that cake! My goodness, I've got to have the recipe for that. That is, if I'm allowed?' Lola said with a laugh and Audrey smiled to see the flush of pleasure on her mother's face.

'Sí... of course.'

They returned to the cool of the kitchen and made their way back through the rooms and up the staircase, turning right at the landing. It seemed to Audrey that the closed door at the end of the corridor beckoned them.

'My goodness, more bedrooms!' Isabel was wide-eyed as they passed door after door.

'Yes,' Lola responded, 'it was quite a community once. Most of the nuns lived a contemplative life here. It was only a handful who taught at the school.'

'When did they leave?' Max said, the deep tone of his voice seeming incongruous in this setting.

'Some of the younger nuns left, went back to Ireland, I assume, but others died here. There's a cemetery near the abbey—quite beautiful really...' Lola's voice trailed off as though she was lost in the thought.

'I believe the abbey was abandoned earlier,' Max said.

'Yes, that's right. They were all called back to Ireland, though I'm not sure why that was. Once they'd established a foothold, they moved on—not so unusual. Anyway, the nuns were left to take care of the parishioners.

'Here we are,' Lola said brightly. Her hand was on the large brass doorknob, and she was facing them, building a moment of suspense.

Audrey glanced across to her parents and Max flicked his eyebrows up and down in anticipation.

When Lola opened the door, light poured into the corridor, bathing and temporarily blinding them. She ushered them in, and Audrey could feel her excitement like a hit of static electricity. Once her eyes had adjusted, she stood transfixed by all that was before her.

The wall that had been secured in plastic was now an expanse of reinforced glass panels extending from the floor to a height of around six metres and almost the width of the entire wall. The view was breathtaking, confirmed by the soft grunt from Max, and a gentle '*Dios mio*,' from Isabel. To the left, dappled light glinted from the wetland as though reflected in a hundred small mirrors. Ahead, dairy cattle grazed on grass that was already browning in the warmth of the late spring days and, in the distance, white caps on the ocean flashed in a Morse code.

Audrey turned to take in the rest of the room. The wooden floorboards that had been covered in dust on her last visit only three weeks earlier, were polished now and shone with tones of rich honey and dark oak. The marble altar, cleaned and oiled and returned to its former dignity, overlooked the space from its platform and behind it, so spectacular that they almost overshadowed the view through the glass panels, the three stained-glass windows were triumphant.

'What do you think?' Lola's voice was soft with uncertainty.

Audrey turned to her, but was momentarily speechless, her emotion almost akin to standing in front of a beautiful painting. She didn't know why but hot tears spiked her eyes. 'It's... oh Lola,' she struggled to contain them, 'it's magnificent.'

Max and Isabel murmured in agreement and Audrey suspected that they, too, were overwhelmed with the beauty of this space.

Lola blinked forcefully as though trying to hold back her own tears.

'It is, isn't it?'

They stood in silence a moment longer. Audrey imagined the yoga mats positioned to take in the view. 'This is going to work' she said to her new friend. 'It has to. Believe me, I'll be spreading the word.' She paused before continuing with the question that had bothered her. 'The eco-lodge... will it be in competition?'

Lola smiled warmly, still unconcerned. 'Oh, I'm sure they'll offer yoga, Pilates, meditation, massage, you name it, so, yes, it will be in competition, but it won't have what we have here,' she said, waving her arm slowly to encompass the space.

Audrey noted the "we" and felt a warm rush of protectiveness for the woman in front of her and her dream. What Lola said was true, but she'd forgotten the most significant asset at The Sanctuary, and that was herself.

'Do you have plans for the afternoon?' Lola asked.

Max had moved to the windows and was taking in the view. He turned to his wife and daughter. 'Any thoughts?'

Audrey considered. 'Well, we're not expected at Rosa and Beppe's until tomorrow, so... I'm curious now about the eco-lodge site. What about you?'

Max had joined Isabel and they nodded in agreement.

'Would you like to join us, Lola?' Isabel said.

Audrey was touched by how much her mother had taken to their host. Isabel was reserved and though she exuded natural warmth, she was not as quick to make friends as her husband.

Lola thanked them but declined. 'I've got a few things to do before next week when Jake and Phil begin the refitting of the rooms. I thought we might have a pre-dinner drink in the sunroom this evening, if you'd like?'

Audrey's response was immediate. Just the thought of that vibrant room filled her with joy.

'Oh yes,' she said.

Audrey elected to drive. Isabel sat beside her and although there wasn't much room in the back, Max seemed content, his body angled so that he could stretch his legs. He'd taken out the notebook from the backpack that housed their bottles of water, spare jumpers and insect repellent, and was recording something in it. His smile was restful as he wrote and it wasn't hard to imagine him on one of the many field trips he'd undertaken over the years, sometimes being away for two or more weeks. She now wondered if, as much as he missed working, he missed his freedom. Isabel and Max were a successful coupling, but Audrey wondered if being constantly in each other's company was eroding that happy formula.

She glanced at her mother beside her. Isabel's head was angled away from her as she looked out the window. What dreams did her mother once have? Still have? Audrey realised with some shame that she had never asked her. Her mother had just... been there; always there, when she was a child and even now. She was the person that her husband and her daughter came home to.

Audrey knew that Isabel had been a keen photographer and had studied for three years at the Universitat de Barcelona, until she met Max. Some of her work from that time still hung in the Ballina house, but the vibrancy of the images had become faded, merging into the background of their lives.

'Mama?' Audrey said, her voice breaking slightly over an emotion caught in her throat.

'Sí?' Isabel turned to her daughter with the expectant look that she was about to be asked for something she would try her best to deliver.

Audrey steadied the car on the road with one hand and clasped her mother's with the other. 'Thank you.'

Isabel responded with a gentle squeeze—a moment between mother and daughter that required no further explanation.

'This eco-lodge,' Max said, his tone suggesting he'd been ruminating on it for a while, 'it could divide the island, you know.'

Isabel and Audrey agreed.

'I've seen this sort of thing before,' he continued, 'with some wanting progress, others wanting conservation. Still... if it lives up to its name, it shouldn't cause concerns.'

Audrey nodded into the mirror. In theory, it seemed to be a good compromise and she just couldn't imagine that the Quin O'Rourke she'd met would be involved in anything that would put the wetland at risk, but Lola didn't seem like a reactionary, or a gossip dredging up untruths to spice up her life. If anything, she appeared to be the opposite—worldly and open-minded yet wanting peace.

They veered off the main road in the direction Lola had instructed, the crunch of the gravel beneath the wheels providing the comfort of being off the beaten track.

Slowing to accommodate the uneven surface, Audrey glanced at their surroundings. The scenery so far had been unspectacular—cleared fields right and left, a scattering of dairy cows and, in one field, several alpacas that raised their heads high to acknowledge the passing car.

As they approached the coastline, the sea all but disappeared behind a dense woodland.

The road began a slight decline as Audrey navigated the road between the trees, a mix of Redgum and Silverbark. A kilometre or so in, they were replaced with the shorter tea trees, and beyond them, the wetland comprising low tea-tree, Salicornia, and mangroves, rare at this latitude, nestled in a bowl of land and stretching towards the sea. Sighs of pleasure filled the space between them. Two headlands, rising out of it like arms extending from sleeves, embraced the cove that Lola had mentioned.

Audrey brought the car to a stop. From their vantage point, they could see that the waves struck a submerged reef further out, but by the time the sea entered the cove they had been tamed and lapped timidly on its shore. They could understand, they conferred, why this site would be chosen for the eco-lodge; it had it all, just as Lola had said. The problem was that access to it was through the wetland that now, to Audrey's eyes, seemed so vulnerable.

'They could do it,' Max said. He was leaning forward with a hand on the back of her seat, 'but...' he paused to take it in, 'mmm... they'd need to...' His voice petered out as it often did when he was mulling over a problem.

'This is an estuary, yes?' Isabel asked.

'You're right, Is,' Max said. 'You can see the river snaking its way through over there.' They turned to the left to where he was pointing. 'Looks like it goes back a way. Let's take a look?'

Outside the car, they were buffeted by the wind that was funneling through the headlands. As they walked further forward, they glimpsed the silver trace of a small river making its way to the sea. From here, they could see how the land declined from the cliffs in the east, to end in this bowl where the tide and river met.

'It would be a shame,' Audrey turned to her parents, her words returned to her ears by a gust of wind, 'to have anything else here at all.'

Max's brow furrowed in agreement.

'Why not just stand here? Why not just *look*, not touch?' Isabel said suddenly with emotion and Audrey saw the look of distress on her mother's face that surprised her; it had always been Max who'd vocally championed the environment. Audrey thought of Isabel's permaculture garden in Ballina where plants grew in their right place, supported by each other. What her mother would see in front of her would be a garden of perfect relationships, something self-sustaining and to be admired from a distance, or at least tended by soft-footed care-takers. The eco-lodge would be a foreign weed.

'I agree,' Max said, 'but I think it's a foregone conclusion. Over there,' he pointed to the headland on the left, 'they've marked that out. It's the best vantage point, but... I can't see how they're going to...'

Audrey followed her father's pointed finger and her eyes tracked back down the slope of the headland, through the dense wetland grasses and shrubs at the lowest point, and up the incline on which they stood. She noticed that here and there the vegetation seemed to be abruptly separated. A slight movement to her left caught her eye and, nudging Max, she indicated towards a patch of tea-tree. Squatting behind it, binoculars fixed ahead, was a middle-aged man sporting the almost clichéd look of a birdwatcher—cap, check shirt and waterproof pants. A backpack was slung over one shoulder, causing the thermos in the side pocket into a dangerous angle. She shifted her gaze to the right of the car and saw a deep, thick tyre tread that disappeared amongst the vegetation.

'I think, she said, 'it's already begun.'

There was silence in the car as they made their way back along the gravel track, each absorbed in their own ruminations.

Audrey glanced in the mirror and saw that Max held the end of his pen beneath his teeth as he frowned at the notepad in his lap. Isabel, with folded hands resting in her lap, was looking straight ahead. It was strange, Audrey thought, how quickly they had all become protective of this island.

Ahead, a four-wheel drive clipped the top of the rise. Audrey began to veer to the left to give enough room for it to pass. As it did, she glanced at the driver and felt her breath catch in her throat. Quin O'Rourke. His face was caught in a sullen moment but lifted in surprise when he recognised her, and he nodded in acknowledgment. She returned it half-heartedly.

In the rear-view mirror, she saw that the sun reflected off dried mud on the thick and heavy rear tyres.

The old abbey was on the opposite side of the island. From the road as they approached, it was difficult to determine its position, despite the road sign that had rather curtly read: *Old Abbey and Cemetery. 300 meters. On the left.*

'There's a section there.' Max had reached forward, his pointed hand shoulder height between Isabel and Audrey, indicating the hill on the left just ahead.

Audrey slowed the car and peered past her mother towards what looked to be the rectangular outline of a large building. Here and there, oversized bluestone blocks that would have formed the base of the walls were still clinging to each other, held together with mortar, while other sections of the wall, made of sandstone blocks it seemed, had been reduced to rubble. Only one building, indisputably a chapel, retained three of its walls and was positioned as though to oversee the surrounding land. Despite its decay, it retained an air of authority.

The ruined abbey sat snugly in the side of the hill facing the road and was surrounded by a grove of conifers, which was surprising as the cliffs at the top of the rise would have provided a spectacular view of the ocean, but there was something comforting about the site; closeted, yet welcoming. On one side, in an area that was either naturally or artificially flattened, about thirty weathered grey headstones were angled like irregular teeth. Beside and in front of it, the land began to flatten and was dotted with the remains of what looked to be stables and sheds. In its time, Lola had told them, the abbey had been a productive farm and the monks had been instrumental in introducing to Hibernia the rare Irish Moiled cattle breed reared for both its milk and meat.

There was little left of it all except for the chapel, but as the dark clouds released a sheet of rain, they resolved to return on another trip to wander amongst the tombstones.

On the opposite side of the road the land was broad and relatively flat. In the section closest to the road were one large and one smaller sandstone building, both of which appeared to be in good condition.

With the windows of the car down, they could hear the low hum of a generator and, as though on cue, a man stepped out of the smaller building and seemed to be heading for the car.

Audrey quashed the immediate sense of embarrassment that they'd invaded someone's privacy, but that, she thought, was probably a hangover of paranoia from city life. She felt these things deeply stitched into her bones and was slowly unpicking them.

The man was tall and slightly built. Beneath a bright red beanie, his dark hair was almost to his shoulders and thick stubble shadowed his face that lit with a warm and attractive smile as he approached.

'Hi there,' he said, in a voice that held the lilt of a Canadian accent. 'Are you lost?' Close up, he looked to be in his mid to late forties and his face, like Quin's, didn't have the weathered look of someone who had spent his years outdoors.

Max extended his arm through the open window of the car. The two men shook hands.

'We were just having a look at the abbey,' Max said. 'You've got a good-looking place there.'

The man nodded in welcome to Audrey and Isabel.

'Yes, it's a fine place,' he said, turning his head to take it in as though he couldn't believe his own luck.

This, Audrey thought, is a man comfortable in his own skin.

'The buildings,' Max continued, 'are they the old dairy? They're in good condition by the look of them.'

'Yes, the larger one was the milking barn. Other than some of my stuff in there, it's empty at the moment. To be honest, I'm not sure what to do with it. The other is my home at the back and a cheese shop at the front.'

'Cheese shop?' Isabel was leaning further towards the window where the man was now leaning in.

'Well,' he said with a warm laugh, 'a "shop" is probably stretching it a bit. Really, it's just a room and... would you like to come in and have a look for yourselves, and a taste?'

The three of them looked at each other, but Audrey already knew what her answer would be. And Isabel's.

As they stepped inside, their senses were sharpened by the sight of the deep burgundy walls, polished wooden shelves and the warm ambience created by down lights strategically placed to highlight the glass cloches covering wheels, slabs and quarters of different cheeses, with their sharp, earthy odour.

The room was prepared for customers and, once again, Audrey wondered where they would be coming from. An image came to her of Alex, Lola, Dion and Quin waiting for people who never came, and it made her uneasy. It wasn't a new sensation—there'd been many times when a new art exhibition failed to draw in the public, at least in the first week. Audrey's heart would sink at the loss of hope in an emerging artist's eyes, but, to her own credit, and with a good deal of strategic advertising, they usually succeeded in making sales, and the gallery chain made its profit.

Isabel asked the question.

'Bus tours,' Alex said, making his way behind the richly polished mahogany counter. 'Hibernia's not quite the backwater it might seem. Once a month, a food and wine club includes the island in their bigger trips. They come to sample the hidden gems—Joe Heppell's duck pâtés and cured meats, Barbara Roche's pastries and breads, and Beppe Cazoni's fresh produce and wine, and...' he smiled with pride, 'my cheeses.'

Audrey was stunned, her ears pricking up at the mention of Beppe. She hadn't heard any of this before and said so.

'There's a group of us,' Alex said, lifting down one of the displays. Shaving off a slice from the wheel of brie, he offered it to Isabel first, then to Max and Audrey. 'And there are others who produce good stuff on their properties, but they're reluctant to sell... just do it for themselves. Old Ernie Drinkwater's got some interesting breeds of chickens and quail, but, other than what he eats himself, they're his pets. I've bought some eggs from him to make soufflé. Amazing!'

Audrey savoured the creamy coating left by the brie before speaking. It was wonderful. 'The bus ... It comes across on the ferry, I suppose?'

He nodded. 'You might've heard the plans to scrap it...
replace it with... well, we're still not sure of that one.'

'But the bus... it couldn't come, no?' Isabel said, her eyes
wide with the ramifications.

'That's right, I'm afraid.'

'Then how the hell...?' Max said, accepting a small spoon of
feta that Alex had taken from a slab covered in brine.

Alex shrugged. 'We're not big enough for the local council
to be concerned. A few wheels of brie and tubs of pâté aren't
going to keep the economy in the black.'

'Bloody beautiful,' Max said, still enamoured with the feta.
'But what about you, mate, won't this affect your business?'

'Oh, this isn't my main source of income, but it is... one of
my loves.'

'And the other?' Audrey was intrigued by this man.

Alex's eyes widened and there was a glint of mischief.
'We've still got some time before the bus. Would you like to
see?'

For the third time that day, their voices were in unison.

They crossed to the shed beneath a portico with sandstone
columns that supported a new colour-bond roof. Alex pulled
open the heavy door and they stepped inside. The temperature
drop was marked. It was a large, vacant space that Audrey estimated would be thirty metres long by ten metres wide, with a
concrete floor and sandstone walls. The space, though, was
filled with light from large panes of reinforced glass frosted
with age and set high into the walls; the roof was corrugated tin
roof supported by Blackwood beams, still sturdy despite the age
of the building, which, Alex told them, was over a hundred
years.

The area closest to the door to their left was fitted with a
long trestle bench. Power tools and a circular saw sat amidst a
coarse powder of wood dust and shavings. Here, the smell of

wood was both warm and bitter, and reminded Audrey of the factories in Melbourne where she'd order frames and supports for the exhibitions. She felt an emotion akin to excitement though she wasn't sure why.

At the far end of the bench, something was shrouded under canvas. Alex took up position behind it and, facing them, lifted off the sheet and gently raised a mandolin still in foetal form. The wood was raw, but when they moved closer to it, they could see the grain like the ripples in a seabed. 'Western Bigleaf Maple,' Alex said with pride. Max and Isabel stepped in to take a closer look just as Audrey's phone vibrated. As Max asked Alex a question, she took the opportunity to check the screen. Two voicemail messages—one from Poppy and the other from Campbell. She felt her heart sink at that one. Excusing herself, she stepped outside under the portico in the hope of some signal.

'Hi. Are you still on the island?' Don't know if you'll get this ...' Poppy's voice had trailed off and Audrey became concerned. They were so far away from each other. 'Babe,' Poppy's voice had continued, 'I'm coming home. Call me when you get this.'

A rush of joy was felt viscerally. Audrey checked the reception bars—two and fluctuating. She went back inside the shed resolving to call her friend as soon as she could. Isabel had moved away from the men who were deep in conversation over the mandolin and was standing in front of a faded photograph hanging precariously on the wall near the door. As Audrey moved behind her mother, she saw by the sepia tone that it was old. Thirty or more cows were corralled in individual wooden stalls and were being hand-milked. In one stall, a woman had turned to face the camera. Her hair was tucked under a white cap, and she was smiling broadly, as though she'd just shared a joke with the photographer. In another, a teenage boy was standing and leaning into the adjacent corral and was speaking to someone just out of view. Others, all wearing the same cap as the woman, were carrying heavy-looking buckets brimming with milk. Light filtered through windows set high in the walls. It was the same barn, now empty of that life, they were in.

'Poppy's coming home,' she said over her mother's shoulder. Isabel half turned towards her, still eyeing the photograph, but Audrey saw the smile on her lips.

'Yes,' she said. 'This is good news.'

There was another message that Audrey needed to listen to, but this was a moment she was not going to let Campbell spoil. He could wait until she was ready.

As they left the shed, Max turned to Alex as he was closing the barn door. 'You've got a gift there, mate. I can see why it's a passion. Getting back to the other one, where do you make the cheese? I thought it would be in the barn, too.'

'Seems a logical place, I agree. But I didn't think the sawdust would be a good flavour inclusion,' Alex said with his easy laugh. 'There's a section at the rear of the shop with a cellar. I'll show you.'

They headed back into the shop and Alex guided them through the door at its rear, the pungent smell of cheese greeting them even before they'd stepped in. The room was small and contained four stainless steel vats of different sizes and a machine with an electronic thermometer. On a bench to one side of the room was a cylindrical container of fermenting cheese that Alex explained was caciotta, a simple rural cheese from Tuscany. With Max's curiosity piqued, Alex took them through the process; the addition of the raw milk—'Goat, from my friends grazing out the back,' he told them—the setting of the temperature of the pasteuriser, addition of fermenters, then curd and the manual curd cutting. At the far end of the room was an open, narrow doorway with a small staircase. Alex beckoned them over and they took it in turns to survey the small cellar, where wheels and cylinders of various types of cheese were ripening.

With the arrival of the bus imminent, and aware they had taken up Alex's time, they gave their farewells, not before taking two business cards—one for the cheese shop, and the other for instrument-making. Max was certain that an old colleague, who was proficient on the ukulele and still played regular gigs on the New South Wales coast, would be interested in Alex's unique designs.

For Audrey, the lasting impression was that of the shed—its dimensions and structural integrity, the play of natural light through the windows and, though clean, the rich, organic smell of cattle dung and milk that had embedded itself in its structure. Far from being unpleasant, it added to the authenticity of the shed's original purpose. She recognised the stirrings of an idea.

'If you come back to Hibernia, you're always welcome here,' Alex said, and his manner was so warm and genuine that Audrey hoped that she could return soon.

Max offered to drive back to The Sanctuary.

Audrey opened the back door to accompany her mother, but Isabel smiled and gestured to the front. 'Sit with your father, corazón.' She seemed pensive, and Audrey wondered if the shift in afternoon light had prompted a low mood. At such times, Audrey knew, from her own experience too, the best therapy was to get busy, or to meditate. Her mother's term for the latter was to 'gather' herself, a form of conscious meditation. This afternoon though, the expression on her face was more wistful than sad.

Once settled into the front seat and on their way, a flash of insight had Audrey turning towards her. 'Mama, do you still have your camera?'

Isabel seemed surprised, a soft 'oh' unspoken on her lips. 'Yes... but so old now,' she said.

'If you had a new one, would you take photographs again?' Audrey was aware of Max's glance towards herself and the rear view, waiting for his wife's response. She could see that her mother was on the verge of dismissing the idea.

'You should, you know, Is,' Max interjected. 'You've got a great eye. Your photos...'

As usual, his voice trailed off, but in the silence of what was not said, Audrey heard a note of something akin to guilt.

Isabel didn't respond, but as they drove on, Audrey knew exactly what her next gift to her mother would be, and she couldn't wait to give it.

As they turned on to the surfaced road that would take them back to Lola's, the small tourist bus passed them. With a quick estimate, Audrey had the number of passengers at around twenty; hopefully, she thought, all had the intention of purchasing Alex's cheese.

'Welcome back.' Lola's warm greeting at the door of The Sanctuary brought a smile to Audrey's heart. The late afternoon light was waning, and the air had cooled considerably, but stepping into the entrance was like being embraced. The ruby window still held a gentle rose tint, a softer version of its earlier display. Salt lamps and candles in traditional holders usually found in Catholic churches in front of stern or sorrowful-faced statues, glowed cheerily red and blue. But it was the temperature that surprised Audrey. She'd thought that it would be difficult to heat this space, but it was perfect.

'It's lovely, Lola,' Isabel said. 'And so warm!'

Audrey marvelled at how her parents voiced her own thoughts. Their time spent together in these last two weeks seemed to have fostered a synchronicity between them. She considered the delicate frame of her mother, knowing how much she suffered in the cold.

Lola, on the other hand, dressed in fine silk—violet top over a paler full-length sarong—looked ready for summer. Her hair was loose and fell past her shoulders in thick white locks. The effect was stunning.

'Ah, hydronic heating,' she said, 'installed in the '70s, I believe. Still works like a charm, thank goodness.' A furrow formed on her brow. 'None up in your rooms though, I'm afraid. That's on the list in time for next winter.'

She accompanied them to the foot of the staircase. 'You know the way to the lounge room, Audra, when you're ready. I'll bring up some pre-dinners and you can tell me about your day.'

As she left them, Audrey noted that, beneath the elegance of her outfit, Lola's feet were cushioned in hand-knitted slippers.

Inside each of their rooms, Lola had placed a fan heater that had already filled the small space with a welcome warmth. Audrey wondered at the stoic nature of the nuns who'd inhabited these rooms. While on one hand she admired them, on the other, she couldn't understand that someone would choose a life of such self-denial. *I must be getting soft,* she thought.

Ten minutes and a change of clothes later, they met in the corridor and Audrey ushered them towards the room at the end that had featured in her daydreams since she'd first seen it. It had been daylight last time and she wondered, as they stood at the closed doors, if the vibrancy of the room would be muted.

When they stepped in from the cool corridor, they were immediately wrapped in heat emitting from an open fireplace set in the wall beside them and there was a soft scent of pine emanating from large cones glowing in the grate. Audrey was surprised, as she'd not remembered seeing this feature before, but surmised that it had been obscured by the collection of small potted palms now sitting at a distance to protect their leaves from the heat.

The room had lost none of its vibrancy. If anything, the glow from the fire and the light from large candle stands placed around the room enhanced the colour of the cushions and the Persian rug between the two sofas that were set at right angles to each other. Outside on the balcony behind the closed glass doors, glowing cast-iron lanterns of Middle Eastern design hung from its ceiling, and two larger ones, the height of a small child, were positioned like sentinels in the balcony's corners.

Isabel had moved towards the doors and Max came to stand behind her. 'Reminds me of Granada,' he said, 'and that place where we met near your home.'

'Sí,' Isabel replied, turning to him, a gentle and loving smile playing on her lips.

Audrey looked away. She knew well the story of their meeting. It had been the university summer vacation. Max was sampling more of Europe while doing his PhD at Leeds University, and Isabel had returned home from Universitat de Barcelona. The young Max had been walking along the Carrera del Darro in Granada when his attention was caught by the sway of long black hair and the shapely legs of a girl walking ahead of him. The further they walked, the more infatuated he became and, when she paused to cross the street, he mustered the courage to speak to her. 'More beautiful front-on,' was all he could say in that moment.

Isabel was not so easily flattered, but she thanked him and crossed the road to a bakery. Max waited on the other side and when she appeared from the shop, discreetly followed her home. The next day, he waited where he first saw her, hoping this was her regular route. To his joy she did return, she saw him, and they chatted. On the third day he invited her for dinner, and she agreed.

'Why didn't you wait outside her home? You knew where she lived,' Audrey had asked him.

'Ah,' Max had said,' I'd reckoned your mother wouldn't give me the time of day if she'd thought I was stalking her, but I would've resorted to that if need be!' They'd all laughed at that one.

Audrey saw, first-hand, the street, the bakery and Isabel's family home in Granada on several visits with her parents during her youth. Although she'd not returned there in recent years, she remembered well the famous Moorish architecture, but above all, it was the scent of spices that formed the most enduring memory, as though it had unlocked something inside her—a genetic memory.

Max returned to stand by the fire and Isabel and Audrey settled into the sofas. There was a soft thud of what sounded like the front door downstairs and a low resonance of voices that became louder and clearer as it progressed upstairs.

The door to the lounge room opened. A tray, gripped in a man's hands, appeared first, edging through the opening, followed by the rest of the body of Quin O'Rourke. Lola, who'd been holding the door open for him, followed quickly behind.

Quin paused, self-consciously it seemed to Audrey, who could feel her heart pounding in her chest. He stood with the tray still in his hands, waiting for instruction.

'We have a guest,' Lola said to them, then turned to Quin. 'Just on the table there, thanks.'

He moved to place the tray laden with glasses, a bottle of wine, a cut baguette, olives, a small bowl of dark green olive oil and one of za'atar, on the coffee table in front of the sofas. As he moved, Audrey felt an agitation in the air around her. She was aware of all eyes on her, except Quin's as he had backed away and was caught in a no-man's land between the fire and sofas.

Lola made the introductions to Max and Isabel and Max moved forward to shake his hand. Audrey stood and proffered her own. 'Nice to see you, Quin,' she said, trying to sound nonchalant, feeling anything but. The words felt dry in her throat as she voiced them, and she wondered about her own sincerity.

Lola had drawn forward an armchair and offered Quin a seat.

'I must be going. I thought that I saw you on the road to the wetlands.' He looked down at that point and then up again. 'I had some work to do at The Island and took a punt you might be here.'

'How's Dion?' Audrey felt a need to rescue him when she saw that colour had risen in his cheeks and heard his voice falter.

'He's very excited to see you. And you, Isabel. I don't know if he'd arranged this before with you, but he seems to be expecting you all,' he paused and turned to Lola to include her, 'for dinner tomorrow evening at The Island. By the look on your face, Audrey, I'd say he hadn't? Ah, I thought as much, which is why I thought I'd better drop in to check.' He looked around to them all. 'If you don't have any other plans, would you come?'

The question seemed to Audrey to be loaded with meaning. This man, she thought, knows what the rumours are, and the fact that they had seen him at the wetlands this morning was, perhaps, causing him discomfort.

There was silence, as though everyone was thinking the same.

'Well, I'd love to meet Dion,' Isabel said, with a volume that took her husband and daughter by surprise. 'I'd love to go.'

'Count me in,' Max said, with a joviality that was both genuine and considerate.

'That sounds settled,' Audrey said, still aware of the battle of conflicting emotions and the prospect of meeting Quin's wife, Marion, but the anticipation of what Dion might cook excited her.

Quin looked relieved. He turned to Lola, who had not yet spoken.

'Lola? Would you do us the honour? We'd love to welcome you to Hibernia. It's well overdue.'

Audrey held her breath, but Lola's smile was genuine. 'I'd love to, Quin. Thank you.' She turned to Audrey, Max and Isabel and her face suddenly changed to mock anger. 'But I have a bone to pick. Why on earth didn't you tell me your name isn't, Audra!'

The bed was much narrower than her own. The mattress dipped slightly in the middle but, combined with the very subtle scent of jasmine in the sheets, Audrey felt comforted in a way that reminded her of being wrapped in the arms of her grandmother, Florence.

She slept deeply, woken only by the absence of morning traffic. Reaching for her mobile, she wondered if it was the first electronic device ever to be in this room.

7:00

A faint chink of crockery suggested that Lola was already in the kitchen.

Snuggling back down into the bed and lying on her back, she savoured the heavy feeling of her body sinking into the mattress and noted that her breath was already established deep in her abdomen. Her thoughts drifted to the previous evening and, though she tried to resist, they circled around the image of Quin O'Rourke standing awkwardly in the living room with the tray in his hands. Immediately, Audrey felt a shift of her breath to her chest and throat and noted how her pulse began to accelerate. Lola's voice echoed in her mind. 'Bring your concentration back to the breath...'

They'd had dinner at the long table in the dining room near the kitchen—a hearty vegetable soup with the rest of the baguette, fresh salami, olives and a wheel of brie that Isabel had bought that afternoon from Alex, followed by homemade apple pie and thick custard. They'd recounted the events of the day to Lola, who was aware of the group of artisans living on the island but had yet to meet them all. Audrey was surprised. Their host was gracious and friendly yet hadn't connected with the locals, something that was confirmed by Quin's invitation to a welcome at The Island Hotel. The salami, she'd said, was from one of the people that Alex had mentioned but was sold in the small bakery in Main Street. Audrey had seen the bakery sign on the shop but had thought it was empty. There'd been no sign of lights or customers on the two occasions she'd travelled along that road.

'Only open for a few hours in the morning,' Lola had explained. 'That's when most of the locals shop for basics. No point otherwise, there's no one around.'

Though they related to Lola the journey to the wetlands, nobody broached the topic of having seen Quin there, nor his visit to The Sanctuary, except to say that they were curious to know what was going to be on the menu. Audrey was relieved. It seemed from everyone's body language that they somehow saw herself, and Quin, at the centre of a melodrama, and couldn't understand where that might have begun.

It was after Audrey had observed Isabel and Lola talking in depth that Lola offered them all a relaxation session in the chapel. Max declined, on the pretext of having things to think about back in his room. Audrey knew that he'd be happy on his own and was pleased to see how this new interest in the eco-lodge and wetland seemed to be keeping his depression in check, at least for the moment. Isabel, on the other hand, looked grave, and Audrey wondered what she and Lola had discussed that had prompted the invitation to the chapel. She considered the contrast between the women. Though around the same age, Lola's vitality and strength accentuated a frailty in her mother that Audrey hadn't noticed before. Isabel had always been slight of build, but wiry. She could spend strenuous hours in the garden and had never seemed to tire. Other than her melancholic episodes, Audrey had never known her mother to be ill, but now she wondered.

Lola had gone ahead to prepare, so that when Audrey and Isabel arrived after changing into comfortable clothing, the chapel was candle-lit and warmed by six radiator heaters attached high up on the walls. Ahead of them, the altar, supporting two gold candelabra with six tall candles each, glowed under their light with an almost translucent sheen that revealed deep veins of blue and pink in its marble. Audrey could see how the quietness and beauty of this space might have evoked emotions of deep faith in the women who had inhabited it. When she turned to look out the plate glass window, she was met with a dark, blank canvas of the night punctuated now and then with the lights of distant sheds.

Purple yoga mats with a cushion and blanket at one end had been placed on the floor ready for their relaxation. Though Isabel had not demonstrably practised her Catholic faith for years, Audrey wondered how she felt about the chapel being used in this way. She turned to her, but Isabel was already seated on the mat as though eager to begin.

Lola invited them to lie down, advising them to cover themselves with the blanket should their body temperature drop. She instructed them into savasana, the yoga position of relaxation, and once comfortable on their backs, slowly guided them through a breathing meditation beginning at the base of the spine, then ascending and pausing at each of the energy centres —the chakras—in turn. Within each pause, the silence of the chapel was broken only by the tick-tick-tick of the radiators that added to a deep sense of relaxation.

It was at the chest, in the 'heart centre', that Audrey's breath caught. 'Pause here... observe the breath,' Lola's voice drifted across her consciousness like fine silk. 'It's here that our deepest yearnings reveal themselves. Listen to your heart... What is it saying to you?'

She could feel herself resisting Lola's instruction to linger and, at one point, had to embed the nail of her index finger into the flesh of her thumb to stop a tremble of emotion. The trouble was, she didn't know anymore what her heart was trying to tell her. Sometime, somewhere, she'd stopped listening.

Across the gap between the mats, Audrey thought she heard her mother's breath catch in a sob.

Out in the corridor, she heard her mother's soft tread and a waft of sandalwood soap slipped beneath Audrey's door as she passed. Was her father still asleep or had he gone out for a morning run? She hoped it was the latter—a positive indication of his mental health.

Audrey's mobile vibrated on the table beside her.

Cam. Another voicemail.

Her breath had risen to her throat and was short and sharp.

'Aud, where are you? We need to talk. Call me.'

She manoeuvred a pillow behind her and leaned back, debating whether to get it over and done with, but the grid was too erratic for a conversation, no matter how brief she intended to make it. *What could he possibly want to talk about?* she wondered with a rising sense of irritation. His tone was not soft and yearning as it had been only a few weeks earlier; instead, it sounded cold, detached. They would be divorced soon, free of each other, but she wished it was over. She remembered then that her solicitor, Beatrice, had also tried to call that morning. Audrey sensed something impending, and it was making her feel unsettled.

After breakfast in the vibrant kitchen, they chatted for a while over a tea poured from the new pot. Rosa and Beppe were expecting them around eleven as Beppe had an appointment on the mainland later that they couldn't reschedule. They had plenty of time and Max offered to fix a door on one of the sheds and to look into the logistics of installing hydronic heating upstairs. Isabel, who had eyed the garden, offered to help Lola plant herbs newly acquired from a nursery on the mainland. Audrey took in her mother. She looked as though she'd slept well and was pleased to see that there was colour in her cheeks.

Content that they would be occupied, Audrey left them to it and decided to take a walk and, if she was able to pick up reception, give Poppy and Beatrice a call. Campbell could wait.

In the street, several older people were converging on the church next door, confirming to Audrey that it still held a purpose here on the island. She paused to take them in. Perhaps they had gone to the school across the road, she thought, and it occurred to her that their lives would have played out here—the baptisms, weddings, funerals. She felt suddenly envious of a life settled in the one spot, something she hadn't thought about before. Her life to date had included many moves, sometimes because of her own restlessness, but more often because of Cam's. As she continued, she watched as the churchgoers clustered on the broad step outside the doors and saw how they greeted each other with the warmth and ease of old friends.

Rounding the corner into Main Street, she saw twenty or more cars parked in the street. People were going in and out of shops that she'd previously thought to be empty.

As she approached, she was aware of glances in her direction. The effect was mildly unsettling, made more so by her years of anonymity walking streets in Melbourne. It wasn't the fault of city life. She could have become more involved in the local communities where she lived but couldn't see the point when another move was inevitable. Life in the warehouse had held more promise; she'd thought she'd live there for a long time, but the closest she came was a nod of acknowledgement to a familiar, but usually nameless face. Cam had been better at it, but on reflection there seemed to have always been some self-interest involved in whom he associated with, herself included.

Cam. She paused and took out her mobile. Three bars. Her finger hovered over his number...

Beatrice's number rang through to the voicemail. Audrey left an apology for the delay in responding and gave a potted version of where she was. She took a punt on Poppy and had already pressed call when she estimated it would be close to midnight in Paris.

'Babe!'

Audrey smiled to herself, marvelling at how much her

friend always lifted her spirits. She hoped that she returned it in kind.

'Pop! You're sounding bright for this time of night. I'm sorry I've rung so late and in your—'

'Condition, you mean, my love?' Well, I'd be cursing you if I was still in Paris,' she said with a laugh, 'but guess what? I'm home!'

'Home? Where...'

'The folks, of course. I'd called you from there yesterday, but it got... hmm... pretty intense here when I shared my news, as you can imagine, so I didn't have time to call you back.'

Audrey knew that her friend's face would be contorted with displeasure. She laughed.

'I'm so pleased, Pop. How're you feeling?'

'Mmm... good, though so many of my favourite things, like food, clothes and sex, are grossly unappealing now. And, of course, no booze to buffer the angst.'

Audrey was impressed. Self-denial had never been a part of Poppy's modus operandi.

'You're still on the island, I gather. So... how's it going?' The shift in her tone held an implication.

'Having a good time with Isabel and Max.'

'Aud... what a pair we are. I'm living back with the folks, and you're on holiday with yours. There's something very wrong with this picture, babe.'

Audrey laughed along with Poppy, but she had to admit that she was loving this time and had never viewed her relationship with her parents the way so many others did—including Poppy. Though she'd visited Max and Isabel frequently over the years of her marriage, there was always an unstated tension at both ends—concern from them, and resentment from her husband. Now was an opportunity to rectify all of that.

'I'm so glad you didn't go to London, babe.' Poppy's tone had subdued and sounded emotional.

'Me too. Hey, are you feeling okay?' Audrey felt the need to repeat the question. Poppy was adept at deflecting intimate conversation away when it involved herself. She heard the hesitation before the response.

'I'm scared. I don't know what I'm doing.'

She pictured her friend—the large, dark eyes, the black hair with the shock of red, and her belly beginning to swell. She would look magnificent, but Audrey couldn't deny her concern for Poppy and the baby's future. While Poppy's parents would take good care of her in the interim, a longer prospect would be a disaster for them all. Though Poppy had made a substantial living from her art, her generosity, extravagances, and sometimes foolishness had caused wild fluctuations in her finances, a fact that she shared openly and with her characteristic, 'c'est la vie'. How would this change, Audrey wondered, with someone else to consider? Moving away from the hub of the Parisian artistic life, she'd need to re-establish herself in Australia. Poppy could count on her to help, and told her so, but it wasn't going to happen overnight, and there was no guarantee it would happen at all.

'Babe, when are you home?' There was a wistful note to her voice, and Audrey could relate. For too long, their friendship had been conducted long distance. Now they were both at a point in their lives when they needed each other. The idea sat well with her.

Audrey related the plan, to return to Melbourne in two days, and promised she'd visit as soon as possible, though the thought of returning home felt hollow. Other than Poppy, and her parents, all of whom were still a distance away, what did she have to go back to?

After their goodbyes, Audrey continued along the street

taking in the shops as she passed—a butcher with a tray of loin chops and one of sausages lying on fake green grass in the window; a pharmacy boasting 70 *years of service* in a banner across its doorway; and a shop double the size of the others that served as a newsagent's-cum-post office. There were fewer people in this section of the street, but even before she reached it, the constant ping of the door of the Bread of Life, advertised on the billboard sitting close to the curb, heralded a different story.

Feeling out of place, Audrey joined the slipstream of the man ahead of her, pleased to sabotage the door's announcement of her entry. Though she had no idea what she would buy, she took up her position behind four others waiting at the counter. There was a rumble of conversation between them and a greeting to the man she'd shadowed, the same light-hearted bonhomie of the churchgoers. One woman, who stood side-on to address the man next to her, acknowledged Audrey with a smile but resumed the discussion on the weather. Audrey relaxed.

The air inside was warmed from the oven she could just see beyond the bread racks behind the counter and held the earthy smell of baked bread and the sharp odour of freshly ground coffee beans. Though she had just eaten, her stomach rumbled in appreciation. As she got closer to the counter, she was able to take in various breads in the racks, the pastries, sweet Danish, and the standard pies and pasties in the display case to the left. On the right, though, in a separate display, was the produce she had come to see—long, thick rolls of salami, sliced prosciutto— Beppe's, perhaps; wheels of cheese with the branding she recognised as Alex's duck pâté, blue vein cheese and organic yoghurt.

The door pinged and Audrey was aware of the voices of two women behind her, one older than the other, whose conversation had continued from the street. The older woman's tone held a forced calmness and she spoke slowly as though to a child.

'It's... *good*... for Hibernia. Isn't your generation all about progress?'

Audrey could sense the other's frustration even before she responded with a forced whisper.

'It'll *ruin* it, Mum. It's not about progress. It's about saving what we have.'

'But it'll bring people here. We need it if we're going to survive.'

Audrey's attention focussed.

'As if the eco-lodge isn't bad enough, but a bridge will be a disaster.'

A bridge? Audrey wondered if she'd heard correctly.

'What's that you say, Ingrid?'

It was the man ahead of Audrey and now she felt caught but transparent in the middle of them. She stepped to her right and positioned herself neutrally.

'They want to build a bridge... across the estuary to Wilson's Point.'

Audrey noted that Ingrid seemed to think it was a fait accompli.

'Who? Who wants to do that?'

The woman who had smiled at Audrey turned to face him. 'Jack, you must've heard. Who d'ya reckon?'

Jack looked bewildered and shrugged his shoulders. The woman sighed. 'Bloody Quin O'Rourke, of course.'

Audrey slipped out behind the mother and daughter, the sound of the door betraying her sudden departure. In the street she paused, once again aware of her heart's acceleration.

. . .

On her return to The Sanctuary, she reflected on what she'd just heard. A bridge would provide better access to the island and increase tourism opportunities; that could be good. Hibernians who worked on the mainland could consider returning to their home and commuting instead; businesses such as The Sanctuary, The Island Hotel and those small artisans like Alex could benefit; the eco-lodge would attract more people and the spillover could improve all businesses—the bakery included. But Hibernia would become an extension of the mainland and would be a prime development opportunity requiring infrastructure to support it. The estuary, the wetlands would be at even greater risk, and bigger businesses would overtake the smaller.

Both sides of this issue had compelling arguments, but Audrey had already come to appreciate that Hibernia was unique; its disconnection from the mainland had created a microculture, a reminder of what a simpler life could offer. But she knew, too, that her perspective was born out of her own dissatisfaction. She was becoming jaded by the fast-paced life-style of the city, and she wasn't alone. Hibernia could be at risk of becoming a novelty. It might experience a tourist boom, only to fall out of fashion when the next "in-place" was "discovered". Audrey thought of Ingrid's mother in the bakery. There would be others who agreed that the island would benefit from the bridge. She was faced then with her own arrogance—how could she, an outsider carrying the emotional and mental baggage of urban life, know what was best for this place?

The convent's front door had locked behind her when she'd left. Audrey made her way along the tiled verandah and followed the driveway on the right-hand side towards its rear. As she came to the driveway's end, she could see the light blue of Max's jumper moving behind a thicket of tall shrubs in front of one of the sheds. As she got closer, she saw that he was measuring the width of its doorframe, and the movement of a flat carpenter's pencil held between his teeth provided a visual clue to his mental activity.

'Aud,' he mumbled, removing the pencil from his mouth.

'Having fun, Dad?"

'I am, actually. Reminds me, though, of how many jobs I've neglected at home.' He raised his eyebrows, but his eyes held hers knowingly.

'Well, you might be up for that when you get back.'

He nodded, without conviction, and she wondered how he would be when he returned to Ballina.

She glanced across at the central herb bed. The soil had been recently turned and there was steam coming up in patches where the warmth from beneath had been released.

'Where's Mum?'

'Inside, with Lola. Secret women's business, I think.' He laughed but looked a little bit lost.

Audrey told him what she'd heard in the bakery.

'Mmm, well, yes, that's a bit of a surprise. It'd be quite an undertaking. Doesn't really make sense if it's just for that eco-lodge, though. Sounds like the council is in on it somewhere, surely.'

He turned back to the shed, but Audrey could tell that he was still ruminating on what she'd told him. The pencil was returned to his mouth.

'I'll see what Mum's up to,' she said.

Her father's reply was a distracted mumble.

She'd expected to find them chatting in the kitchen. The kettle on the slow combustion was steaming and the pot stood with its lid off in anticipation on the bench beside three mugs.

As she passed through the dining and sitting rooms, Audrey paused to take it in. The stillness here was dense, and had she been of a different mindset, she might have been convinced that the ghosts of the nuns still occupied these rooms.

Above the staircase, dawn had risen in the background world of Teresa of Avila and glinted through the eye of the dove in her hand. The grandfather clock struck ten am. At the landing, Audrey followed a hunch and turned right towards the chapel and saw that the door was ajar. As she came to it, she paused and positioned herself so that she could see her mother and Lola without disturbing them.

They stood face-to-face, a metre distance between them. Lola was demonstrating a movement—gentle, flowing—that looked like a type of Tai Chi. Her hair hung loosely past her shoulders and swayed around her as she moved. Isabel was watching intently. Lola paused and began again, inviting Isabel to join in.

Audrey watched as her mother commenced the movement. She faltered, and paused, her face stern in its concentration. Lola moved smoothly back to the start, encouraging her to follow. Isabel began again, her face relaxing as her body found its way as she mirrored Lola's visual instruction. The motion was subtle at first then, each cupping an imaginary ball between their palms, they began to lean from leg to leg, rolling the ball between their hands and widening and widening the space between their hands until both women were moving their arms in wide arcs. Isabel had closed her eyes as Lola had, and her face had shed the concentrated furrow on her brow that she so often wore.

Audrey was hypnotised by their rhythm. There was something primal in their dance and, as though for the first time, she saw her mother as a woman, at home in her own body.

Lola murmured an instruction, and they began to slow down, their hands contracting again around the imagined sphere that they then held in front of their belly.

'Breathe into the ball of chi,' Lola said. 'Let it expand and contract with the breath.'

Audrey turned away towards her bedroom, conscious that she had witnessed her mother in a personal moment, disconnected from family.

Thirty minutes later, she joined the three of them in the kitchen, which seemed to have become the designated meeting space. She heard Max mention 'the bridge' before she entered. He was standing by the sink rinsing a glass. Lola was standing next to him with a tea towel in hand. Isabel was seated at the table by the fire, her handbag ready at her feet. She was intent on what her husband had been saying.

Lola acknowledged Audrey as she came in. 'I've only heard a couple of rumours,' she said, looking at each in turn, 'but thought they were just that.' Her expression shifted and it was apparent that she was concerned.

As Audrey moved to join her mother, she recounted the incident in the bakery, and expressed her own competing mental arguments. 'What's your feeling about it, Lola?'

'I agree with you, Audrey... there are two sides to any decent argument, but personally, I hope they don't build it. I know Ingrid, and there are others here who feel the same. She might come across as a hippie... "feral" or a "greenie" as I've heard others say... but I believe she's right. The island's ecosystems are fragile enough as it is.'

'But what about you... and The Sanctuary? It would bring people here.'

Lola paused and placed the tea towel on the bench.

'Yes, you're probably right, my love, but... sometimes a sanctuary has to be hard won if it's to deliver its promise.'

As Max and Isabel murmured their agreement, Audrey saw a flicker of sorrow cross Lola's face and she knew then that she was talking from personal experience.

Again, they invited Lola to join them, but again, she declined.

'Actually, I've never met Rosa and Beppe, I'm ashamed to say, though I've heard a great deal about them from Dion.'

'But we haven't met them either,' Max said.

Lola shook her head, laughing. '*One* outing today will be enough for me. I am looking forward to this evening, though,' she said, her tone lightly dismissing any further discussion.

It was only a fifteen-minute drive to Rosa and Beppe's and Audrey recalled how, on the last trip to see them, she'd spontaneously turned right towards The Island Hotel and had seen the two of them, Quin and Dion, covered in dust as they emerged from the reconstruction site and, in particular, the sumptuous lunch overlooking a portion of the wetland. She remembered how the young boy had nestled into the neck of his uncle, the warmth and love they shared and, the memory that now perplexed her, the sincerity with which Quin had spoken about the wetland. She'd believed him, but that section behind the wetland was so small in comparison to what they'd seen yesterday, and she wondered now if he'd been deceiving her. 'Bloody Quin O'Rourke, of course.' The woman in the bakery had implied that, not only was he responsible for the bridge, but that he had a negative history in Hibernia. Audrey wondered what Rosa and Beppe knew but didn't feel it was her place to ask.

As she turned into their street, she saw ahead a new *For Sale* sign on the old white house. She hadn't spoken of it to Max and Isabel, thinking that it had no place in her future, but now... She slowed down and pulled over in front of it.

'Is this their house?' Isabel said from next to her.

'No, Mum,' Audrey said with a laugh. 'They're a bit further

along. It's just that... I don't know. I saw this house on the first trip here and...'

'It's charming... but darling, what is your interest?'

Audrey shook her head. 'Nothing, Mum. It was just a fanciful idea.'

'To buy it?' Max's attention had been derailed from his notebook.

The vine's tentacles had wound their way around the posts of the verandah, obscuring the poor condition of the wood and softening the facade. Audrey noticed that the lawns had been re-mown, this time with more care, and the hedge supporting the gate had been trimmed. On cue, parrots darted from between the palm fronds at the side of the house, squawking as though in the middle of an argument.

'What's that sound?' Max said, winding down his window. Isabel did the same.

'It's the ocean. See how the land rises towards the rear? There's a spectacular view from the end of the back garden, and from Rosa and Beppe's house, too.

They sat in silence for a moment, listening to the thud of the waves against the cliffs, and the arguing parrots. A shadow tracked across the car and when Audrey leaned out her window to look, she saw a sea eagle in languid descent. She watched as it hovered over the empty fields next to the house, its presence causing a cacophony of alarmed bird calls.

'I wonder what they're asking for this place,' Max said. 'Any idea, love?"

Audrey related what she'd seen in her online search.

'Interested, Dad?' she said, smiling at her father in the rear view.

He returned the smile.

'It's... beautiful in its way,' Isabel said suddenly. 'It just needs... to feel useful... to be young again.'

'Yes, you're right, Mum,' Audrey said, driving slowly away. She couldn't help but feel that there was a subtext in her mother's comment.

It was only an hour later that Audrey found herself standing at the back door of the house.

They hadn't been long at Rosa and Beppe's when, after introductions, a tour of the house and garden that Isabel in particular had enjoyed, and, at the dining room table with the view of the garden, a small glass each of Beppe's wine accompanied with slices of his salami and fresh tomatoes from the garden, that the topic of Harold's house up the road had arisen.

'They couldn't sell it,' Rosa had said. 'Nobody want a house that is full of someone else's memories. It bring bad luck.'

When an offer was withdrawn, Harold's daughter emptied the house of her father's furniture, tidied the garden and tried again, this time in the hands of a different real estate agent on the mainland.

'Still no one want it,' Rosa added. 'The house is waiting for Harold to return.'

Beppe had listened to his wife and shook his head. 'He is old. He was lonely.'

'Lonely? You went to see him every day, Beppe!'

'I not family. He needs family.'

Rosa looked flustered. 'They will let him rot in that home for lonely old people! Tsk!'

Beppe left them, to return a few minutes later.

'You want to look, Audrey?' he said, showing her the key in his hand. 'The agent said I can do this for people interested.'

She'd gone on ahead of the others, wanting to see on her own the garden that had infiltrated her thoughts over the past weeks. As she turned the corner into the back area of the house, she sighed with pleasure. It was almost as she had remembered it, though greener now as though everything had been airbrushed with overlapping shades of sage and peppermint. Blossoms emerging from their buds softened the harsh angles of trees in need of pruning. She looked down at the small and unremarkable key in her palm and then back at the door, distrusting that the rusted-looking lock could deliver any kind of personal renaissance.

Despite the lock's visual limitations, the key slid into the lock and required only a minor adjustment before she heard it click. The door opened with a creak—a note of relief rather than reluctance and loud enough to disturb a nest of swallows in the eaves. She heard the others coming down the sideway, past the palm tree, then heard her mother's gasp of surprise as they rounded the bushes and came into the garden.

They were all behind her, standing at a distance. No one spoke, as though acknowledging that this was her moment. Audrey felt it, too and recalled other times when she'd felt like this—her first home, before Cam; her first gallery exhibition. Moments that she knew she owned. This was one of them.

A spring breeze riffled through the garden, carrying with it the scent of lily of the valley and the unmistakable odour of onion weed and humus. The ocean, crashing against the cliffs, reverberated through her feet as though a reminder of the impermanence of all that appeared solid and lasting.

The others held back as she stepped across the threshold and into the sunroom, stirring dust particles that were spotlit by rays of sunlight angling in from the east. Despite this room's proximity to the garden that sloped down gently from the edge of the cliffs towards it, Audrey was surprised at the absence of mildew, a ubiquitous smell in the houses of this era that she and Cam had inspected in their many house-hunting phases.

Although Rosa had said that Harold's daughter had

emptied the house of furniture, an old brown-leather armchair with deep cracks of wear in its arms was positioned to take in the view through the windows. It seemed an odd thing to leave behind, and Audrey had a rush of sympathy for the daughter who, perhaps, could not bring herself to remove it. She moved to it and turned to take in what Harold would have seen. A light frosting of salt on the wide expanse of windows muted the vibrant growth of the garden and cast an ethereal glow.

'*Mama mia*,' Rosa said immediately, as she stepped into the room. 'Beppe, you must take it to Harold.'

'*Si*,' her husband said. '*Si*.'

The silence now broken, the others became more animated. Max's voice held its trademark enthusiasm as he readied for an inspection, looking for rising damp, sinking floors, and evidence of leaks and suspicious electrical wiring. Audrey knew the pattern as he, and Isabel, had accompanied her to house inspections—that is, until she married Cam. Rosa and Beppe accompanied Isabel as she headed into the body of the house. Audrey held back for a moment. Though she was tempted to sit in the chair, she resisted, feeling that, in some way, she would break the sixty-year connection between this house and its owner.

Taps were being turned on in the next room as she joined the others. The kitchen was a moderate size, and dull, the result of being enclosed by the sunroom wall on one side and the dining room on the other that could be seen through a small arch. One end wall had small stained-glass windows set high on either side of a large Aga that looked to be in excellent condition.

'Hardly used,' Isabel said, running her hand across the smooth green cast iron. On the burnt orange laminated bench next to it, in sharp contrast, was a portable stove covered in a thick layer of grease and dust. Several butane canisters stood perilously close. Audrey's sympathy for Harold's daughter dissipated. She caught Rosa's expression as she shook her head and heard her sigh of distress.

Despite the lack of light in this room and its deteriorating cupboards and benches, gaps where the green linoleum had worn away revealed old, solid floorboards that extended into a passageway at the left of the room and into the dining room through the arch. Audrey's eye followed their line. From where she stood, she could see a Masonite board wedged to cover a cavity in the far wall. This room, too, was dull, but when she entered, she saw that a brown holland blind was covering the large window. On that first visit, she'd imagined a deck outside where she would sip a gin and tonic while she watched the parrots in the palm tree. She rolled up the blind and turned to face the room, marvelling at how the light transformed the space behind her. On the wall facing her, next to the doorway leading to the rest of the house, an old art deco mirror reflected her silhouette like a snapshot. What would be written on its back, she wondered — *Audrey. Dreaming. Again?*

'Ohhh, what do we have here!' Max was kneeling on mosaic-tiled hearth in front of the Masonite board. He'd managed to peel forward a corner and was inspecting it with the torch in his mobile phone.

'What is it, Dad?'

'There's an original hearth... looks like brown and cream mosaic tiles... the cast iron fireplace is still there. Why on earth would anyone cover it over...?"

Isabel and Rosa were still in the kitchen and were talking quietly, though Rosa's voice was still agitated at the sight of the well-used portable stove. Beppe was nowhere to be seen.

The rest of the house held surprises—fireplaces like the dining room's in the two smaller bedrooms that were served by a good sized, though tired-looking, bathroom; the large black marble surround of the fireplace in the living room she'd seen through the window. It was a larger room than she'd thought and the condition of the Westminster carpet, and the lack of indentations created by the bases of furniture, suggested it had rarely been used.

Audrey paused at the doorway to the main bedroom at the front of the house. Though she took in its size—the same size as the living room opposite and with its large fireplace once again behind a Masonite sheet, its high ceilings and ornate cornices consistent with the rest of the house, except the sunroom, and its proximity to a second, smaller bathroom on the other side of the wall—it was the coaster depicting The Island Hotel, lying as she'd first seen it, that held her in the doorway. She moved in to pick it up, but hesitated. It had embedded itself in her neural pathways like an idea, an obscure dream that she'd tried to bring to life on the apron and tie she'd given as gifts to Quin and Dion. As she stood here now, the reality of it struck her. It was just an old, stained coaster lying on the floor of an old and tired house.

The others moved from room to room, pausing and discussing some small curiosity. Predictably, Max was kneeling, tapping floors, walls and flicking switches. Isabel and Rosa had become like a single unit, deep in conversation. Audrey had noted her mother's easy relationship with both Lola and Rosa and wondered if she had always sought female companionship, though she could not remember her having significant relationships in the past. Audrey had always assumed that her mother was self-contained, a loner other than in her relationship with her husband and her daughter. Now she wasn't so sure.

Beppe finally appeared in the sunroom where they had all gathered. Though he was a quiet man, Audrey had noticed his absence in the house. In the centre of a clean handkerchief spread across the palm of one hand was the bulb of a flower that he angled towards them all in order that they could see.

'*El azafran*', Isabel said suddenly, her eyes widening with pleasure as though she'd just spotted an old friend.

Beppe smiled but looked perplexed.

'The saffron crocus,' Audrey said, hoping he would understand. She remembered how she'd found its wilting leaves in the garden on that first visit and how the sight of it had conjured memories of her mother's cooking. How strange, she thought now as she witnessed Beppe and Isabel's interactions over the bulb in his palm, that her mother was actually here.

Something stirred in her then, the knowledge that good things, good imaginings, could still manifest and were sometimes better in reality than when first conceived.

It was then that Audrey made a decision that she'd not expected to make.

'While we here,' Rosa said as they stood out the front next to the cars, 'Beppe would like to take you to... to Dion's farm.'

Beppe, standing beside his wife, nodded, but Audrey noticed the flicker of grief that crossed both of their faces.

'I not go,' Rosa continued. She turned to Audrey, 'I see you again soon,' then to Max and Isabel, 'and you again, I hope.' Her smile to Isabel, in particular, was warm and the two women nodded in acknowledgement of each other.

Audrey saw how tenderly Beppe guided his wife to the car, helping her to climb into the high seat of the 4-wheel drive.

When he returned, Max offered to accompany him. Beppe looked pleased with the offer and, as Max slid into the passenger seat and closed the door, Audrey saw that the two men were already engaged in conversation. Beppe was smiling.

Thank you, Dad, Audrey thought, as she turned onto the road behind them.

'Mum, is everything okay?'

'*Sí, sí* ... we're having a lovely time.'

'Okay, that's good. What I mean, though, is... is there anything worrying you?'

Audrey could feel her mother looking at her and glanced in her direction. Their eyes met for an instant and Audrey was certain that Isabel was on the verge of saying something, but just as quickly turned away.

'Your father seems better,' she said, looking towards Beppe's car.

'Yes, he does. He needs to be busy I think, but—'

'*Sí*, this is good.'

'Mum, I've seen you talking in depth with Lola and... I'm just worried that something's wrong and you're not telling me. I know you've been worried about Dad, and—'

'That's all, darling. Lola has been very kind to us and, I think she needs to talk.'

Audrey knew that to press her mother any further would not get her anywhere and wasn't convinced by her version, though she considered Isabel's words. Was there something that Lola needed to talk about? Audrey was tempted to ask her mother but knew better.

The route to the farm offered a very different perspective of the island than Audrey had seen so far. The high coastline they'd just left petered out to low rolling hills intersected by creeks that looked like silver ribbons in the morning sun.

'The soil is an interesting colour here,' she said.

'*Sí*... a mix of volcanic and sediment,' Isabel responded immediately, taking her by surprise, which must have been evident in her expression as she glanced at her mother. 'Alex told us,' Isabel said with a laugh, 'when you were on that phone.'

There was a small note of disapproval in her voice. Isabel was still uncomfortable with the twenty-first century.

'It was Poppy, Mum, I told you that.' Audrey suddenly felt like a fifteen-year-old defending herself. 'I need to keep in touch with her.'

'You're right. It's just... you get an expression on your face when you look at that phone. Like this...'

Isabel's brow furrowed and her mouth turned down at the corners.

'Whoa! Do I?'

'Sì... Watch the road. They're turning.'

They followed Beppe as he swung into a driveway leading to a farmhouse partly obscured by thick plantings of she-oak and wattles positioned only a hundred metres from the road. Through gaps in the foliage, Audrey could see that the house had a broad, bull-nosed verandah that extended across the front and at least down the side of the house closest to them.

Beppe had parked the car at the rear of the house and she drew up next to him. From this position, she could see that the verandah extended to the back of the house offering a shaded space to contemplate the view—a field of ten acres or more lined with wideset rows of trees in full blossom. The land rose gently towards its back and sides, creating a shallow bowl nestling the farm.

They got out of the cars and stood together, taking it in. The trees were pistachios, she learned from Beppe, and the land rose to a gentler version of the bluff on this side of the island. In the distance, the sea could be heard breaking more gently here.

Audrey glanced behind her to the house as the others were talking. A hammock strung between two verandah posts swung gently in the light breeze that was riffling through the blossoms, and at the doorstep, two pairs of gumboots stood side by side, caked in mud that looked as though it was still drying.

Together, they walked along a line of pistachios. Isabel had noticed that the soil between the rows was free of weeds and looked as though it had been recently planted.

'Saffron,' Beppe said, responding to her query and smiled as though he'd just revealed a precious secret. He indicated for them to follow him to the medium-sized shed with solar panels on the roof in the corner of the field. Once there, he produced a set of keys from his pocket and, undoing several locks, switched on a light inside and invited them in.

On a long table in the middle, a dozen or so empty trays were in small stacks beneath a large fan, but on a long shelf on the wall opposite the door, glass jars glowed with the unmistakable pigment of the saffron stigma. It was as though the room was bathed in a beautiful deep orange-red sunset.

'Oh, *Dios mio*,' Isabel said, bringing a hand to her mouth.

'This is a like a gold mine, mate,' Max said, looking equally surprised.

Audrey was speechless. Under the light, the room glowed, reminding her of treasure caves from the Arabic stories her mother read to her as a child.

'What do you do with them?' Max continued. 'Sell to restaurants? Buyers?'

The older man smiled with pride that was muted by the sadness in his eyes and shook his head. 'Not yet. They had plans... but... we can't...' His voice trailed as he turned his back to them. Audrey saw how his shoulders rose with a forced intake of air. He turned back to them, smiling. 'Come. I show you something else.'

Once outside, after he'd locked the door and checked each of the locks in turn, he pointed in the direction behind the shed. They walked for a few hundred metres, still following the line of trees and crocus plantings, until they came to a cluster of large basalt rocks stacked haphazardly. They followed as Beppe moved to stand on the far side of them, now facing in the direction of the house and saw that the rocks surrounded a pool approximately four metres across. Beneath a soft white vapour, the water held a green sheen.

'A hot spring?' Max's voice was rising with excitement. 'Of course! The island's volcanic in origin.'

Beppe nodded and drew them in closer. Beneath the surface, they could just see that a large rock had been positioned as a seat.

'Beppe... is this why your limp is better?' Audrey asked, in a moment of clarity.

'Sì,' he said, bringing a finger to his lips. 'Is our secret.'

As they returned to their cars, Audrey took another look at the long verandah—its signs of a life once lived—and thought of the boy and all he had lost.

'The bébé... Dion... does he come here?' Isobel asked. Audrey wondered if her mother was thinking the same, and if she'd seen the fresh mud on the boots by the door.

'Not so much,' Beppe said. Audrey noticed that he hadn't looked at the house since they'd arrived.

'Does he help you with the planting?' Max had turned back to take in the field.

'Sì... but is hard for him here. He worry about me... that it is too much for me. But I'm okay.'

Audrey could understand Dion's concern, but Beppe seemed more than capable of looking after the farm, in fact, he seemed to be more agile than last time she'd seen him. Nevertheless, the harvesting of the stigmas would be labour-intensive.

'Who knows about the spring?' Max asked suddenly. Audrey was surprised at the question, but thought she knew where he was going with it.

'Most on the island.' He shrugged as though it was of no consequence to anyone else.

'You know about the eco-lodge, Beppe?' he added.

'Si... they build it just over there.' He pointed towards the neighbouring property, and they could see the headland where the eco-lodge was to be built. They'd come almost full circle to yesterday's drive to the wetland.

'Do you know who's building it?' Audrey held her breath as she waited for the answer.

Beppe raised his hand in a gesture of uncertainty. 'Quin's company.'

Max met Audrey's glance and raised an eyebrow.

'I have a surprise for you.' Lola's face was creased with a broad smile as she fastened her gold pashmina at the neck with a sapphire brooch.

Audrey waited but was perplexed. She already felt that they'd taken advantage of her generosity, though there'd been no indication of outstaying their welcome. Lola had even tried to convince Isabel and Max to stay on longer. Audrey could see that they would have liked to take up the offer, but there were practical matters that needed to be dealt with in Ballina.

'I had a phone call from your friend, Poppy,' Lola continued. 'What a character! She was wanting to know when The Sanctuary would be officially open... and,' Lola's face became more serious as though suddenly unsure of herself, 'I invited her to stay. I hope that's all right? She's arriving tomorrow.'

'Tomorrow?'

Lola's face lit with pleasure at Audrey's reaction. 'She'd been trying to reach you on your mobile but asked me to tell you... in case you'd decided to leave early.'

'But Lola, you've done so much for us already...'

'Well, love, she's in need, isn't she?'

Audrey was surprised and wondered how much her friend had told her, though she could see that it would be very easy to confide in Lola. Poppy, herself, had the capacity to magnetically attract and sometimes repel people with an almost violent force.

'It's not hard for me to read between the lines of bravado, love. Lord knows I've been good at that myself.'

Audrey felt she would know about the older woman's past in time. Isabel already knew, she was sure of it.

As though on cue, her mother came down the stairs, Max just behind. They both looked refreshed and relaxed and, as they reached the floor of the entrance, Isabel linked her arm through Max's.

'Poppy's coming tomorrow.' Audrey couldn't wait to tell them, and she noticed that they both reacted with relief.

'That's excellent news, Aud,' her father said. 'Pity we'll miss her, though.' His expression shifted and she wondered if he didn't want to go home.

Though The Island Hotel was only walking distance from The Sanctuary, they decided to drive as dark clouds were promising rain later in the evening. Main Street was deserted once again, though above the pharmacy, the only two-storied shop in the street, Audrey saw the silhouette of a man moving against a background of lamplight.

'Someone lives there?' she said to Lola, who was next to her in the back seat of the car. 'The pharmacist?'

Lola shook her head. 'No, Joseph and Yvonne live on a property near the jetty; you've probably passed it. They've recently leased it to a fellow from Sydney. I've seen him a couple of times in the street... about my age... backpack and hat. Heading off somewhere.'

Her brief description rang a bell. 'Oh, we saw him, I think. Yesterday at the wetland. Mum, Dad—remember the man with the binoculars?'

'Yes,' Isabel half-turned towards her to answer, 'the bird-watcher. He was very intent on something.'

'That's right,' Max said into the rear view, 'took us a while to spot him. Very experienced, I'd say.'

'Francis, I think his name is,' Lola said, drifting into her own thoughts.

As they came to the end of the street, Audrey gave directions to her father to park around the corner of the hotel. As they pulled in next to Quin's Land Cruiser, she could feel her blood pulsing in the pit of her throat.

'I'm glad to see Dion,' her mother said, 'and Quin, without the ideas from rumour.'

'Hear, hear!' Lola added.

Max rubbed his hands together. 'Can't wait to see what's on the menu. I'm starving.'

'Max! You never starving. Don't say that.' Isabel's scolding was muted by the smile on her face.

As they rounded the rear of the building, the table and chairs were still in position, a reminder of that day when Audrey had felt so relaxed in the presence of Dion and his uncle. This time, there were no festive splashes of colour from the Moroccan plates, the water jug and glasses. Instead, she saw that the setting was rusted and old. Audrey's skin prickled with goosebumps as a cold breeze whipped up the slope from the wetland and rustled through the trees.

'Welcome, everyone.' Quin's greeting was warm as he stepped out from the back door onto the patio to greet them. Despite the cold night, he was dressed in a light cream shirt rolled to the elbows, black trousers and boots. His face was shadowed, but the light above the doorway caught and glinted in the corner of one eye.

Max moved forward to shake his hand and the others followed in a light exchange of greeting. Audrey, knowing that, unlike him, her face was fully illuminated, hoped that it didn't reveal her anxiety. She tilted her chin forward in mock courage.

'Come in. It's a cold one tonight,' Quin said lightly, stepping aside for them.

As they entered, they were greeted by sounds of action in the kitchen on the right and a curse rang in the air. Quin raised an eyebrow and excused himself, leaving the kitchen door ajar as he went in.

Audrey looked around her, wondering if Quin's wife was going to appear.

On the day of the lunch, she hadn't been able to view the interior of the hotel while the reconstruction was underway so she had no "before and after" comparison, but from her position in the passageway she could see that the softly lit room ahead was the dining room.

Quin returned, followed quickly by Dion who was wiping his hands on a towel. He was wearing the apron Audrey had given him. The look on his face made her smile.

'Audra!' He stepped around his uncle and moved towards her with both arms wide. Just before making contact, he hesitated as though he'd heard his grandmother scolding him.

Audrey moved towards him and gave him a light kiss on the cheek, which seemed to render him speechless for a moment.

'Dion, you know Lola,' she said, taking control.

The boy smiled broadly and nodded his head.

'And this is Isabel, and Max.'

He leaned forward to shake Max's hand, but his eyes quickly turned to Isabel.

'My sincere apologies,' he said, glancing at each of the women, his face earnest. Audrey saw that he was standing with his head slightly bowed as though in an act of contrition.

Isabel and Lola looked at each other and back to him, clearly bewildered.

'Why's that, love?' Lola asked, in a tone that reminded Audrey of her favourite primary school teacher.

'For my poor manners in using an... an ex...' He looked to his uncle for support. Quin nodded and wore an expression of mock gravity.

'Expletive,' Dion said, the broad smile reducing the apology to an almost comedic routine.

Isabel moved forward and placed both hands on Dion's upper arms. It was a position that Audrey knew preceded an enveloping hug, and she wondered what would happen, but Isabel kept her hands there and looked up to meet Dion's eyes. 'I'm so pleased to meet you at last, Dion,' she said. 'We are cooking soul-mates, I think, you and me.' Her head was tilted to the side and Audrey saw in her mother's face that this was no platitude; she meant every word of it.

Dion hadn't moved, but his expression was as though he'd received wonderful news that he was still trying to digest.

'Soul-mates?' he said.

'Sí, almas gemelas.'

He nodded in acknowledgment, his face flushed scarlet. 'Almas gemelas.'

'Oh... my commiserations,' he said suddenly to them all. 'I need to return to the pot!'

Audrey wondered if the formality of his speech was due to his position this evening as head chef. She saw that despite the wrong word choice, Quin made no move to correct him.

'Isabel, would you accompany me?' Dion called over his shoulder as he was leaving.

'*Sí*,' she said without hesitation, as Dion held the door open for her to enter the kitchen.

'Let's go in,' Quin said to Audrey, Lola and Max, gesturing ahead.

The dining room spread left and right of the entrance to form a large, but intimate space enhanced by soft overhead lights. The tone created by the soft furnishings was luxurious, but warm and inviting.

'It's stunning,' Lola said, and Max and Audrey concurred. Audrey was relieved to see that he hadn't chosen a modern, minimalist decor, but doubted that the old hotel had ever seen a dining room quite as discreetly opulent as this. It seemed that no expense had been spared, and at some level it disturbed her. Audrey doubted that Quin would act on a risky philosophy of "if you build it they will come", but rather, the room in front of her seemed as though it was ready for the arrival of a predetermined clientele. When she turned towards him, he was watching her.

'I've set up this one,' he said quickly, directing them to the far side of the room to the only table that was set. Along the length of this wall that ran parallel with Main Street outside, the tables were sectioned into booths separated by narrow black bamboo partitions. On the wall to the left, an open fire had settled to a soft orange glow and threw out warmth that wrapped itself around their legs.

Audrey and Lola slipped in behind the table onto the black leather bench that ran beneath the window and settled back into the comfort of the thick, olive-green cushions at their back. Max sat opposite in a dining armchair that subtly contrasted in rustic gold. Cutlery and crystal glasses between them reflected the light from a medium-sized chandelier of modern design in the centre of the room and from the candle, nestled in its glass with an etched gold rim, in the centre of the table.

Quin returned to the kitchen, leaving the three of them to take in their surroundings.

'He's done a wonderful job, hasn't he?' Lola said.

'That's for sure.' Max turned in his chair to take it in.

On the walls were old photographs of Hibernia, and one enlarged one featured The Island Hotel. Main Street was just a dirt road and the hotel stood alone, with no neighbouring shop as it had now, nor any across the road.

The overall effect of the room was luxurious, yet it maintained a sense of local authenticity. This refurbishment was a tribute to the hotel and to the island, but Audrey knew from her travels with Campbell that, generally, the locals were not so enamoured with their local hotel becoming gentrified. Perhaps it would be different here, she thought, but she doubted that Quin had the locals in mind when he bought The Island.

Quin returned with Isabel and seated her in the chair next to Max.

Isabel's face was alight with enthusiasm. 'Darling boy,' she said, 'he's cooking a recipe for me!'

Quin, who'd moved to the end of the table, was smiling. He looks handsome, Audrey thought, categorising it immediately as mere curiosity and wondered again when his wife would appear.

'Our liquor stock is rather limited at the moment,' he said, 'but we have some wine in mind that should accompany the meal very well, or there are some other options I brought in as well.'

'If it's the same wine I had last time, I'll definitely have it,' Audrey said, but Quin was shaking his head in apology.

'I'm afraid not. It was a sample at the time and I... there's been no customers...' He spread his hands to take in the room. 'Sorry. It was a special one, I agree. But we have another, a red recommended by Beppe for tonight.'

149

'Beppe made it, too?' Max said, 'Aud, you haven't told us about this skill of his.'

'Yes, he's our master wine maker,' Quin said. 'In fact, he's our only one.'

'Well, I'll be in for that,' Max said, and they all agreed. Audrey was disappointed not to be able to taste that honey silkiness again, but she was curious to see what else Beppe could produce.

'So, welcome to The Island Hotel,' Quin said, with the tone of a maître d. 'Our first customers. We're grateful for the opportunity to trial a menu, though we won't be up and running for a couple of months yet.'

Though he looked relaxed, there was a rehearsed note to his spiel as though setting the parameters of the evening. Audrey wondered if it was a way of avoiding more open conversation and the chance of uncomfortable topics. Had the invitation been Dion's idea and his uncle was acquiescing for his sake? But he'd been warm in his greeting, and his face crinkled into a genuine smile as they reacted to the items on the menu.

When he excused himself to organise their drinks, they turned to each other, sharing their assessment of the renovation so far, though Max, Isabel and Audrey acknowledged they had nothing to compare it to.

'I came here a couple of times when I first moved here,' Lola said. 'When Bart and Noeleen owned it. But it was a very different place then, believe me. I only came to look sociable,' she said with a laugh, 'but soon worked out it wasn't for me. Bart and Noeleen are lovely people, but... it was a man's pub, if you know what I mean. Sorry, Max.'

Max laughed. 'Oh, I do know what you mean, Lola. Don't fancy them myself.'

Lola nodded. 'Yes, I think you'd be a fish out of water. Quin and Dion have done a great job. I can hardly believe it's the same place.'

'Do you think it will attract the locals?' Audrey hoped her question wasn't too transparent.

Lola's eyes met hers and held them briefly. She seemed to be on the verge of saying something but reconsidered. She lifted her shoulders lightly. 'Who knows, my love? I've stopped trying to guess what people want. After all, it's the same for The Sanctuary, isn't it? The locals are unlikely to want to pay to stay in what they still see as their convent.'

'How are the locals reacting to your conversion?' Max said, dipping a portion of bread into the oil and za'atar that had been placed on the table before their arrival.

'Oh, some haven't liked it and, believe me, they've expressed their feelings. They think I'm being disrespectful, sacrilegious. But they're few in number. Others... well, there's a general malaise here that I find even more disturbing, to be honest. It's as though they've given up or just don't care that much anymore. Trouble is, that leaves Hibernia open for...' she hesitated and looked towards the kitchen, 'for who knows what.'

Quin returned from the bar with a tray and placed a glass of red in front of each of them.

In a communal gesture that felt like contrition, they each took a sip then extolled the virtues of the wine. If they sounded too exuberant, Audrey thought, it was no lie. Beppe had done it again.

'Will you join us, Quin?' Isabel said.

Audrey had noticed that the table had been set for only the four of them.

'I will,' he said, 'after I've helped the boy with the first course. He's excited, but a bit nervous, I think. Especially because you're here, Isabel.'

151

'I can help!' she responded immediately and was already beginning to stand. There was a note in her voice that held authority. Audrey knew it well. Though her mother was gentle and refined, she had a quiet way of insistence that you just didn't argue with. Quin must have felt that, too. His smile was warm and appreciative, and he conceded quickly.

When Isabel had gone into the kitchen, he drew in a seat to the end of the table with Lola to his right, and Max to his left.

Animated conversation burst from the kitchen, causing them all to grin.

'Sounds like they're having fun already,' Max said, looking pleased.

Audrey could see that a healthy colour had returned to her father's face. This time on Hibernia was doing him good, she thought. And Isabel, too.

'It's a remarkable relationship already,' Lola concurred. 'They've never met before, have they?'

'No,' Audrey and Quin responded in unison.

'They've only spoken on the phone,' Audrey added, 'but they hit it off immediately.'

'Dion... attaches quickly,' Quin said, 'but only to those he considers worthy. In my view, his discernment is excellent,' he glanced at Audrey and back to Lola and Max, 'but if he doesn't like you... well, that's another story.' He rolled his eyes in mock exasperation.

'And Quin, if I may ask,' Lola said gently, 'how are you both coping?' Though the question might have sounded presumptuous coming from anyone else, coming from Lola, it invited honesty and openness and, by the look on Quin's face, he thought so too. His face was relaxed, but there was that furrow again between his eyebrows.

'All things considered, he... *we're* doing well. Working on the hotel has been a great distraction and Dion's very excited about the restaurant.'

'Will there be enough trade, do you think?' Max asked.

Quin paused, as though considering his response. 'There will be,' he said.

Audrey could see that he was uncomfortable. She wondered if her father had noticed or if he'd pursue the conversation.

'Aud's got her eye on a house here,' he said instead. 'She could be Dion's neighbour. You know the one I mean?'

Quin's face was hard to read, a mix of surprise and something else Audrey couldn't determine.

'Harold's house. I know it.'

'It could do with a bit of work... quite a bit!' Max said, laughing. 'But, what a position! That's got to be prime real estate.'

Quin nodded, but his expression hadn't changed. 'Yes, it's an amazing view there.'

'Someone had planned to buy it,' Audrey said, 'but they've withdrawn the offer.'

'Do you think you'll make an offer?' His voice was measured as though restraining some emotion.

Audrey didn't need long to consider her answer. 'Yes, I do,' she said, surprising herself with the commitment.

The conversation was suspended as Isabel and Dion came from the kitchen, each holding plates and sporting satisfied smiles. Quin met them and relieved Isabel of the plates before distributing them.

When Isabel was seated, Dion stood next to his uncle and cleared his throat. 'Mushroom tarte with feta and leeks. All locally produced, of course.'

Quin returned to the bar, but Dion stayed, his eyes bright

with anticipation. Audrey sensed this was the cue to eat. Dion watched closely as they followed her lead.

'Oh, it's exquisite,' Lola said, and they murmured their agreement as they finished the first mouthful.

'Enjoy!' Dion said, flushed with pride but remaining there to watch them eat.

'I can't wait for the main,' Audrey said.

'Audra. You're looking particularly beautiful tonight. The soft lights make your eyes sparkle, but I can't be tempted into telling you what you want to know. The main will be a surprise. Only your mother may know.'

Max's laugh was spontaneous, but he quickly drew it back to himself when he realised the boy was serious.

Dion didn't seem to have noticed and had turned to address Lola. 'You also look beautiful, la-la-la-la, Lola. I'd never considered an older woman that way, but...' he turned back to them all, 'I must say I've changed my mind tonight. Audra, you have competition.'

Quin had returned to the table and was standing behind him. He looked apologetic, but Audrey smiled at him for reassurance.

'You're such a gentleman, Dion,' Lola said. 'Thank you. You've made me feel quite... spirited.' She was grinning broadly, and Audrey saw how radiant she was. Her mother, too, looked elegant and happy. The stay at The Sanctuary seemed to have revitalised her, and the acknowledgment of her expertise in cooking, seemed to have rekindled her energy.

When they'd finished the first course, Quin cleared their plates and, on his return, invited Max to have a look at the rooms under construction, warning that there was considerable dust and debris that might be difficult to negotiate. Max was enthusiastic, Isabel said she'd return to the kitchen, while Lola and Audrey said they'd be happy to relax at the table.

When the others had gone, Lola sat back and turned towards Audrey. 'Well, full marks for what they've done here,' she said. 'It would be nice to have a man around The Sanctuary to help me out. I've loved having your father there, actually.'

'You're doing a fantastic job of the renovation, Lola,' Audrey said, and added that in the short time since she'd last seen it there'd been significant transformation.

'Yes, I'm happy with it and really, there's no rush. It's not as though potential guests are waiting in line.'

'Oh, I don't know about that. When Mum and Dad leave tomorrow, Poppy will be filling a bed.' Audrey felt a rush of warmth and excitement to see her friend.

They talked further of the plans for The Sanctuary, and the outstanding jobs that needed to be done before the opening in January.

'And you might be here, too,' Lola said, 'if you buy the house. I hope you do, my love, you and Hibernia... seems a good fit, I think.'

A good fit. That was what it felt like, Audrey had to agree.

'I'm excited about the garden. Such a wonderful idea. I don't know why I hadn't thought of it before.' Lola's tone suggested that Audrey knew of the plan. 'The paradise garden,' she continued. 'Oh, I can tell by the look on your face you don't know what I'm talking about!' Her laugh sounded like a soft chime. 'Isabel suggested it this morning when we were working out the back. I'd assumed I'd recreate the original——the quintessential monastic herb garden, but... we got talking today and, it turns out we've got a lot more in common than just a convent education.'

Audrey was fascinated and was starting to feel as though Lola was talking about someone other than her mother.

Lola turned her body further to face her. 'I think I've told you that I'd lived in Morocco. For a number of years, actually.'

Audrey saw an expression of sorrow flicker in her eyes.

'Where I lived was the most beautiful garden, a paradise garden built on the traditional Islamic design. Somehow or other I got talking to Isabel about it. She knew the style very well. She'd seen them in Morocco, as you probably know.' Audrey didn't know about Morocco but didn't interrupt to say so. 'But she knew them even better from the magnificent gardens of Alhambra in Granada. She said she used to go there to sit and contemplate, to watch the passers-by—mostly tourists, of course—and then she established a friendship with one of the chief gardeners. She said she learned a lot about gardening from him. She took photos, too and one was commissioned by the directors of the Alhambra and used to hang in a gallery there. But listen to me. You must know all of this, and I'm just rattling on!'

Audrey felt as though her mind was shifting through increasing levels of surprise and something akin to guilt, if not shame. Though as a family they'd visited Alhambra several times, her mother had never told her about her history with the place. Lola had learned so much about aspects of Isabel's life within the space of an afternoon's conversation and she wondered what had prompted her mother to tell Lola so much. They were women of the same age, she reasoned, and both seemed to have little contact with other women like them.

'You look disturbed, love.' Lola's expression was concerned. 'Is everything all right for you?'

Audrey took a breath and knew that in its release, she would understand why Isabel had done so. Lola was the rare kind of person who would listen and not make a judgement.

'I'm just feeling a bit lost, I suppose.'

She'd said it—given voice to a gnawing feeling that had

plagued her for a long time now.

Lola didn't speak but was waiting for her to continue.

'It's just... I don't know. It feels like I've been living in some kind of fog for... I was going to say for the past twelve months, but I think it's been longer.'

'Because of your marriage?' Lola hadn't looked away, and her expression was calm, warm, as though she'd heard such things a thousand times.

'Yes, that's a big part of it, you know, blaming Cam again, but even in in my job, the one that I'd nurtured and loved, I felt like I was just going through the motions in the end. It was that realisation that disturbed me the most, to be honest. What was I, if I didn't have that?'

'Mmm, yes, but you saw the problem with both situations— your marriage and your work—and you left. That's very courageous.'

'Or I'm just a quitter, on several levels.'

They both laughed.

'I don't think so, Audrey. Sounds to me that you're perceptive... and strong. What will you do now, do you think?'

Audrey paused to consider her response. It was a question she'd asked herself so many times but seemed no closer to the answer.

'Don't be afraid of uncertainty, my love,' Lola said, patting the back of Audrey's hand that was resting on the table. 'It's natural when significant changes are made. And that's what we would hope if the change is to be truly significant. Embrace it and trust yourself.'

Audrey could feel herself relaxing as though granted a respite from a trial.

Lola continued, 'Do you see Harold's house as figuring in your future? You must, I suppose if you're considering putting in an offer.'

'You know what, I think I do. I can't explain it, it's just...'

Lola waited for her to continue, but Audrey couldn't find the words to express what it was she felt about the house, or why.

'Well, that's something important. It's a gut feeling then, an instinct.'

'Then you think I should act on it?'

Lola paused and seemed to be contemplating something. She looked down at her lap and then up again.

'I imagine I must seem like someone who'd be all on the side of the gut feeling...'

'Oh, I'm sorry, Lola, I didn't mean—'

'No, love, don't worry. It's true. I do believe that those things we know instinctively should guide us, but...'

Audrey waited.

'... the problem is, it can be hard to truly hear that voice. Sometimes, we can think it's our gut feeling talking when it's not. Instead, it's our desires, our hopes.'

Audrey was confused. 'But isn't that what instinct's about? What we truly desire, what we truly hope for?'

Lola considered her. 'There's the important word. *Truly.* But I'd say that deep voice, when we listen for it, is trying to tell us what is truly *good* for us. There's a distinction.'

Audrey contemplated her words. 'Lola, you said when I first came here that going to London wasn't my path. What did you mean?'

'I think you already know. It's just a matter of really listening to yourself. And you have. You've made significant changes already and I'm sure it wasn't the result of the words of this wild-haired woman hiding in an old convent on an obscure island.' Her laugh was throaty, but Audrey heard the note of something else.

'Are you hiding?'

The older woman's expression began as a light-hearted denial but shifted. 'I suppose I am in a way,' she said. 'Not from anyone, but from my past, my mistakes, my grief. I'd prefer to think of it as a renewal, and that's what my last two years have been—a bit like yours, in fact.'

Audrey heard her and chose her next words carefully. 'If you don't mind my asking, have you lost someone very close?'

Though Lola's expression hadn't changed, Audrey saw her chest expand with a breath before she replied, 'Oh yes, my love.'

She was about to continue but her eyes flicked to her left and she stopped. Max and Quin were returning to the table. Halfway back, Quin veered towards the kitchen. 'I'd better see how he's going in there,' he said to Max. The two men were getting along, Audrey could see, and she wondered if her father had broached the subject of the eco-lodge. If so, it would be with genuine curiosity. Max was guileless in relationships and for that reason people loved and respected him.

Isabel gave Quin a smile and a nod in passing as she returned to the table. She looked as she did when preparing a celebratory dinner—birthdays, Christmas, Audrey's graduation...

'How's he going?' Lola said as she sat down.

'Oh, the *bebé* is doing so well. I suggest one or two things, but he doesn't need my help.'

'Mum, you'd better not refer to Dion as a baby,' Audrey said, but knew that her mother meant it lovingly.

'Ah, *sí*, I know, but he's so young in ways.'

'*Hu yuhibuk*,' Lola said, with a smile.

'*Nem fielaan.*' Isabel was looking almost teary.

'Sorry, I don't understand...' Audrey looked from woman to woman, bemused by the language they were sharing.

'It's Arabic, *mi querida*,' Isabel said, her expression wistful. 'Lola said, "he loves you" and I agreed.'

'It's looking good back there,' Max said, oblivious to the conversation and indicating with his head towards the rooms at the other end of the hotel. 'Still got a lot to do, though, but Quin's got a handle on it.'

'Did you ask...' Isabel's brow was furrowed as she waited for his response.

'About the eco-lodge? Not yet... not the right moment. Besides, it's not really our business, though it is yours, Lola.'

Lola raised her hands and shrugged. 'It doesn't feel appropriate tonight, as their guests.'

'So true,' Max said, looking a little embarrassed. 'He seems a good bloke. Anyway, yes, let's just enjoy the hospitality.'

'Cheers!'

Quin and Dion emerged from the kitchen carrying dinner plates that left a trail of steam as they walked. As Dion placed one in front of Isabel, Audrey saw that his hand shook, and his face was locked in full concentration.

The plates were the same ones from the lunch weeks before, and once again their vibrant colour enhanced the richness of the Basque recipe—beef cheeks in red wine sauce—all ingredients locally produced.

'We thought we'd serve it. I hope you don't mind,' Quin said. 'Dion wanted to show you how he could dress a plate, didn't you, mate?'

The boy nodded. 'Excuse me a moment,' he said heading quickly towards the kitchen. 'While I change out of my superman costume,' he called over his shoulder, already manoeuvring out of his apron. He returned quickly, looking more his age—a charismatic and handsome young man. He stood at the end of the table between Isabel and Lola.

The wine was replenished for all but Audrey, who was

driving. Though The Sanctuary was only a few hundred metres down the street, and it was unlikely she'd be pulled over for a breathalyser, but she wasn't prepared to take any chances.

'A kangaroo could bound across the road,' she said, almost defensively. 'I don't want my reaction time slowed.'

With Dion at one end, Quin sat at the other between Audrey and Max. Dion was still standing and cleared his throat.

'Thank you, everyone, for coming tonight,' he said, his expression serious. 'This is our inaug... inaugural,' he glanced at his uncle whose nod was barely perceptible, 'yes, our inaugural dinner at The Island. I, we, couldn't share it with anyone nicer.' He was beaming, but suddenly his smile was replaced with a look of shame, 'except Nonna and Nonno... and...' he paused to steady his speech but seemed to be struggling.

'Your mother and father would be very proud of you, mate.' Quin's voice was calm, though the tightness around his eyes betrayed him.

Dion took a deep breath and looked up. He turned to Isabel. 'I'm highly competitive as you know, Isabel, but I would like your honest appraisal.'

She nodded, with an expression of professional seriousness.

'In fact,' he continued, his eyes lit with an idea forming, 'what if you move here to the island and become my... mentor?' His excitement was building, evident in the increase in volume of his voice. 'Head Chef, if you like...'

Audrey was sure she saw a flash of something in her mother's eyes.

'Whoa,' Quin was laughing, 'let's not get too big for our boots yet. Isabel and Max have a life in Ballina and, besides, we haven't passed the test yet.'

Dion's mouth dropped with disappointment, but he

nodded in agreement. 'Yes, well...' He raised his glass of water, 'here we go. '*Saluti.*'

'*Saluti!*' they all said, raising and clinking their glasses.

Dion took his seat, with Quin now adjacent to Audrey at the other end.

They ate with attention, savouring the fragrance of spices and the tender meat. Dion watched their reactions to each mouthful, but there was no need for platitudes; the dish was exquisite, something which was confirmed by Isabel who had been delegated as the evening's expert. She was generous in her praise and congratulated Dion on his own slant on the traditional dish. 'You've improved it,' she told him and the joy it brought to Dion's expression made all of them smile. It was only then that he ate.

Light conversation between pairs and more generally across the table, punctuated the meal. Audrey felt tense with Quin on one side of her and was grateful that he and Lola were engaged in conversation about the island. A few times she wondered if Lola would ask the question—about the eco-lodge, and now the bridge. Lola and Max were similar in their way, honest and open, but Lola didn't ask. Audrey was burning to know the answer to those questions, and to another that had bothered her.

'Dion told me you've been away. Was it a holiday?' Her tone was deliberately benign, though she justified the question as being reasonable enough.

'Nothing that exciting, I'm afraid.' Quin's answer was immediate. 'Just some business matters.'

'Oh,' she persisted and mentally scolded herself for doing so, 'I had the wrong idea. Dion mentioned your wife and I'd assumed...' She couldn't believe the words that persisted in coming out of her mouth and, by the look on Quin's face, neither could he.

'I... yes, there were some matters that Marion and I needed to discuss.'

The sound of his wife's name caused a sinking feeling beneath her ribcage. 'So, you're in business together. That's lovely. What is it?'

The question was loud in the collective pause of conversation.

'They're building an eco-lodge,' Dion said loudly, for Audrey to hear at the other end of the table. 'Here, on the island. And this...' he gestured to take in the hotel, 'is Stage One of the plan. That's right, isn't it, Q?' Dion's face was lit up with excitement and the silence as they waited for Quin's response was oppressive.

Quin shifted in his seat. 'Yes, mate, that's right.' He wore the look of someone who'd just confessed to a weighty crime.

'And guess what?' Dion continued, buoyed by the topic and oblivious to the awkwardness felt by the others. 'You're going to take over my farm, too, aren't you? Such a relief, for Nonna and Nonno. Wait till I tell them!'

Audrey strained to hold back a gasp. She couldn't look at Quin but could feel him almost sag beside her.

'Well...' Lola's voice eased between them all, 'that sound wonderful, love.'

'You stay there, mate.' Dion had moved to follow as Quin stood up and began collecting plates. 'I'll organise the dessert.'

Lola continued with a light-hearted conversation, encouraged by Isabel and Max.

'Have you been to The Sanctuary?' Isabel asked Dion, who shook his head.

'It's too near the church.' The gravity of his face told them everything.

Audrey thought of her morning walk, the people on the steps of the church and how she'd wondered if the funerals for

Dion's parents had been there. She swallowed hard against the thought of the boy, Rosa and Beppe in their grief.

'It was a beautiful service,' Lola said to him, reaching to pat the back of his hand that was curled into a loose fist on the table. 'Your mum and dad were very loved by the Hibernians. You must be proud of that.'

Dion turned to her and smiled. 'Yes. They were loved, weren't they?'

Isabel, on the other side of him, reached for his other arm and was cooing softly.

'I'm lucky though,' his voice had strengthened, 'Nonna and Nonno look after me so well and Q... he's the best uncle in the world.'

They avoided each other's eyes and nodded in assent.

'And look here!' Dion's hands were raised in front of him. 'I have friends.'

'Hear, hear!' Max said. 'To friends, fabulous food and wine.'

'And love,' Isabel added.

They raised their glasses and resumed the light banter. Audrey joined in but was mulling over two things that disturbed her—the boy's absolute faith in his uncle and, although she knew it to be presumptuous, what she could do to protect him.

'I might see if I can help,' she said, standing and summoning courage. The others, deep in conversation, barely noticed her leaving the table. She paused at the entrance to the kitchen. The door was ajar, and she could see the back of Quin standing at the stainless-steel bench. Dessert plates were laid out in front of him, and he was placing on them quenelles of something that looked creamy and light.

She tapped on the door, and he turned around quickly. She saw his jaw shift when he saw her.

'Can I help?' she said, trying to make it sound as matter-of-fact as possible, though her own jaw felt rigid with tension.

'It's under control, but thanks,' he said, turning back to the plates.

Audrey didn't move. He looked back at her and smiled almost apologetically. 'You could give me a hand taking them out, though.'

She moved forward and stood next to him.

'Ask me, Audrey.'

The statement took her by surprise and now that she was here, she began to second-guess herself.

'You want to know if the rumours are true, don't you?' His tone was calm and patient, rather than irritated or defensive as she might have expected.

Debating whether to play innocent, to draw it out of him, she reminded herself that she had no right to do this.

'Yes,' she said. 'I know it's none of my business, but...'

He half-turned towards her. 'But you're falling in love with Hibernia, and you're worrying about Dion, both of which are... admirable.'

'Are you the developer of the eco-lodge?'

He was facing the next plate, easing a quenelle onto the edge of the peach tart. He paused but didn't face her. 'It's my... our company, yes.'

'And the bridge? Is that true too?'

'There's a plan.' His voice was quiet, flat-lined. He heard her intake of breath and faced her, his eyes downturned at the edges as they'd been that first day she met him.

'And...'

'The farm? You want to know why I want it?'

'Yes,' she said.

Quin placed four of the plates on a large tray and turned to face her fully. 'Audrey, all I can tell you at the moment is that it's true, and that it's complicated.' This time, his voice was strong, authoritative.

She didn't respond but picked up the two remaining plates and followed him. At the door, he turned to her and seemed to be about to say something but reconsidered and headed towards the others. Dion was entertaining Lola and Max with a story about the renovation, it seemed, while Isabel had left the table and was scrutinising the photographs on the wall.

'Q, remember when that bit of the ceiling fell and nearly knocked you out?'

'Oh, I do,' Quin said, positioning the tray on an adjacent table. 'I'm still sporting the bump on my head. Sorry, I still haven't mastered the art of plates up the arm,' he added, as he began placing them in front of them.

Dion jumped up and took the remaining plates from Audrey. 'It's unseemly for a guest to be serving the table,' he said. 'Please sit down, Audra and I'll serve you!'

'Thanks, mate,' Quin said, avoiding looking at Audrey.

'Will staff be easy enough to get?' Max said, as he eyed the dessert with blatant lust.

'I'll cross that bridge...' Quin's voice faded into the collective silence.

'The bridge! Good one, Q.' Dion's face was flushed with pleasure and excitement as his eyes flicked from his uncle back to the others. He tapped his fingers to his forehead. 'I forgot to tell you that. There's going to be a bridge. You'll be crossing it all right.'

'Is that right, Quin?' Lola's tone was even, calm.

Quin visibly sighed. 'There are plans,' he said, as he had to Audrey, 'but nothing's approved as yet.'

'That's a pretty big deal for the island, I'd say,' Max interjected. 'Did the people here get to vote on it?' There was no

166

note of aggression in Max's voice, but Quin's reply was loaded with tension.

'No, it seems the council wants it done.'

Audrey met his gaze in her direction and saw that his expression was pained.

'Enjoy the pear tart,' Dion said, cutting across the tension.

Quin took up his seat next to Audrey. 'Do you think you'll make an offer on the house?' he said to her when the others resumed their conversation.

'I don't know now, to be honest. It sounds as though Hibernia is about to change... in ways I want to leave behind.'

'Audra! You must buy Harold's house. Please. It'll be all right, won't it, Q?' Dion had overheard her comment and his concern was apparent as he looked towards his uncle for reassurance, but Quin gave him a half-hearted nod and smile.

Despite Lola's own interests in whether the bridge would be built or not, she didn't press the matter, but shifted the conversation to the paradise garden she and Isabel were designing.

As the others were discussing it, Quin leaned towards Audrey and spoke softly. 'Audrey, my wife...'

'You don't need to explain anything to me,' she said, almost whispering, but knew that it came out more abruptly than she intended. 'I'd thought she might have been here tonight,' she added, trying to sound only mildly curious.

'We... we don't live together. We separated, not long after the accident with my sister.'

'I'm sorry to hear that.' Audrey felt something physically or mentally shift and wondered if the separation was caused by his move to the island to help look after Dion, though she wondered now if that had been the true reason for his moving there. 'You're still in business together?'

'Yes.' It was said with a note of derision. 'As I said, it's complicated.'

'Audra, I've missed you!' Dion drew in a chair and sat next to his uncle.

'The meal, Dion, it was fabulous,' she said, with sincerity and gratitude for the interruption.

'It was, mate,' Quin said, sitting back and extending an arm around his nephew's shoulder.

Audrey saw the way the boy leaned into him. He needed his uncle, and she wondered if Quin needed him, too. The more she knew about Quin O'Rourke, the more confused she became.

'Audra, will you buy Harold's house? Please? We would be neighbours!'

As she took in the boy and his innocence and genuine warmth, a sensation coursed through her body, expanding the region around her heart. She recognised it but hadn't felt it in a long time—something just for her, not dependent on anything or anyone else. It was something akin to joy.

Outside, their farewells were warm and appreciative. Dion basked in the glow of success, his smile broadening with each compliment. He and Isabel had formed a bond, evident as they stood side by side, her arm linked through his in a motherly gesture.

Promises were made between them, with Max and Isabel already planning a return in four weeks to help Lola prepare for the opening of The Sanctuary. All of this was very good news to Audrey.

'We'll need to be here to help the girl with the house,' Max said, smiling at this daughter.

'Dad!' Audrey laughed. 'I haven't even made an offer yet.'

'Buy it tomorrow!' Dion said.

Audrey laughed. 'I'll try,' she said, wishing that she could have his faith that things would work out so easily. 'You'll be the first one I tell if it happens,' she added, as she gave the boy a hug.

Quin was saying his goodbyes to the others then, when Dion moved to do the same, he came to her. 'When do you go back to Melbourne?' he said lightly.

'In a few days.'

'If... if you have time, I'd like to see you—perhaps I could cook dinner for you here, or at my place, though it's just a rental for the moment.'

She saw the colour rise in his face, the hesitation as he looked down at his boots. 'My friend is coming from Sydney tomorrow, so we'll be spending the remaining time together.'

'I see,' he said, looking at her directly as though trying to gauge her thoughts.

As they walked towards the car, the silence between them was filled with the banter of the others. Audrey felt as though her body was stiffening, her movements uncoordinated. As she reached the driver's door, he opened it for her, and she turned to him. 'Thank you for the evening, Quin. And good luck with your ventures.' She heard the tightness in her tone and trembled internally.

His reserve was betrayed by the slight jerk of his body as he stood with his hand still on the door handle. She tried not to look at him. His vulnerability in that moment hurt her on some level, but the newly pragmatic Audrey reminded her that there was a fundamental issue between them—she didn't like his ethics. She'd made that mistake before.

Max, Isabel and Lola were settling into their seats and Dion was entertaining them with a joke. Quin leaned in towards her.

'Audrey, trust me, please.'

She turned to him, hand on the ignition, wanting to say something, but she couldn't find the words she needed.

'Goodbye, Quin.'

This time, she wasn't going to look into the rearview as she drove away.

That night, Audrey lay awake for hours staring at the ceiling, listening to the distant thump of the waves and the call of the nightjar. When she did sleep, it was riddled with incoherent dreams, snapshots—of standing in the dining room of Harold's house staring into the mirror on the far wall, but try as she might, she couldn't see her own reflection; of Quin's face as he stood at the driver's door. But it wasn't these that had woken her, rather it was a feeling akin to dread, not of something she knew, but of something hovering. When her attempts to breathe deeply became stuck in her ribcage, and the cracks in the ceiling, partly illuminated by the passage light filtering under the door no longer entertained her with their artistic expression, she got up.

As she stepped onto the landing, the grandfather clock reverberated softly in the entrance as it struck three o'clock. A salt lamp glowing pink on the pedestal table near the front door cast an ethereal light on an ethereal scene.

In socked feet, Audrey made her way across the parquetry floor and through the sitting and dining rooms, keeping her eyes directly ahead to avoid her mind conjuring images of veiled figures sitting in their favourite chairs. Her skin prickled at her neck. Ahead, she could see that a light had been left on in the kitchen and the thought of the ambience of that room cheered her. She picked up her pace.

The door was ajar and when she entered, she gasped at the sight of a figure with its back to her, sitting beside the Aga.

'Couldn't sleep either, my love?'

Lola, of course it was. Audrey scolded her own whimsy, but was surprised to see her, nevetherless.

'Sit down and I'll make you a cuppa... or a hot chocolate?' Lola was already out of her chair and was drawing another in by the Aga that was radiating a gentle warmth. She was dressed in an Oriental patterned housecoat. Her white hair was loose and when she looked up to face Audrey, the skin beneath her eyes was puffy as though she'd been crying.

'Tea would be lovely, let me make it for you.'

'Not at all. Sit down, love.'

'You couldn't sleep either?'

Lola moved to the bench and half turned her head as she began to spoon leaves into the new teapot. 'No. I had a mind full of thoughts that wouldn't settle tonight.'

Audrey nodded.

'And what about you?' Lola continued. 'What has you up at the witching hour?'

Outside, jacaranda blooms, devoid of their vibrancy, pressed their faces to the window as though to hear the response. When Audrey shrugged, unable to verbalise her incoherent thoughts, they pulled back, caught in a light breeze.

Lola returned with the pot and poured steaming tea into two mugs. She slid the same one as that first time they'd met towards her, with the slogan *You are entirely up to you*. This time, the message seemed to be resonating even more deeply.

'I thought,' Audrey said into the quiet between them, 'that it might just be uncertainty, or even anxiety, but it's more... it's as though something's waiting, something I can't... oh, I don't know.'

'Sometimes,' Lola's voice was quiet and gentle, 'when things in our lives need to change, and we can't imagine what or how, there's a feeling of... well, I see it as akin to one's own impending death. Is that what you mean?'

'That's exactly how I felt a while ago, before I first came to the island, but this feels different, it's more as though there's something external, and a feeling of dread.'

'Yes, I know the feeling.'

Audrey saw how Lola stared across the steam of the tea as though lost in thought.

'In the restaurant,' Audrey ventured, 'you mentioned that you'd lost someone very close to you...'

'Yes, that's right.' Lola placed her mug on the table and placed her hands in her lap, ready to talk.

'I grew up in Sydney, in a conservative Catholic family who had notions of my entering the convent. I had those notions myself, but I suppose that's no surprise,' she said with a laugh and spread her arms to take in The Sanctuary. 'But,' she continued, 'there was a definite down side to the vows you had to take. Poverty, yes, I could do that. Obedience? No. And chastity? Definitely not!' Lola let out a deep, throaty laugh. 'I did study comparative religion at university, though and fell in love with the whole gamut of belief systems. I'm still fascinated, actually. After university, I travelled with friends to London, the rite of passage back then. Australia just seemed so cut off from everything. It was the late Sixties and was "happening" everywhere else, it seemed to us, but nothing was happening here. It's awful to say, but we were embarrassed about coming from Australia. It was a very different place back then. So, we partied, worked in bars and travelled, and after a year most had returned home, but I decided to stay on. I wanted to see more, to stand in those places where the religions I'd studied had begun.

'My father had a friend, Vincent, a banker in Morocco, in

Rabat, and he asked if I could stay with him and his wife, Ronnie. He was a protective father, my dad.' Lola's eyes shifted briefly to her lap as she remembered. 'Vincent and Ronnie agreed. I'd only been in Rabat a week when Ronnie asked me to attend a function with them at the royal palace to welcome home one of the King's nephews. He'd been studying in London, too, it so happened. What twenty-two-year-old girl was going to knock that back!'

Lola paused to take a sip from the mug. Audrey saw that the brightness had returned to her eyes as she relived this period of her life, and she didn't want to stop the flow of memories. Lola was building to the answer to her question.

'I wore one of Ronnie's dresses,' she continued, 'a stunning turquoise chiffon with matching djellaba, a type of hooded robe. In those days, my hair was black—natural, but with a little help.'

Audrey pictured the woman in front of her in her youth and knew that she would have been stunning.

'Anyway, it was a wonderful night, and the reception room was magnificent. The King's nephew Aamir arrived to great applause. He was so handsome. He was married, an arranged one, and his wife was there, but multiple wives were common back then in Morocco and it was so obvious that the local women in the room were hoping to be the next one.'

Anticipation began to twitch in Audrey's body as she felt the tension building.

'Vincent and Ronnie knew so many people there and mingled for most of the night. They introduced me, but after a while I felt like a third wheel and sat at the table. Once or twice, I saw Aamir looking my way and, though flattered, I thought no more of it until... We were about to leave when one of his minders, I think, came over to me saying that the prince would like to meet me. I gave my apologies, much to the man's horror, and left with Vincent and Ronnie. "He won't take kindly to that," Vincent said. "It's not diplomatic, to refuse a member of the royal family.'"

Lola paused again. 'Am I boring you, love?'

Audrey spluttered over her reply. 'Are you joking? It's like you're telling me the plotline of a movie!'

Lola laughed softly. 'Yes, it is, isn't it? The setting, the handsome star and the reluctant heroine. It gets better... or worse, whichever way you view it. I thought little more about it after we got home. Aamir was handsome, yes, but he was a married man, and a father of four young children, and I had plans. I was flattered, of course, but I'd been around enough by then to not take such things seriously. I'd be forgotten by the time he'd moved his attentions to someone else. And ... well, I wasn't totally inexperienced in knowing powerful, influential men,' Audrey saw that Lola's cheeks flushed as she continued, 'but that's for another time perhaps.

'The next morning, Vincent was visited at work by the same man who'd approached me, saying that Aamir requested his attendance at the palace, and he was to bring "his daughter" with him. Vincent explained the situation to me and, given that I was a guest in his home, I didn't feel that I could refuse.

'We arrived at the apartments in the palace, and I was ushered into a small reception area. Vincent was asked to wait. Aamir was sitting in an armchair facing the window with his back to me. I felt a rise of anger that he didn't stand, didn't move, but simply gestured towards the chair opposite him. I had been summoned, it seemed, and I didn't like it one bit. As soon as I took a seat, I told him so, though I have to admit my heart fluttered at seeing his face again. I asked, too, that Vincent be able to come in. He agreed and looked amused rather than angry and this riled me even more.

'Once Vincent was standing next to me, I relaxed, for his

sake really. I didn't want to create any ill will for him. Tea was brought in and over the next hour or so, my irritation changed to... enchantment, I suppose. Aamir was, in fact, shy, gentle and highly intelligent, and it turned out that we shared some common interests.'

Lola looked away at this point.

'You fell in love with him?' Audrey offered.

Lola's gaze turned back to her.

'Yes. Over time. In the few weeks after that, he courted me. I resisted at first. The concept of seeing a married man, and a father, was abhorrent to me, but...' she smiled sadly, 'but how quickly we, or at least I, can overcome a moral stance when we're in love!'

Audrey nodded, feeling a resonance of truth. She'd felt that during her marriage to Campbell, she'd compromised, not morals so much as personal views, tastes, for the sake of him. For love.

'However,' Lola continued, 'I was in a different culture to our own. Aamir's wife knew of our relationship, and she gave her blessing. Theirs was an arranged marriage and, although I've come to appreciate that they are often more successful than love matches, theirs was purely contractual.'

Audrey nodded, knowing that what she said was true. Her university friend, Sharmi, and her husband had an arranged marriage, and they had a wonderful partnership. 'Did you keep in contact with Aamir after Morocco?'

'No,' Lola said immediately, taking her by surprise. 'Because I never left... until two years ago. You see, I was married to Aamir for forty years.'

Over the next hour, Lola told her about her life with Aamir. Though they'd travelled extensively, she was happiest when home in Morocco.

'Did you have to convert to Islam in order to marry him?'

Lola shook her head. 'Aamir didn't insist, but I did because it was expected by the society. I didn't mind at all. There is much to love about that beautiful religion, despite the bad press. But Aamir knew my love of all religions and we even travelled to India together so that I could train in yoga. He was a devout Muslim and Moroccan, but he was also very liberal in his views.'

While she and his first wife had a courteous relationship, communication with her was difficult, until Lola became fluent in Arabic and French.

'Did she resent you?'

Lola shook her head. 'It didn't seem so at the time. She had three sons and a daughter to Aamir. I, on the other hand,' the muscles in Lola's face twitched slightly, 'was unable to have children. Aamir knew how much that distressed me, but... he was a gentle and compassionate man. 'It is as Allah requires,' he'd said, but I saw how wonderful he was with his children and I wanted that, too.'

Audrey knew that burning and sometimes all-consuming desire to have children. She and Campbell had had intense discussions, and arguments, but he'd refused to consider it. Now she was glad they hadn't. She was stunned by Lola's story —her relationship with Aamir had been an enduring love match. 'What happened, Lola? Why did you come back here?'

The muscles around Lola's mouth clenched slightly. 'Aamir died two years ago. He's been ill for months, but it was sudden in the end.' She looked away and spoke to the jacaranda blooms that were pressed once more to the window. 'I was devastated. Still am.' She turned back to Audrey. 'After his death, his wife and his children—all adults now with children of their own— turned against me. They said I had no rights. It seems that there had been more resentment than I'd thought. Had we had children it might've been different, but... in my grief, I left. After Aamir died, I no longer felt that I belonged in Morocco, despite it being my home for forty years.'

'But you must have rights, surely? Financially, at least?' Audrey felt a rush of protection for this wonderful woman.

'Oh, they paid me off in a sense, but new laws have been introduced very recently and, even though members of the royal family might see themselves as being outside legal jurisdiction, my lawyer seems to think that I'm entitled to something. In fact, I heard from him today and have an appointment in Melbourne this week. Audrey, if it's not too much of an imposition, I was wondering if you, and your friend Poppy, would look after The Sanctuary for a few days.'

'Of course.' Audrey reached for her hand. 'Oh, Lola, I really hope that you're entitled to something.'

Outside, the birds began a tentative chirp in anticipation of the morning. It was four-thirty on the kitchen clock and they both agreed it was time to try for a few hours' sleep.

'Thank you, my love,' Lola said as she stood. 'I feel better for talking about it. I hope you didn't mind.'

Audrey stood and embraced her. 'It's a remarkable story, and Aamir sounds like a remarkable man. Thank you for sharing it with me. Have you spoken of it with anyone else?'

'Your mother knows.'

Audrey nodded, realising then why a bond had formed between the two women.

'See you in the morning, love.'

'You too.'

As Lola was heading towards her room, she paused and looked back over her shoulder. 'By the way, my name's not really Lola,' she said with a chuckle. 'It's Bernadette, but don't call me that.'

CHAPTER FIVE

Audrey woke to the sound of her parents preparing for their journey home, the soft murmurings between them as they moved from bedrooms to bathroom. She wondered how she would deal with the quiet over the next few days, but reminded herself that it would be anything but, once Poppy arrived. A rush of pleasure and energy at the thought of seeing her best friend woke her fully, despite her late night, and she leapt from the bed eager to begin the day.

By the time Max and Audrey arrived downstairs for breakfast, Isabel was already in the kitchen helping Lola. The two women worked convivially, and Audrey thought of what Lola had told her last night and noted that the heaviness in her eyes had been replaced with the more familiar spark.

Rather than there being a sense of goodbye, breakfast was bright with discussions of Max and Isabel's return, earlier than the four weeks they'd initially planned—he to help with some of the smaller renovations, and she to help with the planting of the paradise garden.

'I've just the thing in mind for the centre-piece—the fountain,' Lola said, 'and I'll order one from the Moroccan importer in Melbourne that I know.'

'I'll source the new door handles,' Max said. 'You're going to need quite a few of them, so it'll be in bulk. That should keep the cost down a bit.'

Audrey watched and listened to the flow between them and felt, in that moment, that she was content. 'We'll celebrate when you... when we're all back.' For a moment she'd forgotten that she, too, would be returning to Melbourne by the end of the week.

The ferry was just docking as they pulled into the car park. At this time of the morning, only one car was coming in from the mainland, though Bill would have off-loaded a number of Hibernians going the other way in the earlier trip—these were the islanders who'd resisted moving and still travelled across to work at the dairy.

Audrey was helping Max get the luggage out of the boot when she saw two pedestrians alighting. The black hair of the taller one with its shock of red was unmistakable. Handing a bag to her father, she all but ran down towards the ferry to embrace her friend.

'What's this? You're here so early!' she said, stepping back and holding Poppy by the shoulders to take her in.

'I know, I know. There's little left of this ol' gal's ways now,' Poppy said, smiling broadly.

Audrey couldn't help but notice how drawn she looked, more so than when she'd last seen her in Ballina. She stepped in and held her closely, feeling the slight bulge of Poppy's belly that was a sharp contrast to the bony points of her shoulders. As she drew back, she saw that the other pedestrian was retrieving his bicycle. Though only his profile was towards her, she recognised his hat, check shirt and vest—the bird-watcher.

The others joined them. Even though Poppy was in flat shoes, she towered over everyone, but Max. Audrey introduced Poppy, who was still held in a dual embrace between Max and Isabel, to Lola. She couldn't miss the look of concern on her mother's face.

'Welcome to Hibernia! You have Audrey and The Sanctuary all to yourself, but I look forward to seeing you when I came back in a few days' time,' Lola said, with genuine warmth.

Max kissed Poppy's cheek and returned to the luggage as Bill joined him to take them to the ferry. Isabel still had a protective arm around Poppy's waist and seemed reluctant to leave her. The two were in close conversation together and both were looking down at Poppy's belly, where she rested her hand. Audrey looked for Lola and saw that she and the bird-watcher were engaged in conversation. She couldn't hear what they were saying, but he was laughing at something she'd said.

Audrey turned at the sound of the tyres crunching on gravel. A light grey utility vehicle came to a stop and the driver alighted quickly, slinging a backpack over one shoulder. He was tall and lean, and Audrey recognised him immediately by the flaming red of his beanie. Alex. He jogged down to the landing and stopped when he came to the four of them.

'Hello again!' he said, the lilt of his Canadian accent adding another layer of colour to his presence. Alex greeted them in turn with a broad smile. He'd remembered their names but paused with a look of slight confusion when he saw Poppy.

Audrey made the introductions and at the mention of her name, his face lifted. 'Poppy Varidis? You're the artist.'

Poppy had coloured slightly, much to Audrey's surprise and she nodded rather than spoke in reply. Her red stripe and his red beanie seemed even more vivid, as though some kind of pheromone was at work.

'I was in Paris last year and went to your exhibition. I love your work. But I must say I'm a bit surprised to see you here.'

'Thank you.' Poppy's eyes held his. 'I've come to see my friend, Audrey.' Her hand moved protectively to her belly. Alex's gaze followed but flicked away quickly.

He turned to Audrey. 'Have you moved to Hibernia? I hadn't picked that up...'

'No,' Audrey said with a laugh. 'Well, not yet anyway.' The suggestion in her reply stirred her and she felt an urgency to see the old white house before someone else fell in love with it.

'All aboard!' Bill's cheery voice drifted towards them.

Max and Isabel began to make their way to the ferry. The birdwatcher had gone, and Lola joined them.

'Hope to see both of you before you leave,' Alex said to Poppy and Audrey. 'I'm back this afternoon. Come to the farm. Do you eat cheese?'

Poppy looked at Audrey and shrugged her shoulders. 'I'm not meant to, am I?'

'I think it's only soft cheese,' Audrey said, thinking that she would need to bone up on her knowledge of diet and pregnancy. 'We just might take you up on that offer. Thanks, Alex.'

'You're on,' he said as he made his way to the ferry.

The two friends walked to the end of the gangplank and gave their last goodbyes. Isabel and Max would be picking up a hire car on the mainland and driving to Melbourne airport, dropping Lola off in the city on their way.

'I'll call you tonight,' Audrey said, giving her parents a last hug. 'And I'll tell you how I got on with the house,' she added as Max was opening his mouth to speak.

'Sí... sí.' Isabel kissed her daughter's forehead.

'Good luck, love.' Max's bear hug wrapped her in confidence and certainty. Kisses were exchanged between them once again. Isabel held Poppy in close to her. 'I don't want to go,' she said, lightly stroking Poppy's face.

'Mum, you'll be back soon. Besides, you've got some planning to do for Lola's garden.'

Isabel's eyes brightened. 'Yes... I have things to do.'

'Come on, love,' Max urged his wife. He was already on the ferry with Lola, who was chatting with Alex. Isabel joined them and they all turned to wave. The gangplank was drawn in with a thud and the old ferry eased away from the dock.

Audrey picked up her friend's bags despite her protest. 'Ready to see Hibernia?' she said.

Poppy nodded. 'My darling Pop, I'm so happy you're here.'

Poppy wrapped an arm around her shoulder, drew her close and kissed her hair.

'So am I, babe. So am I.'

On the drive back to The Sanctuary they filled in the gaps in their phone conversations. Poppy railed against living with her parents but was grateful to them, too. 'It's all my fault, of course,' she said. 'That's not their words, by the way, but mine.'

'Not a fault, Pop,' Audrey said glancing at her friend. 'B's a gift... for me as much as for you, to be honest.'

'Really?' Poppy's eyes were moist, and her voice was soft.

'Yes, really.'

Audrey paused, once again, at the crossroad.

'In a hurry to get to The Sanctuary? Need the loo?'

Poppy laughed. 'No... not at that stage yet.'

'Okay, I'll show you the house first then. Can't wait to see it again myself.'

'Great! Let's go for it.'

Audrey smiled to herself. Poppy, her partner-in-crime. What a pair they were!

'I'll take you to meet Rosa and Beppe later. He's left the key in a spot for me at the old house,' Audrey said, as they drove past the villa.

When the chimneys of the old house became visible through the vegetation surrounding it, her heart began to pound in her chest, and when she pulled into the gutter in front and turned off the engine, they both sat silently taking it in.

'Wow,' Poppy said at last, still turned away to look out the passenger window. 'It's... old.' Audrey felt a wave of disappointment. 'And bloody fantastic,' she added, turning back towards her, her eyes bright with excitement. 'It's yours, babe. I can tell... it has you written all over it... Aud, what's up?'

Audrey leaned into Poppy's open arms and allowed her tears to flow freely. It was as though her friend's presence had released something.

'Babe? Are you okay?'

'Yes...' Audrey sniffed back her tears as she sat up, 'when I'm with you, I'm very okay.'

'That makes two of us,' Poppy said, releasing her. 'C'mon. Let me check this place out.' Once outside the car, she paused. 'What's that sound?'

'Well, let me show you.'

Beneath the palm, Audrey told Poppy of her dream for the decking and how, on that first visit, she'd pictured herself there with a gin and tonic, watching the parrots. And because it was Poppy—outrageous and creative—nothing seemed impossible. The garden delighted her, the ocean enthralled her and, inside the house, she envisaged things that Audrey had not, saw things that Audrey hadn't seen and believed in possibilities that

Audrey had only hoped for. In her presence, Audrey's senses were alive.

At one point, after they'd both gone in separate directions to investigate rooms, Audrey had sought out her friend and saw, through the salt-streaked windows of the sunroom, that she was wandering in the garden, pausing every now and then to inspect a budding fruit tree, then kneeling carefully to inspect something at ground level, a protective hand across her belly. Her face was relaxed in concentration and Audrey was surprised to see her like this. The Poppy she knew had never expressed an interest in nature, had always been restless to be in the thick of things, more comfortable surrounded by concrete, asphalt and the cacophony of the city. Now, as she bent into the garden, she looked as though she wanted to lie down amongst the plants.

Audrey joined her and they walked again to the rise to watch the waves striking against the cliffs. 'What should I do?' Audrey said.

Poppy breathed in the salty air before turning to her friend in response. 'What I think is that you should buy this place immediately. If you don't, Aud, I will.'

Audrey gaped with surprise. 'Really? You love it too?'

Poppy had turned back to the ocean and was nodding.

'Well, if I do buy it,' Audrey paused to consider her next words, but knew in her heart it was right, 'would you come and live with me?'

Poppy turned, her startled expression difficult to read.

'That is, if you want to,' Audrey said quickly. 'Even if just until you're sorted...'

'Oh, babe.' Poppy stepped in and wrapped her long arms around her friend. 'Would I ever! But only if you're very, very sure. I can be a bitch, but you already know that.'

To see the spark return to her friend was all Audrey needed.

'Yes, I do know that,' she said with a laugh and stepped in closer to rest her head in the crook of Poppy's neck.

As they walked arm-in-arm towards the car, they were startled by a figure standing between the house and the palm as though waiting for them.

'Who the fuck's that?'

'Quin O'Rourke.'

'*The* Quin?'

Audrey sent a warning glance her way and received a shrug of mock innocence in reply, but the incongruence of him standing there rattled her.

'Hi, Audrey,' he said as they approached.

She made the introductions and could feel her friend sizing up the man in front of them. He shifted his gaze quickly from her to Poppy and nodded a hello.

Audrey wondered what he would think of her friend, who matched him in height, and her fierce red streak. She smiled to herself. 'Hi, Quin. What can I do for you?'

'I was on my way to pick up Dion and saw your car. You're serious then? What you said last night... about buying the house?'

'She sure is.' Poppy's voice was a welcome intrusion between them.

Quin smiled with warmth at her enthusiasm. 'That's good then,' he said and looked back at Audrey, 'but I suggest you put in an offer quickly. I know Harold's daughter and... she's very nice, but she'll take the highest offer, of course.'

Audrey was alert and her pulse began to race. 'Someone else is interested?'

'Possibly.'

There'd been a hesitation before he'd replied.

'Do you know who?'

He went to answer but hesitated as though reconsidering. 'It's prime real estate and...'

'Prime for development, you mean?' Audrey was watching his reaction carefully.

'Yes.'

'Who the fuck would...'

Audrey touched Poppy's arm beside her. 'Thanks for letting me know. I'll put in an offer today.'

He dipped his head as though satisfied with the answer. 'I'd better be on my way. Can't keep the boy waiting, as you know,' he said, his voice sounding lighter.

Audrey took him in. The man was a conundrum, she decided. 'Give him my, er, love.'

He nodded. 'Nice to meet you, Poppy,' he said, extending his hand.

'You too.'

'Hope to see you both again and Audrey... good luck.'

'Thanks, Quin.'

As he walked away, Poppy leaned down towards Audrey's ear. 'He's got it bad for you.'

Audrey scoffed as she watched him walk away. 'How can you tell from that conversation? The trouble is, you're a romantic.'

'True, so I know one when I see one.'

'You're nuts.'

'True again. And hey, I kinda like him, though he's not as hot as that cheese guy down by the ferry, though.'

'Alex? Yes, he's good-looking for sure.'

'"Good looking"? Sex-on-a-stick, babe. Sex-on-a-stick.'

Audrey couldn't contain her laugh. 'Remember your condition.'

'Oh... I remember how I got into this condition.' Poppy

adopted a dreamy look and winked at her friend. 'Come on, you're gonna buy a house!'

'Tired?'

Poppy was leaning back into the seat and opened her eyes. 'A bit. B's not, though,' she said, with a weary smile.

'Meaning? Not kicking already? Can you feel it?' Audrey's eyes flicked from the road to Poppy. She could feel her smile widening of its own accord.

Poppy laughed. 'Not yet, babe, wishful thinking. It's more like... a flutter, or a ripple of wind, really. Maybe that's it... I am a bit hungry.'

'Okay. We'll stop at the bakery for supplies on the way back. You do look like you could do with a nap, though.' Audrey could see that dark circles were forming under Poppy's eyes. Although, as far as she knew, her friend hadn't abused her body over the years, but she hadn't looked after it, either. And they weren't getting any younger. Poppy wasn't yet past the critical three months and there was still a long way to go. Looking at her now, Audrey feared for her and the baby's welfare.

'I've got something to show you when we get there,' Poppy said.

'Oh?'

'B's first happy snap.'

Audrey pulled quickly into the side of the road. 'What! Where? Show me now!'

Her friend's smile was broad as she retrieved an embossed envelope from her otherwise chaotic handbag. Carefully, she slid the image out and held it on the windscreen, pointing to a smudge in a sea of smudges.

'Meet B, Auntie.'

Audrey looked closely. She couldn't determine the shape of an embryo, but she trusted it was there. Her eyes began to prick with tears. 'And is everything okay?' she said, turning to Poppy who was still looking at the image with an expression of love.

'Yes. I was scared, though, so that's why I asked. The doctor sized me up and agreed, especially as I was planning to fly home. But I saw that tiny, tiny heartbeat and... I fell in love, Aud. I need to look after myself, for B's sake.'

Audrey watched her friend as she slipped the image back into the envelope and saw how gently she placed it in the pocket of her bag. She would look after them, she resolved— Poppy and B, all together in the old white house.

'It's amazing... but kind of spooky, too.' Poppy pirouetted slowly, taking in the large entrance hall bathed in the light emanating through Teresa of Avila. The grandfather clock struck one.

Audrey had shown her the other rooms on the bottom floor, and the jacaranda blooms had nodded their greeting at the window. She could tell her friend was tiring as her usual dynamic and often boisterous comments were tempering.

'Wait until you see upstairs.'

Audrey took her first to the chapel and was relieved and happy when Poppy stood in awe of the renovation and the view.

'Oh, wow! It's just perfect. I've seen a few yoga spaces, believe it or not, but this... this is magic.' Her voice had become subdued and there was a look in her eyes that Audrey couldn't quite fathom—longing came close.

Lola had made up Isabel's room for Poppy before she'd left. As they deposited her bag, Audrey wondered how she would react to the tiny space.

'It's not much smaller than my bedroom in Paris,' she said, sizing it up. 'Strangely, I'm rather comforted by the confines of it, as though it'll rein in my... distractions.'

Audrey nodded with understanding. 'I'll settle you in the room at the end of the corridor and get some plates from downstairs for lunch.'

'Do we need them? Let's just eat those babies out of the paper. I'm starving!'

As they entered the sunroom, Poppy let out a long sigh. 'Oh God, it's gorgeous.' The sun angled across the verandah, picking out the pattern in its mosaic floor and beamed through the glass doors, laying kisses of light on the tips of the palms in their pots, the brass candle holders and spotlighting the array of colours in the cushions and settees.

'Lola really knows what she's doing,' Poppy said, and Audrey nodded her agreement.

'Here.' Audrey pulled in an ottoman close to the settee. 'Put your feet up while I organise these pastries.' She held up the bag that was still slung across her shoulder. The pastries were still warm and the odour of their spicy fillings and rich, buttery coating was making her stomach rumble.

Poppy removed her sandals and sat with an exaggerated slump into the couch, causing her belly to look larger. Audrey thought of the smudge in the ultrasound taken weeks before and wondered how different B would look now. She hadn't been particularly good at Biology in school so couldn't remember the developmental stages in the flow diagram from fertilised egg to full-term baby. But she did recall that the weeks before transition to the foetus were critical and felt some relief that B had reached that significant milestone.

As they chatted between bites, Poppy's eyelids became heavy and she finally fell asleep, the empty brown paper bag now filled with pastry flakes still in her lap. Audrey reached across and placed it on the table carefully so as not to spill them on the floor.

Stepping out on the balcony, she checked the reception on her phone. There were enough bars to make the call. In the other hand, she held the slip of paper with the agent's number that Beppe had tucked into her hand. She took a deep breath as she tapped it into the phone.

'Brian Elsden Real Estate. Brian speaking.'

Audrey had anticipated a series of scenarios—a receptionist first, or a "leave a message', or 'the agent handling that one is out at the moment'–giving her time to shape her thoughts and words. Her introduction sounded jumbled, and she faltered over the address of the house.

'You're interested?'

Did she hear a note of surprise? Audrey assured him she was and was keen to get to the crux of the matter, the price, but Brian began to wax lyrical about the property: its position, its potential, so much so that she began to wonder if they were talking about the same run-down house she knew it to be.

'It's still available?" she asked, hoping to contain his enthusiasm and get to the point.

'Yes, but there's another party interested and...'

'What are you asking for it?' Her breath had moved into her throat now and a small tremble was beginning somewhere deep in her body.

When he told her the price she nearly laughed. Though it was still very affordable by city standards, it had gone up by ten thousand dollars since she first saw it in the online search. She could have bargained, but the tremble was beginning to grow.

'And the deposit? How much would you require?'

Ten per cent. She could do that with her savings fund. She'd already calculated that the balance would be covered by her share of the sale of the warehouse and supplemented by the funds in the trust account Florence had established for her as a child. There'd be enough for renovations, and to provide her with a small, but adequate income for two years if she was careful, enough time to re-establish herself—in what, she still hadn't yet determined.

'You've seen inside?'

'Yes. I know Beppe and...'

'Oh yes, the key. Of course. Well, you know what you're up for then.' There was still that note of surprise in his voice. 'The other potential buyer's only really after the land. The house, I'm sure you realise, isn't worth anything really. It's the—'

'Position. Yes. It's special.'

'Well, Audrey, it is a special little place, Hibernia, and it's drawing quite a bit of attention. Now's a good time to get into the market before...'

There was little sincerity in his tone, but Audrey couldn't miss the rise of enthusiasm before he trailed off, as though catching himself from revealing too much. If Hibernia was to be connected to the mainland, it would be this estate agent's wet dream.

'Will they accept the offer, Brian?'

There was a hesitation at the other end. Audrey could feel her pulse pounding from her fingers into the phone.

'The vendor wants it sold, so I think so. I'll run it by them now and I'll get back to you ASAP.'

'Okay, thank you. I'll wait to hear your answer. Perhaps let Harold's daughter know that I can pay the deposit immediately. Today, in fact.'

'Right, yes, that might be good. I'll do that.'

Poppy was still asleep, a soft snore escaping her mouth that was hanging loosely.

Audrey settled herself amongst the cushions on the floor by the doors in a patch of sun and began a calculation of her funds. With the warehouse settlement due in a few weeks, the timing would be perfect. Although she didn't want to tempt fate, she couldn't help doing a rough estimation of renovations. The kitchen would be first. The wall between it and the dining room and the wall to the sunroom would be removed, perhaps requiring a beam for support. This would let light into the space, as well as a skylight over the kitchen if needed. The Aga looked to be in excellent condition, but she'd also need an additional stove—an industrial sized one, perhaps in the centre of the kitchen in an island bench, and a range hood overhead. It would all need to be painted, white, perhaps, for light and space and...

Feeling a return of the creative energy that she'd felt whenever designing the setup for an exhibition, she suddenly pulled herself up. *What if something goes wrong? What if Harold's daughter prefers the other contender? What if there's a problem with the finances?* Something was niggling at her and she remembered the feeling of impending doom she'd spoken about to Lola. Beatrice.... she needed to call her solicitor.

Audrey got up and moved to the balcony, shutting the door behind her. With still enough bars to make a call, she re-dialled Beatrice's personal number.

'Audrey, thank goodness.'

'Is something the matter?'

'Well... Campbell's solicitor has contacted me. Seems he wants to make an adjustment to the settlement.'

'Oh?' Audrey swallowed deeply as she waited for Beatrice to continue.

'He's claiming half your savings, and... half of your trust account.'

A tremor began in her feet, and she sat down on the wicker

chair in the corner of the balcony. 'But... but they're mine! He can't claim them, can he?'

'The savings, perhaps, though I'm still looking into it. I'm fairly confident the trust is safe.'

'Fairly confident? But I need the savings for...'

'I'm afraid they're frozen for the moment. Until we sort this out.'

Audrey rested her hand with the phone in her lap then brought it back to her ear. 'How long?'

'A week, perhaps. Things move slowly, I'm afraid.'

'I can access the trust, surely?'

Beatrice was quiet at the other end. Her voice was gentle when she spoke. 'I'm afraid not. It's just while we sort this out.'

There it was. Doom no longer impending.

'I'll call you as soon as I can. Will you be okay in the meantime?'

No, she wouldn't. 'Yes, thanks, Beatrice. And please... if you can push it along...'

'I'll do my best.'

When she ended the call, Audrey sat back in the chair, her mind blank with shock.

Poppy was just stirring as she closed the door behind her and looked over the back of the settee. 'Aah... went out like a light. Babe! What's wrong?'

Audrey sat down next to her and related the conversations —the one with Brian first.

'But that's fantastic, isn't it?'

And then with Beatrice about Campbell's claim.

'Fuck that arsehole!' Poppy's face was flushed with rage.

Audrey shuffled in next to her. 'Shhh... calm down, it's not good for you or B.

'Truly, Aud,' Poppy said more softly, 'what did you ever see in that c... that guy? Okay, I know you don't need to hear that right now, but...'

'Yes, well...'

'What can you do? What about the house?'

Audrey shrugged, still numb. 'Just have to wait, I suppose. Hopefully, Beatrice will get back to me quickly—with good news. It's just that I won't be able to pay the deposit right now and, if Campbell's successful, I'll just have to...'

Leave Hibernia. Go back to Melbourne. Go back to work. These were the words, but she couldn't say them.

'Hey. Hey! Look at me.' Poppy had grabbed her hand and was staring into her face. On closer inspection, the red stripe seemed to be fading and had broken its rank while she'd slept and had merged with the black. Highlighted by the sun coming in through the doors, Poppy looked as though she was surrounded by an amber halo. 'You're gonna get that house. You *have* to. You need it, Aud, and it needs you.'

Audrey smiled at her friend and placed a hand on her belly. 'It needs us,' she reminded her, feeling a rise of strength and determination.

'I can't sit around and wait, or I'll go crazy,' Audrey said in the kitchen, after giving Poppy a tour of the rest of the convent. 'Anything you'd like to do?'

Poppy's smile was mischievous. 'Oh, well... I feel like a bit of cheese.'

Audrey couldn't help but laugh at the look on her face. 'My God, you're...'

'Insatiable? Sexy? Irresistible?'

'Not to me, you're not.'

'Double negative, babe. Does that mean you think I'm hot?

I might need to know this if we're going to share a house together.'

'I don't fancy you.'

'Ohhhh.' Poppy adopted a look of pained disappointment. 'I don't fancy you either, by the way. Not that I'm averse to...'

'Okay, I know,' Audrey said, still laughing. Her friend's diverse sexual preferences were well known to her. 'So why don't you fancy me?'

'Well... you're more like my—'

'Confessor? Uptight sister?'

'Sister, yes.' Poppy's face had settled into a soft smile. 'What do you say we go for a drive then, sis?' she added with a wink.

Audrey checked the time on her phone. 'I doubt Alex'd be back yet. What say we go for a tour of the island, have a look at the wetland maybe and circle back to... buy some cheese if he's there?'

Poppy suddenly leaned forward and kissed Audrey on the cheek. 'Sounds like a good plan.'

Audrey wondered how she would cope with her outrageous "sister" for the next few days, let alone living together. The thought brought a smile to her face.

'That's The Island Hotel,' Audrey said, giving it a cursory look from the car.

'The den of iniquity?'

'Whooh! You make me laugh, Pop.'

'"She who laughs last, laughs loudest".'

'What does that mean?'

'How the fuck would I know? You're the educated one.'

'Mmm, well...' Audrey glanced at her friend and back to the road, 'and look where that's got me. No job, no home and, if *he* gets his way, no money. Oh, I've done really well with my education, haven't I?'

'Babe. Come on. You're so smart. And creative, by the way.'

'No, I think that's you.'

'Ha! Listen to us. Okay, I'll take creative, but I'm definitely not smart. Take a look at me!'

Audrey glanced her way again. Poppy had exaggerated the curve of her back so that her belly protruded even further.

'B's going to be smart,' Audrey said.

'Well, B's got a dickhead for a father and a fool for a mother.'

'Lucky I'm here then,' Audrey said, feigning sincerity.

Audrey's mood lifted. They both knew they were avoiding the big dilemmas each of them faced, but, for the moment at least, they could still laugh with each other.

Large tyre treads became evident in the dirt road as they neared the wetland. Audrey had already filled Poppy in on the proposed plans.

'Yes,' Poppy said. '"Bill" is it, on the ferry? He mentioned he'd brought a couple of large graders across last week. Against his better judgement, he said, but he didn't have much of a choice. I forgot to tell you that.'

As they came to the top of the rise, they couldn't miss the graders on the promontory, already scouring the earth and leaving deposits like large age spots on the hill. Though they were at a distance, their hum and vibration were loud in the amphitheatred wetland.

'Far out,' Poppy said. 'It's not just a "proposed" plan anymore.'

'Yes, true.' Audrey became distracted by a movement to their left. Though he was crouching in the shrub, the bird-watcher's hat and check shirt gave him away. She could tell that his binoculars were trained on the graders.

'You've got to admit it's a great spot for an eco-lodge,' Poppy said, with an almost guarded tone to her voice. 'If I didn't see what it took to build it, I'd probably sign up for a program there myself.'

Audrey had to agree. 'Dad says it could be done with minimum impact on the ecology here, but it would take great sensitivity and considerable expense to ensure that the wetland wasn't compromised.

'So... what's the actual problem then?'

'Rumour has it that the developers don't have that kind of sensitivity.'

Audrey could feel Poppy's eyes on her, knowing exactly who she was referring to.

'Maybe the rumours are wrong, babe.'

'Well, we'll see, I suppose. That is, if we're ever back here to see it. C'mon. Let's get out of here.'

The conversation became more subdued as they made their way to Alex's farm. Audrey followed the coastal road, pointing out Dion's farm and recounting the boy's announcement about Quin's "takeover bid" as Audrey now thought of it. They both agreed that a natural hot spring in such proximity to the eco-lodge would be an incredible boon to its business and they both knew how others like it had been commercialised and, sometimes, exploited.

'But the guy seems really nice... from my brief meeting, anyway... and you said his nephew loves him, right? Surely he's not that two-faced?'

Audrey nodded. 'Yes, Dion does, and Quin seems to genuinely love him in return.' She thought of Quin's plea for her to trust him. 'It's complicated,' he'd said, but these were only words and, so far, the evidence was beginning to stack up against him.

Further along, she pointed in the distance to where the

house and Rosa and Beppe's would be. From this angle, she realised that she had traced a line connecting the eco-lodge to Dion's farm, and now to here. As far as she knew, there were no other properties between them except for the old abbey, the cemetery and Alex's farm.

As they approached, they could see Alex's Ute parked at the end of the drive. The front glass doors of the cheese shop were open and two men, sitting at a table on the patio at the front, seemed to be just finishing some business between them.

Alex stepped out of the shop to collect their cups, but his expression was far from hospitable. The men stood. One, dressed more as a local in comparison to the other in a suit, had his head bowed slightly as though in an act of contrition as he shook Alex's hand. The other man stood formally, waiting.

Alex went inside. The others walked to their cars parked in the paddock to the right and shook hands as they parted.

'Oh dear, Alex didn't look very happy,' Audrey said, as they parked in a bay. 'Perhaps now's not a good time.'

'Something's going on, for sure,' Poppy said, already unbuckling her seatbelt. 'Let's test the water first. He's probably heard us pull up, anyway.'

It seemed that Alex had, as he was coming out of the shop and heading towards them.

'Oh... I would show him a good time,' Poppy muttered under her breath, prompting a "look" from Audrey in return.

They greeted Alex outside the car and Audrey took him in, looking for a sign to gauge his mood, but he smiled broadly and, she noted, wider still as he greeted Poppy.

They walked three abreast towards the cheese shop. Poppy, it seemed, was mildly tongue-tied again. If Alex was attracted to this version of her, Audrey thought, he would be in for a surprise, if not a shock, when she relaxed into herself.

Inside the shop, they were greeted with the same ambience

Audrey had experienced on the first visit, though this time the open concertinaed doors to the patio added a sense of light and space. Alex, who seemed subdued, had moved to the other side of the display case and Poppy was surveying its produce. When he offered them both a sample of cheese, she hesitated.

'I think it's okay,' he said, beginning to colour slightly. 'I believe hard cheese is fine... not as much water for the listeria to grow.'

Poppy matched his smile and took the proffered chard of cheddar. 'You sound very knowledgeable about it. Do you have children?' A tiny crumb rested on her lip as she spoke. Audrey was tempted to wipe it off for her, knowing she'd be mortified if she knew, but the crumb was accommodating and fell to the floor.

'No... no children,' Alex said. 'I'm assuming this is your first, because you weren't sure about the cheese,' he added hastily.

'Oh, I'm a novice in many ways,' she said. 'This is a big surprise all round.'

Alex was watching her closely. 'Is your partner joining you?'

'Whoooh!' her loud response startled him. 'I don't think his wife is up for the trip.'

Alex's eyes widened as the meaning became clear and he looked as though he was straining to contain a smile. 'I see,' he said, moving back around the counter to join them. 'Would you like a coffee or a soft drink outside?' He gestured towards the patio.

Audrey looked at Poppy for confirmation but knew her answer. 'Love to, but just wondering if you'd be happy to show Poppy the barn... and your instruments?'

Poppy turned to her and then to Alex, her eyes wide. 'Instruments? That sounds...'

Alex and Audrey laughed at her expression.

'It's okay,' he said, 'they're still in production.'

Poppy didn't look comforted. 'Okay, but if you go putting on a leather mask, I'm outta here.'

'Ha! I promise I won't,' he said, 'this time at least.'

The interior of the barn held the scent of oiled wood and sawdust. As Alex directed them to the workbench on their left, in a moment of déjà vu Audrey's phone vibrated in her bag. Brian Elsden's number appeared on the screen, and she mouthed an apology, thinking of how her mother had given her a disapproving glance last time this happened. She stepped back out into the digital hotspot.

'Hello, yes, this is Audrey.'

'Good news. The vendor will accept your offer.' Brian's voice was loud but affable.

This should have been a moment of joy, but Audrey almost wished that he'd said the other bidder had been successful, as that way it would have been out of her control, a sign that this was not her destiny.

'Audrey? Are you still there?'

'Yes... that's wonderful news.'

'Well, the immediate deposit certainly helped. If you can manage that today... but tomorrow is—'

'Brian, something unexpected has come up and, I'm not able to pay the full deposit, just yet at least.'

'Oh?' His voice had lost its joviality and was now pitched lower. 'Well, I'm not sure how the vendor will feel about that. I'd reassured her. Based on what you'd said.'

Audrey took a deep breath. She needed to buy time and knew from her experience with estate agents that there was usually room for negotiation. 'I can put down a holding deposit tomorrow.' She waited anxiously for his reply.

'Ahhh ... and the rest? Just so I can discuss it with the vendor?'

'What are your usual terms?'

'Two thousand down now and the remaining deposit in ten days.'

Audrey's thoughts were scrambling. It was a risk and if there was a delay in the release of her funds, she'd lose the holding deposit. If Cam won, she'd have no hope of securing the house. 'Okay, that would be fine with me.'

'I'll need to check with the vendor first.' Brian's tone was reserved. 'But I think I can get onto her now.'

'Thank you, Brian. I'll wait for your call.'

She walked back inside the barn, to see Poppy and Alex standing close together on the same side of the work bench. He'd removed the mandolin from its case and was showing her the engravings on the neck and she was clearly impressed.

'There you are,' Poppy said, looking up. 'Any news?' Alex was looking expectantly at her, too. Poppy, she assumed, had told him.

Surprised at how quickly the two of them had ventured into more serious conversation in her short absence, Audrey related the conversation with Brian. Alex put the mandolin onto the bench and covered it with a dust shroud. 'I really hope you're able to sort this issue out, Audrey. Poppy's filled me in,' he added sheepishly.

'Me too. It's hard to know if there really is another interested party, or if it's just a realty ploy. Either way, it mightn't make any difference, if my soon-to-be-ex is successful.'

'I'd say it's very likely they're real. You saw the two men here before? The guy in the suit is from a development company buying land in this area. The other guy is my landlord.'

'Alex has to find somewhere else to go,' Poppy said. Audrey noticed the small step she took in next to him.

'Oh, Alex, I'm so sorry to hear that.' Audrey was struck with a thought. 'Do you know the name of the development company?'

'Sure do,' Alex said immediately. 'Foster-O'Rourke Holdings.'

Audrey felt as though her stomach was plummeting to her feet.

'They're the ones behind the bridge proposal, if you've heard about that,' he continued. 'Right in someone on the council's pocket, I believe.'

'Wait! Aud... isn't that...?' Poppy's eyes were wide with disbelief.

'Yes.'

'You know Quin O'Rourke?' Alex said. Audrey nodded. 'He's been here a couple of times,' Alex continued, 'seemed like a really good guy. Showed real interest in what I'm doing here, said all the right things about the conservation of the island's heritage that includes the dairy barn. I must be losing my discernment. The guy's actually a... a prick, it seems.'

'Is that Canadian slang, too?' Poppy said smiling.

'Nah...' Alex had exaggerated an Australian nasal tone, making them all laugh.

'What will you do now, Alex?' Audrey said. Poppy was intent on the answer.

He shrugged. 'I've got some time to find something. Six months from the contract being signed, I believe. As far as I know, that hasn't happened yet. Arthur, the landlord's, got a conscience. He was certainly apologetic about it. He'd bought this property a few years back when the dairy went into liquidation. He and his wife, Carol, planned to hang onto it, for their grandchildren he said, but I think he's been offered a lot more than he'd ever thought he'd get for it. Carol hasn't been well apparently, so they're thinking of retiring to the Gold Coast.'

'Why this land?' Poppy asked. 'It's not that close to the eco-lodge, is it?'

'Well,' the muscles around Alex's mouth flexed slightly, 'the rumour is that they want this area for a golf course.'

'What!' Audrey's and Poppy's voices echoed around the barn.

'Bloody hell,' Poppy said. 'Aud, where's your house in relation to here?'

Audrey wasn't sure what she was meaning, but Alex's voice interrupted her thoughts.

'I know Harold's place. It's parallel to here, that way,' he said, sweeping his arm to indicate the land behind them.'

'And what's between it and the eco-lodge?' Poppy continued.

'Dion's farm,' Alex and Audrey said together.

There was silence as the three digested it.

'It's perfect for a golf course,' Alex said at last. 'Plenty of flat and naturally undulating land, rising towards the coastline.'

'But the cemetery and abbey...' Audrey paused, unable to completely digest the information, 'surely they're heritage or something?'

Alex shrugged his shoulders. 'I'm not sure, but they should be.'

Dion's farm, Alex's farm and Harold's house formed a substantial parcel of land adjacent to the eco-lodge. Audrey could feel the blood rising into her face. She'd tried to think better of him, but she was beginning to despise Quin O'Rourke.

. . .

'Hello, Brian.' Audrey pulled over to the side of the road. 'That's great... yes... ten days... I understand.'

Poppy waited while she ended the call. 'Aud, are you sure you can do this?'

'No.'

'You've got the holding deposit, yeah? If not, I can—'

'Thanks, Pop, but I'm fine. Fortunately, I took a portion of my savings out to come here. The island still runs on cash.'

'Why? In case you decided to splurge on Parisian fashion or something?'

Audrey smiled. 'I need to go across to Wilson's Point to pay it, though. Okay for a trip tomorrow, or do you want to stay here?'

'Mmm, let me see. A bit of cheese fondue'd be nice,' Poppy feigned a dreamy look, 'but I'll sacrifice and come with my bestie. A macchiato would be heavenly. I could kill for a decent coffee.'

'You and Alex seem to get on very well,' Audrey said, knowing that the almost sly tone of her voice was betraying her. 'He's nice.'

'Yes, he *is* nice.'

Poppy's own tone was tempered, more serious than when she'd spoken of other potential love interests in the past. Audrey wasn't sure what to make of it but suspected that her friend might well be actually and really falling in love.

Out on the bricked patio of the cheese shop, Alex had told them of his life in Canada, of how he'd studied journalism, but had abandoned it to perfect his craft as a luthier, a trade taught to him by his grandfather. He'd been in a committed relationship for twelve years but 'it wore itself out,' he'd said and hadn't been helped by the financial difficulties they faced as he tried to establish a reputation. 'And I did build it,' he said, but he'd looked pensive as he spoke. Two years ago, a fire that had started in a nearby forest destroyed his workshop, including the instruments ordered that he'd been working on.

'Fortunately, I had enough savings to start again, but I was shattered by that fire and so... I decided to give the luthering away, too and turned to my interest to cheese instead! Except, of course, I couldn't really give it up, could I?' His eyes had softened then.

'And bloody good job you didn't,' Poppy said. 'What you just showed me is amazing. By the way,' she hesitated as though considering her words, 'what happened to your girlfriend?'

'She decided to give *me* away.' A smile stretched broadly across his face and Poppy looked very satisfied with the answer.

Alex had then prompted her to talk about her own art, her inspiration and life in Paris. As Audrey listened, she heard another side of her friend. She knew that Poppy was not just talented, but was a gifted painter and sculptor; however, it was how she viewed her own talent and the sources of her inspiration that surprised her.

'I start in a dark place, I have to admit,' she'd said. 'Somehow, that negative energy, I'd call it, seems to draw something out of me and out of the medium I'm working with. But what I find is that as I work, as I begin to shape, and that means to remove rather than to add, I find a type of... purity, sometimes godly, sometimes even darker than when I began. Either way, it heals me, restores me...'

She'd blushed as she said it and Audrey had noticed how intently Alex was listening to her, as though he understood. 'But it's thanks to Audrey and Bruce that I got my break,' she continued, looking to her friend with deep appreciation. 'Aud's not going to blow her own trumpet, so I will instead.' She turned to Alex. 'That girl there, she's gifted, so ignore her shaking her head. She is. Audrey sees what others can't, or won't. She sees beauty where others see darkness and even decay. The gallery spaces she designs are bespoke for each artist exhibiting and always, always reflect the artist's vision. I've exhibited in a number of galleries here and overseas and I can tell you that she's the best. The absolute best.'

When she'd finished, Audrey linked her arm in hers. 'Thank you. It means a lot to me to hear that, and especially now.'

Poppy squeezed her hand. 'I mean it, but what a pair we are. For such "gifted people", we're in a real mess. Both knocked up in one way or another by arseholes. Sorry, Alex.'

Alex laughed. 'Oh, they sound like that for sure. You can add me in there, too. I'm about to be done over by one myself.'

'Well,' Audrey said, 'that will be you and I bowled out by the same guy. Not a good club to join, Alex, but welcome.'

'How're you feeling?' Audrey said as they continued along the road following the coastline.

'Pretty good actually, though every now and then a get a little jabbing pain here,' she pointed to the side of her stomach. 'B's got steel-capped boots.'

'Oh?' Audrey took in her friend. She had more colour in her face than when she'd arrived that morning but was still far too thin. 'Should you see a doctor?'

'No, I don't think so. They're not that bad and I've only had them twice.'

'Okay,' Audrey said, but was struggling to be convinced. 'Maybe we should go back to The Sanctuary, and you can have a rest.'

'I had one before. No, babe, I'm fine. What did you have in mind that we do?'

'Well, we're on the road to the house, though I don't want to go there again until I know what's happening. But I thought we might call in to see Rosa and Beppe, and Dion if he's there.'

'Sounds good. I love the sound of them from what you've told me.'

There was a motive behind the suggestion. Audrey was becoming concerned about Poppy's condition and, as she'd had no experience with pregnancy herself, she felt the need to be with someone who had. She was hoping that Rosa would be alert for signs of any problems. Just the thought of being there in hers and Beppe's company made her feel reassured.

Rosa and Beppe greeted Audrey with their usual warm embrace and, after introductions, extended this to Poppy, who towered above them. Audrey saw Rosa's gaze shift to Poppy's belly and back to her face, and she wore the same look of concern that Isabel had had that morning.

'I have a pot of chicken soup—have some with us, *ragazzas*.'

Audrey wasn't hungry, but surprisingly, Poppy seemed to be as she was nodding enthusiastically. She'd eaten more since she'd arrived, Audrey mused, than she'd ever seen her eat, and mentally thanked the island air for its healing effects. Since being there, Audrey's normally frequent use of nasal sprays had been reduced considerably. She'd noticed, too, that her own eyes seem to gleam in the mirror, and that, despite the hard water of the shower, her hair held a sheen. If only Poppy could be similarly "repaired"... perhaps chicken soup, with its anecdotal history of health benefits, could help.

Rosa directed them to the kitchen. Beppe followed. Audrey had seen him gazing up at Poppy in wonder. Her height, the red stripe, and now the swelling belly created an almost surreal effect, not so far removed from some of her own sculptures.

Poppy was not classically beautiful, but her long, aquiline nose and full lips added a regal look about her, that is, until she spoke. Audrey hoped that she would be able to monitor her language in Rosa and Beppe's company.

Rosa stepped into the kitchen first and began to speak in Italian. There was no mystery to whom, as Dion hooted with pleasure and came immediately to the door.

'Audra!'

The boy embraced her without waiting for his grandmother's approval and stepped back. Dion's eyes followed upward to Poppy's face, and he let out a laugh.

'You're a giant!'

Poppy laughed at his lack of guile. 'I know. I'm a freak of nature, my family says.'

Dion nodded seriously. 'Yes, me too. I like your red-back spider stripe. You look like you're ready to eat a mate.' He looked at her abdomen and back again. 'Or have you already done that?'

Poppy's laugh was explosive. Beppe and Rosa looked mortified.

Audrey bit her lip, hoping that her friend would not pick up on the reference and say something inappropriate.

'Oh, thank you. Dion, isn't it? Audrey's told me a lot about you.'

Dion beamed. 'About me or about my cooking?'

'Both.'

'And what do you do?'

'Dion, this is Poppy, the friend I was telling you about.'

'Ahhh, yes, Pipi. You're an artist, aren't you? I've never met someone like you before. Will you do a sculpture of me?'

Rosa intercepted in Italian, the tone causing her grandson to force his lips together. He turned away towards the table covered in flour, but Audrey saw the small smile on his lips.

'Come in, come in.' Beppe ushered them further forward.

Last time Audrey was here the kitchen smelled of the richness of Italian cooking. Today, the odour from the large pot on the stove prompted memories of Florence's home—hearty and wholesome soup. Despite her earlier reluctance, her stomach rumbled.

Dion was finishing wiping down the table as they were invited to sit. 'So Audra... I can't wait to hear. You've bought Harold's house, haven't you and that's why you're here. Nonno, we need some wine to celebrate!' He'd paused with the cloth in his hand. Though he was smiling, his eyes were tight with what looked to be trepidation.

Audrey and Poppy took their seats. Rosa, Beppe and Dion were still standing together on the other side of the table, waiting for her response.

She raised her hands in an "I don't know" position. 'I'm putting down a holding deposit tomorrow, but...' She told them about the conversation with Beatrice and the freezing of her funds.

Dion began to lightly flap his hands with anxiety. Beppe stepped closer to him and rested a hand on his forearm.

'Tsk... tsk,' Rosa said under her breath, returning to the pot and beginning to ladle soup into two large bowls. 'Dion, cut up some of your bread,' she directed, heading back to the table.

When she'd placed a bowl in front of Audrey, she stroked her hair. '*Non*, this is no good,' she said. 'What sort of man is he?'

Audrey could feel Poppy building up to a response. 'He's an... unpleasant man, Rosa.'

'Audra, you have to choose more wisely next time,' Dion said, looking very serious as he returned from the bench with a plate of steaming bread. 'I need to speak to him.'

Rosa and Beppe, now behind Dion's back, exchanged

bewildered looks.

'Thanks, Dion,' Audrey said gently. 'I don't think he has a case. I'll put the deposit down tomorrow and I'm sure things'll work out.'

The boy seemed relieved. 'If you say so, Audra. I trust you. Things will be all right, you'll see.'

Beppe placed a container of butter in front of them and the three of them remained standing on the other side of the table watching Audrey and Poppy eat, with a look of great satisfaction.

Filled with delicious soup and warm, crusty bread Audrey followed Beppe, on his invitation, out through a gate behind the dense vegetable garden to a large shed. Behind and to the left was the vineyard she'd seen that first day. This time, the long arms of the vines were vibrant in their sleeves of sprouting leaves. Poppy, too full of soup, elected to stay at the table and talk with Rosa and Dion.

Inside the shed were a dozen or more large wine barrels stacked on their sides and crates of new, empty wine bottles. At each barrel, he talked about the wine inside, the process of making it, and what it would accompany best. At one, he paused and picked up a bottle from a nearby crate. 'This one ready,' he said. There was a tap already inserted into the barrel's lid and he began to fill the bottle, stoppering it just short of the top.

'Here, Audrey. For you to celebrate.'

Audrey was touched and took it from him. 'I hope I have something to celebrate, Beppe, and I really hope I get to buy Harold's house. I would love to be your neighbour.'

'Si, sì,' he said gently, 'I hope too.'

. . .

The afternoon was spent in relaxed conversation in the kitchen, surrounded by the fragrance of peppery chicken stock, warm baker's yeast and, from a large pot set to simmer at the back of the stove, the unmistakable and wonderful odour of Bolognese sauce heavy with garlic, wine and garden herbs. Rosa, in what seemed like a desperate attempt to fatten Poppy up, kept producing more and more delights from stacked Tupperware containers in the pantry. Dion was at his exuberant best and entertained them with stories about people on the island. When he'd exhausted the inventory of names, he took a well-used Spanish cookbook from a well-stocked shelf of recipe books from various countries, donned a pair of spectacles that were on the bench next to them, and adopted a very serious expression as he opened the book to a page tagged with an elaborate feather-topped bookmark.

'When's Isabel coming back?' he said over the top of the book. 'She said as soon as she can, is that true?'

Audrey nodded. 'Yes, that's the plan. They want to help Lola at the Sanctuary, but... I suppose it all might depend on...'

'You're going to get Harold's house, remember. Nonno, can you buy it for Audra?'

Beppe, who'd been sitting quietly at the table, content to just watch the goings-on, smiled at his grandson.

Dion didn't wait for a reply as his eyes widened in the waxing of an incoming idea. 'I could buy it for you... when Q buys the farm!'

Rosa and Beppe exchanged looks that Audrey couldn't interpret. 'That's so lovely of you,' she said quickly, 'thank you, but it'll be okay, Dion.'

He seemed to be reassured and returned to the table with the book.

'When Isabel comes back, I'm going to be cooking her *Arroz Negro*—Squid and Rice. What do you think?'

'She'd love it,' Audrey said, wishing too that her mother was there. Dion's attachment to her was sweet and, she realised that, as yet, he hadn't created a nickname for Isabel and Max.

Later, reluctantly, they said goodbye. The afternoon spent in the family's company had soothed her. Lulled by the food and their kindness, Audrey now felt a return of Dion's optimism. As she and Poppy headed in the direction of the house, she experienced a surge of excitement. Surely it would be hers. After a day like today, spent on Hibernia in the company of Alex and now Rosa, Beppe and Dion, and being with her friend who would share it all with her, it seemed as though she and island, and particularly the house, were a match. Surely all she needed was to believe, trust her gut instinct, have faith... all the terms that proponents of positive thinking would assure would bring the best result.

As they approached the house, she saw two cars parked in the curb outside. The closest one looked vaguely familiar, but the other she recognised immediately—Quin's Land Cruiser. At that moment, she saw him and another man coming out from the property to the cars. She slowed to a crawl.

'Isn't that...?' Poppy said sitting forward to get a clearer view.

'Yes.'

'The other bloke's the "suit" that was Alex's place. The developer guy.'

Audrey felt a sense of foreboding. 'I thought I recognised him.'

'Whatever they're talking about, Quin doesn't look happy.'

Audrey nodded in agreement as she swung the car in a sharp U-turn, dispersing roadside gravel in violent projections.

When she looked in the rear view, Quin was standing in the middle of the road with hands on hips as he watched her take off. His expression was dark.

'Hi, Dad, glad to hear you're home safe and sound.'

'Thanks, love. Now, what about you? How'd you get on?'

Audrey filled her father in on the conversations with Brian Elsden, and Beatrice. An automatic reflex had her holding her breath waiting for what he would say about Campbell, but she let it go, knowing that she no longer needed to "side" with her husband and would share any sentiment her father offered. Not that Max had ever said anything. Neither of her parents ever voiced the criticisms and concerns that they would have felt over the years with their only child's choice of partner.

'Well... that's...'

'Pretty consistent, Dad?'

There was a snort at the other end. 'Mmm, yes, you could say that. But Aud, surely he hasn't got a legal claim? The savings... well, maybe he's got a case there, but the trust fund was set aside for you by my mum when you were born. I'll be buggered if he's going to get his hands on that!'

Audrey heard an uncharacteristic tone of anger in her father's voice. She wished she was there for one of his bear hugs. 'Wait until I tell your mother. Issy... Issy...' In the background, her mother's reply of 'Sí... sí' was like a Doppler effect, growing louder as she approached. Though he was on his mobile phone, she heard the plonk of his hand on the screen in a reflex to shield it so that she couldn't hear. She listened as he related what she'd told him to Isabel. There was a loud fumbling sound as her mother took the phone, but Isabel was so irate, she was speaking rapid-fire Spanish that Audrey had no hope of understanding.

Another fumble and Max was back on. 'Right. We've got a few things to do tomorrow, but we're coming back the day after. No, love, it's all okay. We want to and Lola has already contacted us to see if we could give her a hand sooner than later. Seems like good things are happening for her and she's keen to get moving on the project. Mum's already drawn up the plans.'

'I have a new camera, too,' Audrey heard her mother call in the background. They were upset about her latest news, there was no doubt, but she was starting to wonder if she'd just provided them with the very excuse that they needed to justify returning to Hibernia earlier than planned.

'That'd be great to have you here, Mum, Dad. Poppy's fantastic, but your calm support would be appreciated. Dad, have you found out anything more about Foster-O'Rourke Holdings?'

'I'm still working on it, love. I've been given a contact by one of my old colleagues—did I tell you we're thinking of setting up a consultancy business together?—anyway, I can tell you about that later, but this chap apparently has, or had, some sort of connection with them. I'm following it up tomorrow...'

His hand was over the phone again as Audrey heard her mother talking in the background, though she couldn't make out what she was saying. 'Yes, that's good,' she heard him say to his wife in return. 'Aud, you there? Love, Mum and I want to help you out... I know, I know you don't want us to. You've been independent for a long time now, but... well, we'd love to help you. We've got the money there for the full price... No, it's fine, love, we're very comfortable, you know that. If that bloke doesn't have any luck, then you can pay us back, but Aud... it would mean a lot to us to help you get that house. We're probably being a bit selfish, but we love it, too, and the island, and hope that it becomes a big part of our life from time to time... that is, if you're okay with that.'

'Dad. Mum. I don't know what to say. If you're sure, that

would be such a relief. I would hope that the house and Hibernia could be an important place for us all.'

When they'd arranged the logistics of the transaction and said their goodbyes, Audrey felt a weight lifted not just from her shoulders, but her whole body. Tomorrow, she'd be able to put the whole deposit down on the house for now and secure it from the hands of Foster-O'Rourke Holdings.

Poppy had seemed relaxed when they'd returned to The Sanctuary and, after a light dinner of a tinned salmon and mayonnaise sandwich and a cup of tea, had gone to bed untroubled by the pains she'd experienced earlier. She'd shown no sign yet of missing the Parisian life, though it was early days. Hibernia offered little in comparison and that, Audrey knew with certainty, was what they both needed, at least for the moment. How Poppy would cope with it in the long term, and restricted by motherhood, was yet to be seen, but Audrey knew that as much as she loved her friend, and as much as she was prepared to emotionally support her, Poppy's decisions were hers to make.

Tomorrow would be a significant day, she'd thought as she'd snuggled into the bed after setting her phone alarm for an early rise. She wondered whether she should have let Brian Elsden know the positive news about the deposit. The weather was promising to be warm and mild so the crossing would be calm, and she could already taste the pleasant bitterness of the macchiato they would have to celebrate the purchase. Perhaps they'd stretch it to a Danish as well, she thought as she began to drift through the layers of sleep.

That night, Audrey slept deeply. The house would be hers and the future, though still uncertain, held more hope.

CHAPTER SIX

As predicted, the weather was perfect for the crossing—a positive sign, Poppy said, as they stood on the deck watching the island slowly recede.

Audrey felt the best she had in days and sent a mental thank-you to her parents. Campbell would not win, she felt certain; the funds would be released and in just a few weeks she'd be divorced and free of him.

'I can smell that coffee from here,' Poppy said, exaggerating a lean over the rails and sniffing the air in the direction of the mainland. 'Pity that bakery in Main Street isn't open for longer in the day. Perhaps we could encourage them.'

'Celebrate with one after the deposit's paid?' Audrey said, eager to sign her name on the deed.

Poppy smiled. 'Of course. This is so great. We should buy a bottle of Möet while we're at it, that is, if they sell such things over there.'

Audrey laughed. 'It's not a complete backwater,' she said, 'but we've still got the bottle of red from Beppe remember. I think that'll be even better.'

Poppy placed a hand on her stomach. 'It'll be water for me. Maybe I should get some Dom Perrier. At least I'll feel like it's something special.'

Audrey leaned up and pecked her cheek. 'Good girl, you. Proud of you, Pop.'

Poppy grinned. 'I'm proud of me, too.'

'Feeling okay?'

She hesitated in her reply. 'Um, yeah, though I had another one of those pains this morning before we left. A bit stronger than yesterday.'

Audrey took her in. She looked better than when she'd arrived the day before, but this news was worrying. 'I think we'd better get it checked out while we're over there, don't you? When did you last see the doctor?'

'When I had the scan. Everything seemed fine.'

'Pop, I'm not comfortable going back to the island until we know for sure you and B are okay.'

Poppy was shaping a resistance but shrugged her shoulders. 'I guess. Yes, you're right. It has been worrying me a bit, I have to admit.'

Audrey breathed a sigh of relief knowing how stubborn her friend could be. There were a few things about her that were changing, it seemed. 'We'd better do that first. I think I saw a sign to the hospital somewhere when I was passing through.'

'No, no, I'm fine at the moment. Aud, I don't want anything to spoil this moment for you. B and I are fine. When we get off this ferry, you're going straight to "Brian" and buying us all a house.'

'Sorry I didn't get to chat,' Bill said, as they waited for the gangplank to descend so they could disembark. 'Bloomin' pump's bin playin' up. I'll see you later on, or you stayin' in town?'

'Back today.' *Coming home* was what Audrey really wanted to say, but she didn't want to jinx anything.

They waited their turn behind three other cars and a small truck, then drove off the ramp through the marina, where boats of various sizes, ages and condition bobbed in the wash from the ferry. Some of these, Audrey knew, belonged to the islanders—those who worked in the town or were just shopping. The town centre was close enough to walk and Audrey entertained the idea of owning a boat herself and envisaged sitting at the rudder and cranking up speed across the inlet. In reality, she thought, the wind would probably blow her hair into her face.

She looked across at Poppy beside her. 'Sure you're okay?'

'Yes, babe. Can't wait for you to get this done. Then I'm going to relax, as I'm sure you will, too.'

'Oh yes.' Audrey could feel the smile across her lips. 'Of all the places I've owned, on my own and with "him", I think this one's the most special.'

'Agreed! The latest ones had that dickhead's mark all over them and less and less of yours.'

'Well, I'll have you this time to leave your mark. Will you help me decide on the renovations?'

'Physically, yes. I'll help after Bubs comes, but... not sure otherwise.'

Audrey glanced at her, unable to decipher her meaning.

'Aesthetically, you don't need my input, and besides, I'm too "out there". This place has got to be yours, Aud, and you'll do a fabulous job of it. But just don't expect me to love pink should you randomly decide to go there.'

'Pink? Hardly!'

Poppy let out an exaggerated breath. 'Thank God.'

A thrill ran through Audrey's body as she anticipated the changes that she'd make restoring dignity to the old house. The feeling wasn't unfamiliar—every exhibition setup spiked her creativity, but this time, it would be just for her... and Poppy... and B.

'Speaking of which,' Poppy continued, 'I'm betting you couldn't help eyeing off the possibilities of that dairy barn at Alex's.'

'Oh, sure. What a fantastic space for an exhibition. The light in there is great. Did you fancy it, too?'

'Babe, I lusted after everything at that place.'

Audrey shook her head. 'I'm sure you did. Shame about Alex having to leave, though. I wonder what he'll do. Maybe go back to Canada?'

She waited for Poppy's thoughts on the matter, but she was very quiet. *Interesting*, Audrey thought.

'Okay. This is the town centre.' Audrey made a right-hand turn into a wide street that was surprisingly busy at this time of the day. 'Now, where's Elsden Real Estate?'

The traffic was travelling slowly enough to enable them to look more closely at each of the shops that lined the street.

'You look right,' Poppy said, 'I'll look...'

'Left?'

'Hey, there's your boyfriend... and guess where he is?'

'Who? Where?'

'There.' Poppy pointed to Elsden's Real Estate, three shops ahead of them. 'Quick, there's a parking spot just there.'

Audrey indicated and turned into the space.

'There he is,' Poppy said. 'In the doorway.'

They were far enough away from him that he didn't notice them staring through the car window. He was on the verge of leaving and was half-turned, talking to someone inside. They watched as he closed the door and headed along the street away from them.

'Wonder what he's up to?' Poppy said under her breath.

'Buying up someone else's dream, I'll bet.' As soon as she'd said it, Audrey felt a small grip of panic. Surely not, she reasoned. She'd made the offer on the house and the vendor had agreed to the terms. It was a done deal other than actually signing the papers. But she was experienced enough to know that something could go very wrong and that thought sapped her of her confidence.

'Come on, let's go in.' Poppy clasped her hand that was still holding onto the steering wheel, but Audrey was frozen to the spot.

'Aud. Let's go.'

Her offer had been accepted. She now had access to the full price of the house. Then why, Audrey wondered, was she feeling this way? Quin wasn't interested in the house. He'd seemed genuinely relieved that she was serious about buying it, but... really, what did she know about him? He was buying Alex's farm and Dion's farm and Harold's house would be right in the way of a golf course. Suddenly, her anxiety turned to an internal rage. She unbuckled her seatbelt. 'Yep, let's go.'

Brian Elsden looked completely different to what Audrey had envisaged— which was a reed-thin man in an ill-fitting suit, sandy hair slicked back, a ruddy expression with a tendency to perspire. The man in front of her was short, in a dark polo shirt that stretched over his portly body, balding and had a pale complexion.

'Hello, Audrey Spencer, I take it?' When he spoke, she had trouble associating the voice with his body. He was standing behind a counter and when she accepted his proffered hand, she realised, with discomfort, that the tendency of his avatar to perspire was accurate.

'And?' Brian Elsden was staring at Poppy with a look of mild horror.

'This is my friend Poppy Varidis,' Audrey said, fairly confident that her name would not register any familiarity for this man.

He nodded and dragged his eyes back to Audrey but looked nervous. 'I tried calling you earlier, but...'

'We were probably on the ferry,' Audrey said, remembering she'd forgotten to check her phone. 'Is there something wrong?' Her body began to tense as Brian Elsden's eyes refused to hold her own.

'Ah, yes... I'm afraid that the vendor has decided against your offer.'

'What's that?' Poppy had stepped up to the counter to join Audrey and he visibly contracted back into himself.

'The vendor has accepted another offer,' he said, gaining some strength.

'But she'd already accepted mine!' Audrey said, feeling her face flush with anger.

'Yes, but you hadn't paid anything on it and—'

'The other party has,' Audrey finished for him. 'When? Just now? Quin O'Rourke?'

'Well, actually, not yet. There's been two parties, but I'm not at liberty—'

'Cut the crap,' Poppy said quietly and leaned towards him. 'We just saw him walk out.'

Audrey placed her hand on Poppy's arm. 'What's the offer?'

He quoted a figure ten thousand dollars higher. Audrey took a step back in surprise.

'Give us a minute,' Poppy ordered, and Brian obeyed, moving to the rear of the counter to the printer, where he proceeded to tidy a paper stack. 'What can you do?'

Audrey's thoughts were in a spin.

'Mum and Dad said that there was leeway with the price if I needed it, but the extra would require a higher deposit to put down now. More than I've got.'

'How much can you go to?'

'With Mum and Dad's money, another two thousand?'

'Leave this to me, Aud.' Poppy's tone was determined.

'Brian,' she said, almost as a command. 'We'll offer two on top of that. What would that make the new deposit?'

He gave them a sum immediately, his skill in such calculations apparent.

'Done. We can have that to you this afternoon.'

Audrey stood to the side, gob smacked. 'Pop, I don't have that much,' she whispered.

'But I do. No, no argument.' Poppy turned back to Brian. 'Get that "b" of a vendor on the phone and give her the new offer.'

Brian's eyes lit up as though he suddenly realised that things were looking very good for his business. 'Please, take a seat and I'll try to get on to her now,' he said and headed to a partitioned office at the rear.

'And tell her that I can pay the full amount by the end of the week,' Audrey called after him.

Audrey and Poppy took a seat.

'Are you sure?' Audrey said to her friend, still marvelling at how she had come to the rescue.

Poppy placed her arm around her shoulders. 'It's important to me, too, that you get this house. I've never been surer of anything before.'

Brian's smile was obsequious as he returned to the counter. 'Congratulations,' he said, staying on his side of it, 'the vendor will accept your offer. However, I'll need to ring the other party—'

'Listen...' Poppy had gotten up from her seat and was walking towards him. Standing opposite him, she raised her body to its full, impressive height. Audrey wouldn't have been surprised to see her fading red streak suddenly blaze in a surge of maternal hormones. 'You'll wait until we've put the deposit down, then you'll tell her... *them*.'

'But...'

'You didn't wait for us, to give us a chance, so you're not waiting for them. There's got to be a law. Aud?' She'd turned to Audrey, who had stepped up to the counter still in awe of the proceedings. 'You've bought *lots* of properties before. Do you know?'

Audrey hadn't needed to answer before Brian cut in. 'It's okay, I'll wait for you, but you'll need to put down the *whole* deposit today—'

'God, this is the shonkiest real estate agency in the world,' Poppy said.

Even though she and Audrey had agreed on the deal between them, Audrey could tell she was playing with him now. Poppy was right. A holding deposit and a cooling-off period was standard practice. Elsden Real Estate was treading on treacherous ground and, by the look on Brian's face, he knew it. But things worked differently here, legally or not, and Audrey felt the urgency to finalise the deal before Foster-O'Rourke Holdings exerted more influence.

'We'll have it to you before the end of the day, Brian,' she said. 'In the meantime, I'm sure you'll prepare the documents for me to sign when we return.'

'But—'

'It's a breach of practice?' she said, looking him directly and holding his gaze.

He looked away. 'I'll have them ready for you.'

'Thank you. And by the way, make sure you ring the other parties and let them know that the house is mine.'

When they stepped out the door, neither of them could contain their laughter.

'Whoooh! You did it!' Poppy said once she'd gained control of herself.

'No, *you* did it. Thanks, my love.'

Poppy's grin stretched across her face. 'Stuff it. I'm having a macchiato to celebrate. Sorry, B. That is, after I've had a pee.' Her laughter suddenly stopped, and Audrey felt her grip her arm.

'Pop? Pop? What's wrong? Is it that pain again?'

She didn't answer but began to topple sideways and it took all of Audrey's strength to stop her from falling to the ground.

'POP! HELP!' she implored two women walking towards them, who both rushed forward to take some of Poppy's weight as, together, they laid her down on the sidewalk. Audrey, kneeling beside her, whipped out her phone and dialled triple zero; it was answered immediately.

'What's the name of the street?' she almost snapped at one of the women, who was kneeling and gently stroking Poppy's hair. 'Is she still breathing?' Her tone was almost pleading now. The woman nodded. Audrey looked down at her friend. Poppy's eyes were closed and her skin was deathly pale. She recited the address to the operator and answered the required questions, trying to breathe deeply between responses to calm the panic that had pervaded her body.

She was still on the phone when she heard the welcome sound of the siren. By now, a small crowd had gathered around them. She held Poppy's hand while they waited for the ambulance to manoeuvre into the closest position and let out a gasp of relief when two paramedics almost flew out the doors towards them, the crowd parting to allow their access.

As she climbed into the back of the ambulance, Audrey, still in shock and holding Poppy's hand, looked out at the silent crowd gathered on the footpath and spilling onto the road. At the back, near the door of Elsden's Real Estate, a man with a stunned expression on his face was trying to make his way forward, but the paramedics were shutting the doors in their haste to leave. As they drove off, the siren accompanying her internal wailing, Audrey watched through the rear windows as he pushed his way forward. It took her several seconds to register that it was Quin.

It seemed like they'd only just left when the ambulance came to an abrupt halt and the back doors flew open. As the stretcher was lifted out, Poppy's eyes opened and searched for her friend. When Audrey called her name, they closed again as though comforted.

Assisted by a paramedic, Audrey climbed out the back and followed behind to the emergency department entrance, feeling as though she was caught in a silent and sinister maelstrom. Once inside, she was directed to a counter to supply the necessary details, while Poppy's stretcher was herded through the automatic doors that closed with an ominous thud. When she'd finalised the forms and reminded "Margaret" behind the counter that Poppy was pregnant, she crossed the passage to a small but otherwise unoccupied waiting room, painted and furnished in various tones of grey, and sat on one of the hard vinyl chairs to wait. On a small television set high in the wall, a panel of women were in earnest discussion, the tone of their voices fluctuating from sombre, to angry, occasionally punctuated with laughter.

. . .

Half an hour later and still no news. Audrey's state of shock had rendered her unable to think or to feel anything. On one level she knew that she needed to call Poppy's parents, to call her own parents, but she doubted any muscle in her body would enable her to move, to talk, or even to cry. She was sitting like this, in a state of psycho-paralysis, when she saw him come in through the entrance and head for the counter. Her brain registered her own and Poppy's names being spoken. Her eyes recognised him as Quin, but none of it mattered. She watched with disinterest as he drew up a chair and spoke her name again, to which she nodded in confirmation. She watched as he reached out his hand and took hers and saw how the fine hairs on the back of his looked silky in the light from the fluorescent globe above them. She was vaguely aware that she should feel heat coming from his hand, but there was nothing and she saw how her own hand rested in his and that her nail polish had chipped. No matter. The only thing that had clarity for her was a tiny smudge on a photo held against the windscreen, an embossed envelope, and the care in which those fingers with their perfectly applied black nail polish had placed it in...

'The handbag!' Audrey turned to Quin as if he should know exactly what he was talking about. 'Where is it?' She pulled her hand away from his when he didn't answer and almost ran across the passage to the desk. "Margaret" came out from behind the counter and listened intently, nodding and murmuring soothing sounds as she guided Audrey back to the waiting room.

'We have it, dear,' she said. 'It was in the ambulance. You identified it, if you remember, and the patient's ID in the wallet. I've just got to register it and I'll return it to you in a minute,' she said, as Audrey sat down.

'Audrey.'

She looked up and met his eyes at last. His face was so close, she could see the pores of his skin where he'd recently shaven. Beneath his nose, a small, thin scar met his upper lip. His hair, normally back from his forehead, had fallen over it, making him look younger, though the creases around his eyes when he smiled, as he was doing now, seemed deeper than she remembered. His eyes were his dominant feature—kind, wise...

She pulled herself back from the temptation to lean into him. 'Why are you here?'

His body jerked back as though he'd been hit. 'To see how you both are... I saw what happened.'

'Oh yes. Standing in front of the real estate agents. Brian Elsden. Had you forgotten something inside?'

He looked at her, bewildered.

'We saw you leave there earlier... when you'd gone in there to... to do me out of the house.'

Quin's eyes widened. 'But I didn't...'

Audrey placed a hand on his arm. 'It's okay. I won. The house is mine.' She pulled away again.

'Audrey, I didn't go in there to buy the house, I—'

'Audrey Spencer?'

She turned away from Quin towards the voice. A tall woman was bending towards her. 'Yes?'

The woman glanced at Quin in acknowledgment and leaned in closer. 'I'm Anna Rhodes, the obstetrician.'

Quin's voice cut between them. 'I'll leave. I hope everything's okay. Please... let me know.'

Audrey nodded lightly and fixed her eyes on Anna Rhodes. In her peripheral vision she saw Quin leaving through the front doors to the street.

'How is she?' she said, bracing herself for what was to come.

Anna took the seat that Quin had left. 'She's fine. Sleeping now.'

'And the baby?'

Anna placed a hand on Audrey's shoulder. 'There's a strong chance that Poppy will lose the baby.'

Audrey sat silently for a moment. Margaret had come out from the reception booth to stand beside her, and she and Anna Rhodes were offering sympathetic murmurs.

'Does she... does Poppy know?' Audrey said at last.

Anna nodded.

Audrey waited.

'She was... upset, as I'm sure you can imagine, but I'm not sure whether it's truly sunk in yet. She's been slipping in and out of sleep.'

Audrey was longing to see her friend, but she felt the need to arm herself with information. 'Do you know what's causing the pain?'

Anna shook her head as she spoke. 'We can't be certain at this point, until tests are done. It could be that the foetus isn't viable, or Poppy's body is rejecting it.'

'But she saw the heart beating.'

'Yes, but any number of things can go wrong. Poppy's age and... her condition—she's anaemic and very underweight. Really, it's hard to know until the tests come back, and even then, we mightn't really know. She'll need to stay in here for a few days at least, so that we can monitor them.'

Audrey listened and knew that Anna was giving voice to the fear she'd had since she'd seen her friend step off the ferry the day before.

Margaret, who'd been standing close by ready to offer support, moved back to reception with the arrival of a mother and her teenage son on crutches.

'Can I see her now?' Audrey was desperate on one hand to

see Poppy, but on the other, she dreaded seeing her emotional pain.

'Yes, I'll take you.' Anna waited for Audrey to gather her bag and called a hello to the mother and son, who returned the greeting with easy familiarity. 'This way,' she said, directing her through the automatic doors and along the grey linoleum-floored corridor to a room on the right. Audrey paused in the doorway. Poppy was lying in a foetal position with her back to the door, the sheet pulled up close to her ears. Only the black hair on the back of her head was visible and, in its wild state, she looked incredibly vulnerable.

'Hey, you,' Audrey said, sitting gently on the edge of the bed.

'Hey you back.' Poppy's voice was croaky and her smile soft, but her dark eyes beneath her heavy lids were like deep pools of sorrow. 'Sorry, babe.'

'Sorry? What for?' Audrey shuffled closer and had to lean down to hear her.

'For stuffing things up, as usual.'

Audrey stroked the hair back from Poppy's face. 'Don't be an idiot,' she whispered. 'I've already got the title as "stuffer-upper". Pop,' she said more seriously, 'I'm here for you... and whatever happens. We'll work through it together.'

Poppy reached for Audrey's hand and squeezed it softly. 'I'm not losing B, Aud,' she whispered, her lids twitching under the strain to keep them open, and her voice began to slur. 'I promise.'

Audrey looked down at her friend, who was now asleep. If the baby's survival just came down to Poppy's steely resolve, she would be confident, but as both of them knew only too well, no matter how much you might want something to happen, there were no guarantees.

She sat by the bed for another twenty minutes in case

Poppy woke, but when Anna returned from attending to another patient, she confirmed that the sedative she'd been given would help her rest for a few hours at least.

'Have you got some things to do in town? Anna asked as they walked back out to the waiting area.

Audrey hesitated, not sure what to do. At this moment, there was no desire to do anything, and the thought of the house just increased her sorrow. But she knew that if she didn't act today, she was in danger of losing it and, although she couldn't hang on to the chance that Poppy wouldn't lose the baby, she felt she needed to move ahead with that hope. Poppy, wonderful unpredictable Poppy, could decide against living on Hibernia, no matter what the outcome. Audrey, on the other hand, knew that she wanted the island to be her home.

'Yes,' she said firmly. 'I'm buying a house today.' Exactly how she could do it, she didn't know.

Anna's eyes widened with surprise. 'Oh, congratulations!' She took Audrey in and her expression became softer. 'She'll be in good hands here. It's lucky you got here when you did. If you'd been on the island... who knows what the delay might have meant. Do what you need to do. We can always make a bed up for you if you want to stay here with her.'

'Oh, would you? I hadn't thought that far ahead, to be honest, but that would be wonderful.' Audrey could have kissed Anna Rhodes, but doubted she'd be a keen recipient.

Outside, the warm air temperature was a shock. Audrey considered what her next move should be. Checking the hospital's location on Google Maps, she headed back in the direction of the town. Her head was beginning to throb from the stress of the morning, and she realised that she never did have the coffee they'd so been looking forward to.

Eyeing a café that exuded ambience, she crossed first to the grassed square opposite and sat to make the first of her calls. Poppy's parents were startled by the news, but weren't able to get "down there", they'd said. Audrey promised to keep them up to date with her progress and they promised to call their daughter that evening.

Isabel was already packing by the time Audrey had told her father the news. 'We'll be there this afternoon,' they'd said. When she told them the latest on the house, their response was immediate. The extra funds would be transferred immediately. Audrey listened to them talking to each other at the other end, grateful for their love and support. The idea of her parents bailing her out had made her unhappy, a sign that at her age she was unable to look after herself. But she'd come to understand that Max and Isabel wanted, perhaps even needed, to feel a part of their daughter's life again. For too many years, and particularly her more recent married years, they'd begun to feel redundant, and she knew that in her fierce determination to be independent, to live up to their belief in her, she'd been complicit. The time spent with them on Hibernia had gone a long way to restoring their relationship.

Her finger hovered at first over Campbell's number, then she pressed it with determination.

'Audrey.'

'Hi.' Audrey breathed deeply before continuing. Her emotions were running high, but she didn't want to sound hysterical and lose dignity. 'I spoke with my solicitor yesterday and she tells me you're claiming half of my personal assets.'

'Well... yes. That's right. I've been advised by someone. I did try to call you and warn you, though.'

She couldn't believe that he actually thought he was being noble. 'Why are you doing this, Cam, and so late in the whole settlement process? I thought we'd reached a deal that you'd agreed to.'

'It's actually not fair. We were married for ten years. *Married*, Aud. What's yours is mine and what's mine...'

Audrey could feel her blood pressure rising. 'Really? What am I getting that was yours?'

'That's not fair. You knew right from the start how difficult it can be in the creative

world—'

'Creative, my arse.' Audrey bit her lip, thinking that Poppy has suddenly taken over her body. But suddenly it was clear to her. 'Cam, is this a payback? For not getting back with you?'

'Don't flatter yourself, Audrey. I'm just asking for what I deserve.'

There was no arguing with him, she knew from experience. Why she'd bothered to call him, she didn't know. They ended on a bad note, a 'see you in court' threat from him and a dismissive sign-off from her. Taking advantage of the reception, she rang Beatrice and told her what had happened, and about the funds for the house.

'He'll get nasty, you know that don't you?' she said.

'Well, what else can he do? There's nothing else he can get his hands on.'

'Audrey, you didn't tell him about the house, did you?'

'No.' Audrey went cold.

'Don't buy it in your name. Not until this is over. He's out for blood.'

'Surely...'

'I'm still in negotiations over all of this. There's a good chance he can't claim what he's gone for so far, but don't risk anything else.'

Audrey nodded into the phone, finding it hard to believe what she was hearing. 'I won't.'

'If your parents sign for it, it will be okay. Audrey? Are you okay?'

'Yes... I'll be fine. Thanks, Beatrice.'

When she ended the call, Audrey wished she could let out a long and loud howl.

In The Daily Grind, she took a seat by the window. Though it was hours since she'd eaten, she had no appetite, but when the ordered macchiato was placed in front of her, her brain cells began to spark up from its aroma and she felt a surge of strength. Campbell was a first-rate bastard, she whispered into her cup, just as Poppy had always believed.

Here's to you, Pop, she thought as she took her first sip, still not quite able to digest the fact that they should have been doing this together, making plans for the house and life as islanders.

She took a small notepad from her bag and began the financial calculations for the house and projected expenses as a way of giving it all some substance, something tangible that would make it seem real. Despite being proficient with technology, she preferred to work this way, as though by seeing it in her own hand, she was able to exhibit control. Now, however, she knew that such control over anything was an illusion. She hadn't banked on Campbell making more claims as he'd seemed more than happy with the terms of the original settlement. His own contribution to their finances had been sporadic, to say the least, but she had been willing to share the profit on the warehouse evenly, despite the fact that a significant portion of its purchase price had come from her own previous investments.

To be in this position—funds frozen, borrowing from her parents, an uncertain financial future, and now not even able to buy the house in her own name—was not only a shock, but Audrey was beginning to feel stripped of who she was. Who she would be, or could be, seemed so uncertain and obscure that it was beyond her capacity to envisage it.

She checked the time on her phone. The funds for the deposit should be there in thirty minutes, her father had said. She'd go to the bank then and organise the bank cheque that Brian Elsden had specified. Max and Isabel thought they'd arrive in about four hours, enough time for them to sign the contract.

As she savoured the coffee, she took in the view from the window into the street. Wilson's Point was a bustling town, and she was now even more endeared to it when she thought of how quickly the ambulance had arrived and the immediate attention at the hospital. Anna Rhodes had been right. If Poppy had collapsed on Hibernia, who knows how long it would have taken for help to arrive. While she was sure there'd be an emergency helicopter service, she wondered if the bridge was actually a good idea, after all.

The grassed square opposite the café was larger than she'd thought. A number of people— workers from local businesses, she assumed by their office-type outfits—were sitting alone or in groups eating lunch in the sun. She was reminded of her own work routines, her favourite café for lunch and the bright and airy space of her office in a corner of the main gallery, but nothing about the memory was nostalgic; it seemed instead like a distant past and she didn't miss it at all.

A few people were milling around a banner wrapped around a power pole. From where she was sitting, she couldn't see what it said, but it was provoking considerable discussion amongst them, led, it seemed, by two females and two males, all in their mid to late twenties. One she recognised as Ingrid, the daughter in the bakery.

Audrey paid and expressed her appreciation of a good coffee and crossed the road and stood at the rear to see what the banner said. In large letters, it read *SAVE HIBERNIA*, hand-written in thick black Texta. Beneath it in red were the details of a protest march to be staged at the island's wetland on the site of the eco-lodge development in just four days' time. Ingrid and the other three were dressed in green tights and tee shirts, their faces and hair smeared in paint of the same colour. A crowd had started to form around them, and Ingrid picked up a megaphone to be heard over them.

'People of Wilson Point, save your most precious resource—Hibernia. Develop at your peril. Five species of migrating birds and sixty species of native wetland plants will be lost if this development goes ahead. Don't be fooled by the "eco" promise. There's nothing ecologically sound about this lodge. Sections of the wetland will be drained, and the integrity of the rest will be compromised...' She paused. 'What's that?'

Audrey saw her bend towards someone who was wearing a hat she recognised. The birdwatcher was saying something to Ingrid, who nodded, stood up and drew the megaphone to her lips. 'And we have an expert here who says that the Hibernian wetland is unique. Not only is it the most southern mangrove community in the world, it's the only breeding ground left for the blue-footed Banjo Frog.'

Members of the crowd were muttering to each other, some dismissive of 'those greenies', as Audrey heard one woman say, but mostly they looked surprised, evident in the questions directed to the girls.

'There's a plan for a bridge,' Ingrid said forcefully, her face flushed behind the green paint and her eyes wide and alert. 'Did you know that?'

This prompted louder mutterings from the crowd.

'Bullshit!' one man called out.

Ingrid persisted. 'I wish it was, mate. Go to the council and demand to see the plans.'

'YOU, THERE!' an angry voice bellowed from the opposite side of the crowd. A section parted to let him through, and Audrey caught a glimpse of a man in a dark, cheap suit moving forcefully towards the two girls. 'You can't do this! You don't have permission to—'

'Do you, Frank? Do you have permission to do what's she's talking about?' another man called and was joined by a chorus of supporters. 'Love to know who's in your pocket, mate!'

The one identified as Frank looked flustered and waved his hands downwards to quieten the crowd.

'There'll be a meeting next week...'

He's stalling, making it up, Audrey thought.

'... when we'll discuss the proposals... in a civil manner, not like this.'

'So *it's true!*' a woman called out. 'Always knew you were a shonky bastard, Frank Ryan. Just like your father.'

Ingrid raised the megaphone. 'It's beyond a proposal. They've already started work on clearing the site for the "eco-lodge",' she said, scraping the air with two raised fingers of the free hand.

The crowd turned towards Frank Ryan who had begun to pull at the neck of his shirt. 'We'll discuss this at the meeting next week,' he called over them and turned quickly on his heels and headed back the way he'd come.

As the crowd dispersed, snippets of conversation reached Audrey's ear.

'Bloody disgrace. That place is special.'

'Property prices will go up. Sounds brilliant.'

'It'll take years for them to get it done. Like everything here.'

'Yeah, it'll blow over.'

'It'll be a waste of money. Nothin' to see over there, anyway.'

'When were you last there, Ken?'

'Wouldn't waste my time.'

A few people had stayed back to talk with Ingrid and her friend. Audrey waited for them to finish and introduced herself.

Ingrid and the other girl, who Audrey learned was Sal, nodded as she told them what she'd heard.

'Yeah... Foster-O'Rourke Holdings. A strange one, that,' Ingrid said.

'Why's that?'

'Well, Quin O'Rourke owns that company, with his wife— sorry, his ex I think—and he... well, we... my family and friends an' that... we always thought he was a really good bloke. And everyone knows Dion.'

Audrey nodded with a smile.

'Yeah, you know him,' Ingrid continued. 'Strange as he is, he's a good judge of people and, well, he loves Quin.'

Audrey agreed. With everything she was discovering about Quin O'Rourke, the fact that Dion loved him, that Rosa and Beppe respected him, was indisputable. Something just didn't fit.

'Coming to the rally?' Sal asked, as others stepped forward to talk to the girls.

'I'm not sure where I'll be then, but if I'm still here, count me in,' Audrey said.

After saying her farewells, she checked the time on her phone then punched in the numbers to her bank account. *Thanks, Mum and Dad*, she muttered under her breath when she saw the substantial figure to cover the deposit. Taking Beatrice's warning seriously, she found Brian Elsden's number and called.

'Audrey? I didn't expect... how's your friend?'

'She's sleeping at the moment thanks Brian, but... I'm in a

bit of a bind. I'm about to organise the bank cheque for the deposit but need to get back to the hospital. I'm wondering if you could draw up a receipt for the amount. I'll sign it and return later, with my parents. There's been a change of plan and it's to be in their name.'

'Really? Well, I suppose... as long as it's the amount we've discussed, it doesn't really matter whose name's on the contract. Sorry to hear about your friend, though.'

Audrey bit her lip. Brian's sentiment was hollow.

Twenty minutes later, she was standing in front of him with the bank cheque ready.

When he took it from her, his eyes blinked with approval at the amount. 'I'll see you and your parents later then,' he said, his lips forming something bordering on a smirk.

Outside, Audrey called the hospital. 'No change', Margaret told her, 'still sound asleep, love. Hang on a minute.' She heard a muffled conversation, then, 'Just talking to Anna. She says give it a couple of hours. Vitals are good and she's sleeping soundly.'

Audrey thanked her and, once clear of Elsden Real Estate, wondered what she would do. It was only then that the fact she'd just secured the house hit her and she smiled to herself. How she wished she could celebrate with Poppy, but they would, in time. She considered another coffee, and perhaps a Danish to at least acknowledge the moment, but decided against it. Ahead, she saw the faux pillars of the Shire Council offices and, still with hours to kill, decided to do exactly what Ingrid had suggested.

Inside, she headed to an oversized reception desk and was greeted by a woman who looked as though she was straight out of the Sixties—high, almost beehive hair, and glasses with rims that swept up like butterfly wings on the sides.

'Hello,' she said with a nasally twang, her scarlet lips

released of their pucker to form a version of a smile. 'How can I help?'

Her reception was as chilled as the air-conditioned space in which she sat. Audrey introduced herself, explaining that she was in the process of buying a house on Hibernia and would like to see the plans for the proposed development.

The woman looked at her blankly. 'I'm not sure what you mean by "proposed plans", but it's policy that only current rate payers would have that privilege.'

Interesting choice of words, Audrey thought. 'I think you'll find that I do have a right to see them as a prospective buyer.' She was bluffing, but it had worked on a lax council office once before.

The woman sized Audrey up. 'Just a moment,' she said and dialled a two-digit number on the desk phone. There was short to-ing and fro-ing of conversation before a squat and balding man, bearing a striking resemblance to Brian Elsden, appeared from an office at the rear.

As Audrey watched him approach, her attention was distracted towards a flurry of movement in a glass-partitioned office to the left. Two men were standing with their backs to the glass and half-closed venetian blinds, and seemed to be in an animated conversation, evident in the gesticulations that one of them was making.

'Darren Elsden. How can I be of assistance?'

The name was not lost on her. Audrey drew her attention back to the man in front of her, a more insipid version of his brother, who was holding out a hand in greeting as he came around the desk to stand next to her. She took his proffered hand and reiterated her request.

'I'm afraid Jean here is right,' he said, half-turning to include the woman behind the desk whose eyes held a satisfied glint. Darren Elsden explained the regulations.

'Well,' Audrey said, 'can you tell me if it's true that a bridge is planned to connect Wilson's Point to Hibernia?'

'I'm afraid I'm not at liberty...'

In the relative quiet of the reception foyer, the sound of the two men's voices carried forward from the glassed office as the door was opened. Audrey couldn't distinguish whether they were just talking enthusiastically or arguing, but Darren Elsden and "Jean" turned towards them with a look of concern and some embarrassment.

As the two men stepped into the foyer space, Audrey gasped. One was the man at the square—Frank Ryan—and the other was Quin who, by the look on his face, was angry. He paused in surprise to see her, and then walked towards her. Frank Ryan looked as flustered as he had in the town square.

'What's up?' he said sharply, looking at Darren Elsden, who quickly explained the situation. 'For God's sake!' he said, clearly unable to take any more stress in one day.

Quin, who was standing near Audrey, turned to her. His expression was still tense and, in contrast to Frank Ryan's high blood pressure flush, was almost grey with rage.

'Don't waste your time here, Audrey,' he said, loudly and firmly. 'I can tell you everything you want to know.' He cocked an eyebrow to her and the expression in his eyes convinced her that this time he was going to talk, and she was going to hear him out.

'Okay,' she said and they turned their backs on the other three and walked together to the doors.

Once in the street, she stopped. 'Have you eaten? I haven't and can feel my energy dropping.'

Quin looked at her, surprised. 'I'm happy to but I have to admit I'm surprised at the invitation. Thought I might've been on the blacklist.' His smile was warm and colour had returned to his face.

Audrey couldn't help smiling in return. 'Don't get ahead of yourself. Depending on what you've got to say, my reaction could radically alter.'

His eyes widened, but there was a hint of mischief behind them.

For an almost local, Quin was unfamiliar with the eating establishments of Wilson's Point. 'I think I saw a new tapas bar along the waterfront.'

'Really?' Audrey was surprised. She hadn't noticed but thought it an ambitious project in this town and wondered how ready the locals were for the changes that those in power had in mind. She told him her thoughts.

'Couldn't agree more. Things are growing too fast here. Someone in the council, and I know exactly who that is, has big plans for the town. I suspect he's been on a recent holiday to the Amalfi Coast or Spain and thinks he can recreate it here. What he's missing, of course, is that the biggest attraction of this area is its simplicity.'

'Like Hibernia.'

'Yes,' he said, holding her gaze briefly as they walked. 'But that's even more special.'

Audrey was warming to him, but still felt guarded. It was easy to believe him and that his intentions were sincere, but she'd learned the hard way to not be so gullible. She'd hear him out, but she wasn't going to take anything he said at face value. He had some questions to answer and, although it seemed that the growing evidence of his role in the island's development was stacking against him, she also knew that there were times when things are not what they seem. She reminded herself of his tenderness with Dion, and how he's spoken of the wetland that day when they'd relaxed over the lunch table. Surely, she thought, she wasn't such a poor judge of character.

'How's Poppy?' he enquired, as he indicated the road to follow to the marina.

Audrey related all that Anna Rhodes had said and she saw his expression grow sombre as he listened intently.

'I'm sorry to hear that,' he said, placing his palm on her shoulder in a tentative gesture of support.

'Thank you,' Audrey replied, acutely aware of the shot of electricity now humming through her body.

The marina was busier than it had been hours earlier, with boats of various sizes and people milling along the gangplanks. Across the inlet, and in the clean air, Hibernia looked closer than usual. Too close, Audrey thought as she eyed the signs of development on this side of Wilson's Point.

The tapas bar held prime position looking over the inlet towards the island and she wondered how she hadn't noticed it before, as it was painted in red and yellow, though the colours were subtle rather than garish. It had seemed an odd choice for lunch on Quin's part, representative of the encroaching development, and the thought scratched at the irritation that he was complicit in a similar threat to Hibernia.

As they took their seats at a table in the gentle sun on the deck, she felt an uneasiness, her suspicions of him returning. She voiced her concern.

He didn't look surprised but seemed calm and relaxed. 'The development here is the council's doing and, to be honest, I don't know who they're in league with on this project. However...' He paused to acknowledge the woman bringing menus to the table. 'Audrey, would you like a drink?'

'Just water for me, thanks.'

'Same for me,' he said, taking the menus. 'I'm looking forward to this,' he said to the woman. 'Have you been busy?'

She smiled in return. Audrey recognised the ethnic elements of her features immediately.

'Mmm... not so much,' she said, with an inflection that suggested she was not from Granada like Isabel.

'Córdoba,' she said in response to Audrey's question. 'And you?'

Audrey was surprised. 'My mother is from Granada.'

The woman nodded in recognition.

'I'm sure business will pick up,' Quin said, 'I've heard excellent feedback.'

The woman nodded in appreciation and, as though on cue, a group of four drew up to a table further along the deck.

'I hope it does work out,' Audrey said to Quin, when the waitress had left to attend to the new arrivals. 'You were saying?'

'Exactly that,' he said, picking up on the thread of his conversation. 'The proprietors here have bought into this development in good faith, I'm sure. They're here now, and I really don't like to see businesses go under. Especially family ones, which is what this is, I suspect. There's been enough of that on the island since the dairy closed and fishing sanctions were imposed. So, in answer to your question, no, I have nothing to do with this development.'

Audrey believed him, but it wasn't the pressing question she needed to ask. 'But how about on Hibernia?'

Quin leaned back in the chair and his gaze briefly drifted across the inlet. The muscles around his mouth and eyes became tight and the fingers of one hand began to lightly drum on the table.

The woman came out of the bar carrying a water bottle and two glasses that she placed on the table.

'Should we order first?'

Audrey couldn't miss the stall for time but nodded. They each scanned the menu and agreed on the shared lunch platter.

When the woman had left, Quin took a deep breath and began.

Audrey listened carefully as he told her about the company that he and Marion had started and the vision they'd shared for building affordable, eco-sound housing in developing countries, mostly in south-east Asia. It had been a successful partnership on many levels for fifteen years but had begun to fall apart several years ago.

'My sister's, and Michael's, death wasn't the cause of the drift. We'd become different people, with different values. Marion wanted to expand the company into other projects here. She was still committed to the existing ones but felt that we could "ride" the current trend in the health and wellbeing industry by building eco-retreats. I wasn't convinced, but there was someone else in her ear...'

He hesitated as the woman brought the platter to the table and placed the plates in front of them. 'This looks excellent,' he said to her as he and Audrey eyed the tapas selections.

Using the interruption, they each took a selection onto their plates.

'Who was in her ear, may I ask?'

Quin raised his eyebrows and let out a small sigh. 'Our silent partner, Tony. Turns out they'd been having an affair for twelve months. In that time, he'd managed to convince her that we should expand, and she went along with that.'

'Not so silent then, it seems,' Audrey said, before taking a bite of the zucchini flower stuffed with mozzarella and prosciutto and rolling her eyes with pleasure. 'Oh, yum.'

Quin smiled and followed her lead. 'Wow, that's great.'

'You must've been hurt?' she said, watching him for a sign of emotion as he talked about his ex-wife.

'Yes, of course... surprised, I think, more than anything. But we'd been drifting apart anyway—each of us travelling without the other. Obviously in my absence there was plenty of opportunity for that relationship to grow. I found out only a few weeks before the accident. When that happened, I...' His gaze drifted past her but was unfocused as though re-imagining that time. 'I fell into a... a depression, I suppose. My sister and I were very close, and it was her dream to come back to Hibernia to raise Dion. She was so happy on the farm, and I visited them as often as I could. Michael... well, he was a great guy. They were a "perfect couple", if such a thing exists, but in their case, it was true. Anyway, I couldn't see the point in anything really, except Dion. Whether Marion and Tony capitalised on my state is beside the point. I let them buy a major portion of my shares and with it, I almost lost control... in all sorts of ways.'

Audrey had the rising sense that she could see where this was going. If Quin no longer had equal control, then Foster-O'Rourke Holdings would be making decisions over the top of him. But it still didn't explain the signs of his own involvement —buying Dion's inheritance, renovating the Island Hotel for a clientele that was clearly not the locals, his name "attached" to the proposed bridge...

She didn't have to prompt the questions. Quin continued immediately and she sensed that he was finding the process cathartic, evident in the release of the muscles in his face. When he paused every now and then to observe her reaction, she saw a return of that gentleness in his eyes that she'd seen, even fallen for, she had to admit. Her pulse quickened in those moments, but she reined herself back in, determined to not allow her heart rule her head again.

Marion, with Tony's promptings it seemed, was aiming to buy up land on Hibernia under the company umbrella and it was not without help from Frank Ryan, Darren Elsden and his brother Brian, who all stood to gain big commissions from the sale. 'They were after Harold's place too,' Quin said. 'They'd made an offer early in the piece, but when I learned of their plans, I still had enough power on the board to block them, and everything else.'

Audrey was confused. 'If you're still able to block them, how are they managing to buy the farm that Alex lives on and have another attempt at Harold's house?'

'Marion is a wealthy woman in her own right,' he said, 'so she's funding it and the eco-lodge development herself.'

'And the bridge? Surely...'

'Yes and no. It turns out that the council, or should I say its Mayor, Frank Ryan, has had that project under wraps for a while, but it's expensive and ambitious. As you can imagine, a bridge would be a boon for the eco-lodge and any other development in mind on Hibernia. That's where Foster-O'Rourke Holdings comes into it, but again...'

'You've blocked it.'

'I'm trying to, but the rest of the board has been swayed.'

Audrey considered what he was telling her. He seemed so genuine, and it was starting to make some sense. She spread smoky tomato and garlic dip on a slice of crusty bread and offered it to him. 'Would you like some of this? You're doing all the talking and not eating.'

He hesitated and she saw that he coloured slightly before taking it from her. There it was again, that electricity when their fingers brushed. Did he feel it too, she wondered?

While he was eating, Audrey filled him in on the latest with Campbell. 'In comparison to your situation it seems such small fry, but to be honest, it's enabled me to put my problem into perspective. I have such support, Mum, Dad, and Poppy. But I did think you were going to buy it from under me.'

Quin nodded. 'Yes, I know. If you hadn't bought it, I would have anyway.'

'It was becoming a price war,' she said.

'Yes, but I at least have the advantage of knowing Harold's daughter. When I heard about the trouble you were having with your, er... husband, I rang her—Jenny's her name—and told her what was going on. She might live on the mainland, but she doesn't want to see Hibernia destroyed, either. She had no idea who the other interested party was.'

'You knew about Campbell's latest move? But how?'

Quin smiled broadly. 'Dion, of course. When you visited them with Poppy. He was on the phone immediately.'

Audrey laughed. 'Oh, of course. He's very sweet.'

Quin dipped his head in agreement.

Audrey paused before she continued. There were still some things she couldn't understand. 'I hear what you're telling me,' she said at last, 'and it makes sense. But what about your sister's farm—Dion's farm—and why The Island Hotel? It's not for locals, is it?'

Quin took a sip of his water. 'Harold's house, Dion's farm, where Alex is living, and the old abbey form a wedge targeted to be a golf course servicing both the eco-lodge clients and international players—a helipad was planned, too.'

'What?' Audrey became alarmed. 'But I've bought the house and...'

'It's okay,' Quin said. He placed his hand palm up in front of her in an invitation. Surprising herself, she responded. The warmth of his hand as it closed around hers travelled into her chest, making her slightly breathless. 'I've bought up those properties ...' he continued with a shy smile. 'Well, all but yours, thank goodness. Alex can stay for as long as he likes. It wasn't difficult to save the cemetery and the abbey—they're now listed as heritage, though that took a bit of work.'

Audrey was impressed, but there was still a nagging doubt that she had to raise. 'But why would you need to buy Dion's? It was safe anyway, wasn't it?' Audrey slipped her hand out from under his, afraid that he would feel the blood pulsing there.

'They tried to get to him. To Dion. He's an innocent and he thought that if he sold it, he could make life a bit easier for Rosa and Beppe. It's hard for him to go there as you can imagine, but I take him every now and then to get used to it. He's getting there. Slowly.'

'Poor boy,' Audrey said, remembering the two pairs of boots with the fresh mud on them at the back door of his family home.

'And the hotel? I'm sorry if I sound nosy...'

'It's fine, Audrey. I'm so pleased to have the opportunity to explain myself. But... I'm not sure you're going to like this. Hear me out though.'

He told her then that he had voted for the development of the eco-lodge on Hibernia when he knew of the plan, but it had been at a very different site that would have had much less impact on the environment, and none on the wetland.

'We agreed on that site, but let's say while my back was turned, they switched to the headland next to the beach— "more aesthetically pleasing", were Marion's words. I'd bought The Island Hotel partly to offer fine dining for the clientele of the original site, and to give Dion something to work towards. You've seen how he is.'

She did see. Dion was in his element in the hotel, and she understood how this might be a significant reason for Quin's plan. But his admission of agreeing to the eco-lodge had surprised her and she had to ask why.

'Ironically, as a desperate measure to save Hibernia,' he replied immediately. 'So many people have left, especially the younger generation who, quite rightfully, see no future there. Once, there were ten families who fished the coast, sustainably I might add. With sanctions, this has reduced to two. The closure of the dairy killed off the most significant employer. Now, it's only a handful of artisans scratching out a living with the occasional bus tour from here on the mainland.

Audrey thought of the small tour bus they'd passed as they'd left Alex's on the first visit.

'I thought the eco-lodge idea was sound. I agreed to it, I endorsed the bloody thing and even agreed, I'm ashamed to say, to the idea of a hydrofoil, not to replace the old ferry, but as an alternative. What a fool I've been.'

This time it was Audrey who reached for his hand. 'Have an olive,' she said, with a small laugh.

Quin softly clasped her fingers. 'Do you believe me, Audrey?'

She held his eyes with hers. If she was gullible, too trusting, too easily ruled by her heart, then so be it. She'd take the risk on him, she decided.

'Yes. I believe you,' she said.

Rain swept in sheets across the island. By mid-morning, Hibernians and mainlanders were to gather at the wetland in collective protest against the eco-lodge development.

Bill's day would be the busiest in years, he'd told Audrey with eyes brimming with anticipation before he'd left for Wilson's Point. Ingrid, her friend Sal and the two boys, Felix and Josh, had been surprised and encouraged by the mainlanders' sentiments and were expecting a few hundred of them to arrive. How many Hibernians would turn up was a mystery, as

Ingrid and the others' appeals were more often met with a non-committal shrug or nod, and even ridicule.

'It's no surprise to me,' Quin had told them. The locals' ambivalence to change was both its strength and its potential downfall, though he knew that many of the older generation welcomed it if it would mean that their children and grandchildren would stay.

It had been this, he'd told Audrey that day at lunch that had persuaded him to agree to the original plan for the eco-lodge. In the days following, he'd taken her to the original proposed site—closer to the ferry and on a section of farmland cleared many years before. While it had a beautiful outlook with views to the Great Dividing Range on the mainland to the northwest, and to several of the rocky uninhabited islands to the north, it didn't have access to a spectacular swimming beach or the serene beauty of the wetland. Tourism, he'd said, would help to save the island from becoming a forgotten backwater, but the ecological cost was too great. Quin had thought that he'd persuaded Marion and the rest of the Board members, but Tony had other ideas and had successfully convinced her to get another opinion—from someone *he* knew.

'But why Hibernia, anyway?' Audrey had asked. 'What's Marion and Tony's interest in it?'

'Eco-tourism is a thriving industry,' Quin said, 'but the number of suitable "unspoiled" locations with good accessibility were few.' As long as the lodge, its amenities and its food *appeared* to uphold that aesthetic, he explained, most potential clients didn't dig more deeply. The company has been clever with the plans for the golf course and helipad—far enough away from the lodge and hidden behind the bands of eucalypt woodland so that it wouldn't be visible.

. . .

As Audrey and Quin had stood at the ferry ramp waiting for its return with the mainlanders, Max and Isabel joined them.

'How's the girl?' Audrey asked her mother, who was holding an umbrella over them both to shelter from a new sheet of rain.

Isabel nodded. 'Good. Resting in the lounge upstairs and Lola is keeping her company. And that nice boy, Alex, he's called in, too.'

Audrey had been so relieved to see her parents and Lola on their return to Hibernia. When the hospital was confident that Poppy was strong enough, they agreed to her return to the Sanctuary, as long as she had plenty of rest and care, Anna Rhodes had said, directly and sternly. Now, with Isabel, Lola, and Alex, it seemed Poppy wouldn't be alone to brood, or to get restless, though that aspect of her seemed to have quietened, at least for the moment.

As the ferry had approached, Audrey, with rising excitement, craned her neck to see the number of passengers. 'I'm only seeing a couple of cars, and the bus—empty, and few freestanding passengers,' she said to Quin and her parents.

Together, they went down to greet them with Sal as the metal ramp was lowered with a thud. Ingrid, Felix and Josh were waiting for them at the wetland with the locals who were true to their promise to come. When Bill appeared to secure the ropes, his expression had lost its earlier enthusiasm.

He met them on the ramp, the rain trickling in rivulets off his peaked hat. 'This is it,' he said to their yet unspoken question. 'Five all-up. The rest are locals on their daily return.' He returned to ensure the passengers alighted safely.

At the other side of the island, the news was not much better. Ingrid and several others, including Francis, as Audrey now knew the birdwatcher, stood forlornly at the edge of the wetland, the clouds of rain so low and dense that they couldn't even see the eco-development site.

'Ah... *Dios mio*,' Isabel muttered as they joined them with the mainlanders. But they knew there was no point. They'd passed the workers on their way back to the ferry, the construction suspended due to the poor weather conditions.

Audrey took in the bedraggled group that they were. Surely, she thought, there was another, more constructive way.

It was then that she had the glimpse of an idea of how to save Hibernia.

CHAPTER SEVEN

TWO MONTHS LATER

'A few more and that will do it, I think,' Audrey said, holding the small glass container close as she positioned its label with precision. 'How many's that?'

'Three hundred,' Poppy said, finalising the count of lids in the cardboard boxes stacked on the dining room table. 'How many will we take?'

'Mmm... half of that, maybe. I doubt we'll sell that many over the weekend, but that'll leave me enough to fill the orders for the Melbourne and Sydney restaurants. How's Alex going with the cheese?'

'Okay, I think. It's been a sharp learning curve for sure, but he's loving it. His fingers look like he's been smoking a packet an hour, but the colour of the cheese... oh, my God, it looks great—the marbling from the saffron. Where d'you come up with that idea?'

'Mum, of course.'

'Actually, it's given me an idea...' Poppy's voice trailed off and Audrey didn't attempt to interrupt her rumination. In these moments, she could almost feel the creative energy radiating from her, something that Audrey had feared might never happen again.

She considered the label she'd just placed on the jar— Poppy's design—*Hibernian Sunset Saffron* in gold overlay on a photograph of the sun setting over the ocean in a blaze of orange and red that was a perfect match for the saffron threads. Isabel had taken that shot from the top of the cliff behind the house.

'Right... that's it.' Audrey held the container to the light. Behind the amber glass, the threads looked deceptively benign and gave no clue of their potency or their financial value. She placed it in the box and stood with her arm around her friend's shoulder.

'You've done it, babe,' Poppy said, stroking Audrey's hand.

'*We've* done it, you mean.'

Through the open glass doors, the sun filtering through the fronds of the palm tree bathed the dining room in a soft light. Outside, Max was bent over the frame of the deck he was in the middle of constructing, his brow creased in concentration. He looked up and smiled in recognition of someone approaching and straightened for the greeting, startling a small flock of corellas grazing near him in the grass. They screeched their disapproval as they left.

Though he needed to return to Ballina on occasion to prepare the house for the next intake of holidaying guests—an already successful plan hatched by Isabel and Max while they remained in Hibernia for an indefinite period—and to tend to the garden under Isabel's strict instructions, Max's spiritual home, according to Lola, was Hibernia. Whether this was true, or whether it was because he was busier than he'd been after the redundancy, Max's mental health seemed to have improved considerably. He'd even attended a few Qigong classes with

Isabel, Audrey and Lola, something Audrey had never thought she'd see.

Alex's soft Canadian drawl drifted through the doorway. Audrey glanced at Poppy to see her smiling broadly in anticipation. 'He's early.'

'Can't keep away from me,' Poppy said, with a wink.

How she's changed, Audrey thought as she paused and watched her friend moving from box to box, folding down the cardboard flaps that bore the *HSS* logo—again, her design. Her hair, which she now wore loosely, had grown, the shocking red stripe replaced with strands of grey. Her face, though still thin, had more colour, heightened by the vibrant clothes she more often wore—today, an emerald-green blouse and rich red skirt. Audrey stole a glance at Poppy's belly and felt a wave of sadness for her loss, for *their* loss.

For the first few weeks after the miscarriage, she'd barely left the bedroom at The Sanctuary and Audrey had despaired for her friend's sanity. Isabel and Lola had helped to coax her into the sunroom and took it in shifts sitting with her while she wept. At other times, all four of them would gather in the chapel and Lola, in her calm yet practical way, would guide them in deep reflection on the cycles of life—on birth and death —that bonded the four women at a deeper, almost primal level.

Last night, as Audrey and Poppy had sipped a gin and tonic, their chairs placed in between the beams where the decking planks were still to be placed, Poppy had spoken of her grief. 'It's probably for the best, Aud,' she'd said softy, but calmly. 'I'd have been a crap mother.' She'd wept as Audrey leaned across to place her arms around her.

It had been Alex who'd had the greatest impact on her recovery. Every day, he would come to The Sanctuary and sit by her side to talk. Bit by bit, he restored her sense of humour and, in more recent weeks, had managed to reignite the passion for her art. Audrey remembered when she'd found him in the hospital corridor, pacing and on the verge of tears when he'd heard the news about the miscarriage. She'd been surprised at the strength of his emotion, but the quickly formed bond between Alex and Poppy was strong and evident to all. Lola understood it, and so did Isabel. Months ago, when Audrey had never even heard of Hibernia, she would have been cynical; hers and Campbell's relationship had ignited quickly, then died. But now...

'Only you could have had the vision for that old barn,' Poppy had said, changing the subject and breaking Audrey's reverie as she watched a cockatoo shred a palm leaf. 'No, don't shake your head, you're a bloody genius, Aud.'

Though Audrey had laughed it off, a happy warmth rose through her body. From the first time she'd seen the old dairy barn, she could feel the return of the aspect of her work that she'd loved the most—giving spaces new life, not by throwing out the old, but by showcasing it, giving it new purpose. Max, Quin and Alex had reframed the windows, patched weathered sections of the walls, and resurfaced the floor using recycled timber sourced from Wilson's Point. Now, the light through the clean original windows reflected off the sandstone walls and polished floor, creating a sense of warmth and character. But the greatest inclusion was the mezzanine floor sitting above Alex's workshop end. From its vantage point, visitors would be able to observe the displays from different angles and in different lights.

'Thanks, Pop. It looks great, doesn't it? They've done a fantastic job. And did you see the look on Mum's face when she saw it?'

'I know.' Poppy's own face began to colour with a rush of blood. 'She's so friggin' gorgeous, your mum. But wow, those photos! Who'd have thought?'

'Not even me, I'm ashamed to say. Dad looks at her sometimes as though he doesn't quite know who she is anymore... in a good way. Between that and the fabulous design of the paradise garden...well, I think it's reignited a spark, if you know what I mean.'

When Isabel and Max had returned from Ballina and met Audrey at Elsden's Real Estate, she was surprised at how youthful and lively her mother seemed. In just the two days they'd been away, Isabel had sketched ideas for The Sanctuary's paradise garden, collated some of her mother's original recipes for Dion, and was sporting a brand-new camera that Max had ordered for her while they'd been in Hibernia. Whenever Max needed to return to Ballina during the past two months, she stayed with Audrey and Poppy, helping with minor refurbishing and in re-establishing the garden, her knowledge of permaculture practices second to none.

Every few days, she would return to The Sanctuary to spend time with Lola and work on the garden, and to help Dion in the kitchen at The Island Hotel. Isabel's camera was always with her. She had an eye for the making the ordinary beautiful, whether the rear view of her husband as he fixed the door of the shed at The Sanctuary, the morning light swallowed in the weathered paint, or a profile shot of Dion intent on the perfect placing of garnish. These candid moments were as profound as the images captured of the lagoon behind the hotel at dawn and the ocean at sunset.

The paradise garden had become her pièce de résistance. Based on the traditional Islamic design of a rectangular garden split into four sections representing the compass points, each was filled to overflowing with vibrant, green-leafed citrus trees and a carpet of native flowers. At the garden's centre was the oversized, blue-glazed pot that Lola had purchased in Melbourne, spilling with water that trickled over its seductive shape into the pool at its feet. Wooden seats were placed at the garden's edges so that it could be appreciated in its whole. It was on one of these that Audrey would often find her mother and Lola deep in conversation, sometimes in Arabic. The garden provided something else for each woman. For Lola, Audrey knew, it was a connection to Aamir and her many years living in Morocco. For Isabel, Audrey assumed it was a reminder of the Alhambra in Granada, though she sensed that it meant something more. Isabel had never mentioned her friendship with the chief gardener of Alhambra. While Audrey wondered, she would never ask. She'd come to appreciate Isabel not just as her mother, but as a woman, and some things just didn't need to be shared.

'Speaking of spark, what's going on with Lola and Francis?' Poppy asked.

'I know. Now there's a surprise. Something's certainly going on. When I was at the Sanctuary the other day, he dropped in—unexpectedly I'd say, because Lola looked a bit flushed with me there. They were going through that awkward small talk in front of me that revealed so much more. He's lovely, though. I hope it works out for them. She deserves it.'

None of them had seen this potential relationship coming. Lola had only mentioned Francis in passing before she'd gone to Melbourne. When she returned, she seemed to be more sociable, more willing to become involved in the life of Hibernia, as though she finally felt that it was home and that she belonged. The case against Aamir's first wife and children was settled out of court. Although Lola didn't reveal the nature of the settlement, it was, she said, substantial. Certainly, the pace of restoration and renovation of The Sanctuary accelerated, with work teams staying there to overcome the unpredictability of being able to cross from the mainland due to the weather.

Though always full of life and positivity, Lola seemed more

content. She'd admitted to Audrey that, although money could never replace Aamir, the acknowledgement of her rights as his wife provided her with a sense that he was looking after her and, she said, a certainty that he would want her to be happy. She bought a car so that she could source produce for The Sanctuary from the local organic growers who were forming a co-operative headed by Ingrid, Sal, Felix and Josh. She accompanied Francis on his visits to the wetland and was becoming a minor expert on the local and migrating birds.

Audrey and Poppy had sat watching the sun slip to the west and listening to the parrots screech their manic farewell on return to their night roosts. Audrey thought back to the first time she'd seen the house. Of how she had imagined herself sitting on a patio under the tree drinking a gin and tonic and how she'd been struck with the thought that she'd be alone. With that memory, she looked at her friend sitting companionably by her side and marvelled at the sight of her. Though recent hurts, the loss of B, and Campbell's ultimately unsuccessful attempts to sabotage her future, had caused her to maintain her guard, she was slowly beginning to understand that life did not always disappoint, but could bring joy she'd never expected. Hibernia was teaching her that. The island had not just opened her nasal passages, she thought as she filled her lungs with the salt air that drifted in the wake of the waves beating against the cliff below in their rhythmic thud.

'What are you two up to?' Alex stepped through the opening and glanced around at the boxes spread throughout the dining room. 'Aaah... stashing the gold, I see. Would you like me to drop them off in town on our way?'

Poppy moved towards him, and his arm curved immediately to accommodate her.

'It's okay, but thanks anyway. Dad'll help me. You two need to get back to the barn—the gallery, I mean,' Audrey said.

'Deck's shaping up.' Alex turned in the direction of Max who was just out of ear's reach. 'I'll give him a hand with it when the show's over this weekend. I'm surprised, though, that he's not required back in town.'

'Hmm. Between you and me, I think he was "in the way" at The Sanctuary. Lola and Mum have their systems. Dad was feeling like the third wheel, I think. He'll love your help with the deck, though. Quin will help, too. I think Dad's really enjoyed working with you two on the barn.'

'You mean the "Spencer-Varidis Gallery",' Poppy said with mock severity.

'Ha! True. Alex, is everything ready there? Have Rosa and Beppe delivered the canapés and wine?'

Audrey smiled inwardly at the memory of Beppe's expression of pleasure when she suggested the idea of promoting the wine he produced. Rosa, standing behind him, had nodded with satisfaction. Though she could be pragmatic and controlling at times, Audrey saw in that moment how much she cared for her husband. But it was when Audrey outlined a proposal for the saffron grown on Dion's farm that Rosa stepped forward beside him and, to Audrey's shock, they both cried. She was worried at first that she'd offended them, but when they had composed themselves, Rosa embraced her and told her that this would be their son's legacy—and so *Hibernian Sunset Saffron* was born.

Beppe, Rosa, Dion and Quin were happy for her to manage the small company that had been formed. The unpredictability of the internet connections on the island was an issue at first, so she decided to rent a small office space in Wilson's Point. She had to admit that she was loving crossing over to work and home by ferry—and soon it would be Bill's new ferry, Maggie 2, funded by the islanders—but if it didn't run that day, it didn't matter; time was now something she could manage to suit herself.

Alex nodded. 'Oh yes, Dion's at his best with those canapés, I'd say. Even if nobody comes, Spencer-Varidis is a pretty cool place to be. Now the workshop area's done, I'm a bit torn between mandolins and cheese,' he said, holding out his hands as though balancing equal weights.

'You can't help being a polymath, my love,' Poppy said, linking her arm in his. 'Anyway, we'd better get back there. How do I look?'

Alex went through the formal motions of appraisal. 'I think you'll pass.'

Poppy scowled, then broke into a broad smile. 'Bastard.'

'I love your soft talk baby,' Alex said, lowering his lids and smiling dreamily.

'Cut it out, you two. It's not fair.'

'Don't worry, babes, you'll have plenty of shmoozing coming your way when this is over.'

'Let's hope. I haven't seen him for two days. Settling Dion into the farm has preoccupied him, but it's important that they take that slowly.'

'Have you heard how it's going?' Alex's face held genuine interest in the answer. He'd formed a strong bond with Dion and a friendship with Quin who was now his landlord. In order to spoil the plans for the golf course and helipad, Quin had offered Arthur, the owner, a better figure with the possibility of buying a section of it back, excluding the area Alex used, should life on the Gold Coast not be what they'd expected. Being able to stay on the farm, and his burgeoning relationship with Poppy, was the impetus for Alex's creativity to flourish in making both cheese and instruments. It was this that had prompted Audrey to suggest the conversion of the barn to showcase the local artists' work.

'Dion seems okay,' Audrey said. 'The first couple of days were hard on him. Hard on Quin, too, I think—all those memories—but they're both adjusting to it. Rosa and Beppe have been spending time there, too. Rosa hadn't been there since Michael's and Fionnuala's deaths, but she's happy for Dion, and she knows he's in good hands with Quin.'

Over lunch on that day in Wilson's Point, Quin had told Audrey of his long-term plan concerning Dion. In stages, they'd been staying together at the crocus farm, slowly adjusting and sorting through the emotions of their loss.

'He's doing okay, under the circumstances,' Quin had told her, 'though I've found him a couple of times in his parents' room, curled up on the bed.' He'd looked down at his lap and when he faced her again, his eyes were glassed over. 'He's just a boy,' he added, his voice cracking with restrained emotion.

'It must be hard for you, too,' Audrey said, reaching for his hand.

Over the following weeks, Quin and Dion spent longer on each visit to the farm, the raw emotion of being there starting its slow healing, until now they spent most of their time there. Audrey, too, stayed on occasions.

One evening as they sat by the fire, Dion stood up with an exaggerated stretch to say he was going to bed and issued the instruction that they 'get along, if you know what I mean'.

'I don't know what you mean,' Audrey had responded, with mock innocence.

'Audra, do I have to spell it out for you? Q's in love with you.' With that, he'd saluted his goodbye and went to bed.

She and Quin had sat silently for a moment.

'Well,' Quin said with a serious tone. 'I think we'd better "get along" then. What do you suggest?'

'That's going to depend on whether Dion's correct.' She turned to face him more fully. 'Is he?'

Quin nodded slowly. 'I think he might be onto something.'

Audrey nestled into the crook of his arm. 'Me too.'

'The hotel's a fabulous distraction,' Audrey continued, feeling a growing sense of anticipation that she'd try to quell all morning, 'and if the weekend goes well, it'll put The Island Hotel on the map. There's already twenty-six staying there and The Sanctuary's booked out. Lola knows that a few of the guests are wanting to check out the eco-lodge site, but she's happy to know that there'll be jobs for locals and, of course, that its relocation will take the pressure off the wetland.'

While the war with Marion and Foster-O'Rourke Holdings was far from over, they were close to winning a battle—a compromise to consider relocating the eco-lodge to the site that had been originally chosen. None of them, Audrey and Quin included, had anticipated the reaction of many of the islanders, and even more surprising, a lobby group at Wilson's Point; it seemed that the mainlanders had an even greater appreciation of Hibernia's uniqueness than the locals did. That, and their growing dislike for their Mayor, Frank Ryan, had prompted action. This weekend, several investors in the company were staying at The Island Hotel and at The Sanctuary on Quin's invitation. Winning them over this weekend to the relocation would be crucial.

'Let's hope they all like cheese!' Alex said.

'And fabulous art,' Poppy added. 'Anyway, *my new boyfriend*, it's time we got back there and finished the labeling!'

'All done. I did it last night,' Alex said. 'I thought we might... you know...'

'Oh, my God! You're not really thinking what I think you're thinking?' Poppy adopted a look of confusion.

'I don't know now, you've confused me. What am I thinking?' Alex had adopted a look of innocence in return.

'Good grief, you two. Get out of here!' Audrey said, laughing. 'I've got things to do, too. Here, can you load a few boxes in my car on the way out?' She didn't wait for an answer but handed two boxes to each of them. 'You'd be better to go out the front door. Dad's managed to unjam it, but just mind yourself on the verandah, Alex.'

'Dad? Would you like a cup of tea before we go?'

'Sounds good, love,' her father answered from outside. 'I'll be in in a minute.'

The dividing wall between the dining room and kitchen had been the first thing to go when Audrey had moved in a few weeks ago. The three bedrooms and the lounge room at the front had been repainted, the five fireplaces had been opened and the chimneys cleaned. In the kitchen, the wall where the sink and Harold's old stove had sat was already braced and a large hole was knocked out into the sunroom, so that now, as Audrey stood at a rudimentary bench scattered with jars of spices and herbs, she looked straight from the kitchen out the sunroom's windows to the garden. The fruit trees, mulched and tended by Isabel, were thick with leaves and small fruits—apple, pear, quince, lemon and orange were beginning to form. At the top of the rise, the sky met the sea in different shades of blue. Though the new kitchen cabinets, island bench and new oven were still to arrive, the Aga was perfectly functional and the kettle sitting on it was already steaming. As Audrey prepared the teapot, she breathed deeply to steady her nerves, then took it and two cups to the sunroom, placing them on the table between Harold's refurbished armchair and another she'd found in an opportunity shop in Wilson's Point.

'It's ready, Dad.'

'Coming, love.'

Audrey knew that the weekend had so much riding on its success. After the failure of the protest rally and the poor turnout at the council meeting in Wilson's Point, she'd worked hard to garner support for a festival to showcase Hibernia. There'd been the nay-sayers, as Quin had told her, but she'd been surprised at the turnout at the local hall when she and he had put the proposal forward. Over the course of the evening, as Quin answered their questions honestly, and he, Francis, Ingrid and Sal had explained the risks to the island if the eco-lodge and the bridge went ahead, Audrey had realised that so many of those who had come had no idea what they stood to lose. For them, life would go on as it had been for years. The eco-lodge was "over there" on the other side of the island where there were fewer farms.

The bridge... well, that would be good, wouldn't it, they'd said, as the ferry crossing to the mainland was often hampered by the weather. In general, the Hibernians didn't realise that they had what so many others now wanted—a slower existence, an alternative to the stress-ridden pace of urban lives. Gaining easy access wasn't the answer. 'We do need to save the island,' Quin had said in response to the concerns about the loss of industry, the loss of youth to the mainland, 'but this is not the way.'

When Audrey had taken to the floor, she had reiterated Lola's words, 'Sometimes a sanctuary has to be hard won if it's to deliver its promise,' and she saw some heads nodding slowly, as though they were digesting it. Utilising her presentation skills to maximum effect, she'd offered her proposal—a festival that showcased the very best of the island. Colin Gregory's free-range ducks and quail; Ernie Drinkwater still couldn't be convinced to kill his beloved birds, but he was happy to supply the quail eggs; Joe Heppell's duck pâtés and cured meats; Barbara Roche's pastries and Bryce and Colleen Millard's organic, naturally fermented breads and, of course, Beppe Cazoni's wines and olives, and Alex's cheese. In addition, there was fine cuisine at The Island Hotel, yoga classes and Jaz Kennedy's Saori weaving at The Sanctuary, and afternoon mint tea and Middle Eastern fare by the paradise garden.

When she'd discussed the proposal for the old dairy's barn —to be converted into an art gallery, though maintaining the integrity and spirit of the building—she could feel a resistance building. But when she'd shown slides of some of the work to be displayed—Jonah Cowley's metalwork and jewellery, XiXi Chan's pottery, "Uncle" Jedda Mac's wood carvings, Poppy's contemporary sculpture, and Alex's gold-inlayed mandolin, it was Isabel's series of photographs of the wetland at dusk that drew an appreciative sigh. By the end of the evening, two-thirds of the locals were on board expressing their growing resistance to the eco-lodge development.

Afterwards, Quin had cooked a private dinner for the two of them at The Island. When he'd toasted her for the idea and the work she'd done towards making it a reality, his eyes, lit by the small candle between them, were soft and loving. They'd become a pair—working together to save Hibernia, working together to build a new life—he with Dion on the crocus farm, as well as starting an eco-development advisory company with Max and his former colleague, and she with Poppy in the house fittingly named after the island she'd come to love, and a business with Beppe—*Hibernian Sunset Saffron*. In time, in slow time that allowed life to flourish, who knew what would happen between them.

Max drained his cup, then headed out to bring the car up

the drive. Audrey returned to the dining room. As she picked up the remaining boxes, she caught her reflection in the Art Deco mirror still on the wall in its original position. The light in the dining room was brighter than on that day she'd first seen it, and this time she saw herself clearly.

Audrey. Happy. At last.

END

Dear reader,

We hope you enjoyed reading *Hibernia*. Please take a moment to leave a review, even if it's a short one. Your opinion is important to us.

Discover more books by Amanda Apthorpe at https://www.nextchapter.pub/authors/amanda-apthorpe

Want to know when one of our books is free or discounted? Join the newsletter at http://eepurl.com/bqqB3H

Best regards,

Amanda Apthorpe and the Next Chapter Team

ACKNOWLEDGMENTS

This story could not have been written without support –
someone who believes in me, listens to me reading it out in the
car, and who cheers me on. That someone is my partner.
Thanks Chris. This book is yours as much as mine. We've travelled to Hibernia together in our minds for quite a while now.
Thanks also go to my lovely family, friends and acquaintances
who assure me that they're waiting excitedly for my next novel.
Whether you mean it or not, thank you.

Thank you to The Next Chapter Team for considering this
work worthy to be published and for looking after your authors
so well.

And thanks to Helen Goltz – just because.

ABOUT THE AUTHOR

Amanda loves to write. No sooner has she inserted the final full stop on the latest novel and she's already shaping up for the next one. Amanda also loves to teach and to share with her students what she knows, and what she's still learning about writing. She holds a Master of Arts, and PhD in Creative Writing and is active in the national and international writing worlds, presenting at conferences and writing workshops.

Hibernia is Amanda's third novel to accompany *Whispers in the Wiring* and *A Single Breath*. A fourth novel is due for release soon. In addition to writing fiction, Amanda has two published volumes of the *Write This Way* series: 'Time Management for Writers' and 'Finding Your Writer's Voice.'

Amanda is a Melbourne (Australia) based author, teacher and life-long student of yoga.

Printed in Great Britain
by Amazon